IN FULL BLOOM

WILDFLOWER RIDGE 1

ELLE ASHWELL

For everyone who grew up wishing for a cowboy,
and got a Kiwi farmer instead.
This one's for you

AUTHOR NOTE

While this is a sweet, sexy love story, some subjects may be upsetting for some readers.

These include: brief mentions of a toxic ex, miscarriage, car accident causing death and horse riding accident causing child injury; anxiety, farming practises, sexually explicit content and coarse language

Please read with care and reach out if you require further information.

GLOSSARY

Wildflower Ridge is a New Zealand based sheep and beef farm and as such, this book uses New Zealand spelling and language. I've included some Kiwi-isms and farming terms in this glossary to help you out.

Bench - a kitchen counter
Bush - native forest
Gumboots - wellington/rubber boots
Heifer - a female cow that hasn't had a calf yet,
    or is having one for the first time
Hereford - a breed of beef cattle that is a reddish
    colour with white face and markings
Horse float - a horse trailer
Paddock - a fenced off field to keep stock in
Side-by-side - an all terrain farm vehicle
Spotlight - a version of hide and seek/tag, played
    at night. A Kiwi childhood classic
Ute - a 'utility vehicle', commonly referred to as a
    pick up truck in other parts of the world

1

———

KATIE

I CAN'T BELIEVE I'm back in this godforsaken town.

Four years ago I swore to myself that I'd never return, yet here I am, sitting in a slightly dingy bar twirling a glass between my fingers. I wish I stayed home, but I needed a drink and the bottle shop was already closed by the time I realised this. Cheap supermarket wine wasn't going to cut it.

The pub, one of only two in this tiny, back-country town, is much like I remember it from my teenage years. Timber panelled walls, a floor that's permanently a bit sticky, a weird fake bison head mounted on the wall—which makes no sense since we don't even have bison in New Zealand. There's a jukebox in one corner, vinyl booths along one wall and pool tables at the back of the room.

It's not airy or modern with a cocktail list the length of my arm and the bison is giving me the creeps, but it's still a far better choice than the shady bar on the other side of town, or sitting at home alone while my thoughts spiral in my head.

And I've got to give it to this place, they mix a good drink.

Rowdy laughter breaks out behind me. I don't need to turn around to know where it's coming from—who it's coming from.

I can't believe on my first night in town I came across the very last person I want to see. I'd rather set fire to myself than have to have a conversation with him—the main reason I swore I'd never return.

I should have known though. Kauri Creek is not a big place. I knew when I drove back here this morning that eventually I'd see him.

I just didn't think it would be on a Wednesday night when I'm exhausted and emotional from moving into my grandmother's old house.

I wish she were here. She'd make everything better. But she died when I was eighteen and I have no other family left.

I left Kauri Creek not long after, making one of the worst decisions of my life. That was six years ago.

If I was allowed, I'd sell Grandma's little cottage on the edge of town and never look back. I inherited it with her passing, but I'm not allowed to sell it until I turn twenty-five. Until then, it's held in trust so while I can live there, I can't take the money and run. I mean, move on.

Maybe she knew that I'd need to come home, and that running out of money was going to be the final domino in a line of events that saw me return. It's not the only reason I'm back, but a pretty major part of my decision.

I take another swig of my drink and let the icy liquid cool my emotions.

Heavy footsteps stop beside me and I suck in a breath. Has he finally recognised me? Come to have a go?

"Hey, man. Another round for that lot, please."

A voice I definitely don't know. I risk a peek out of the corner of my eye. He's one of the few guys from the corner I don't recognise.

He's wearing boots and worn black jeans, a chambray shirt with the sleeves rolled to his elbows, displaying strong forearms that are resting against the bar, and dark blond hair cut short and neat. He works his jaw from side to side.

His real sharp jaw.

He looks like he strolled right off the set of a cowboy movie. Based on his company, I'm guessing he strolled right off Constellation Station, the largest sheep and beef farm in the area.

"Hey." The guys voice is quieter now than when he called for more drinks and I wonder who he's talking to. "Is this seat taken?"

I risk another glance and find him looking down at me. I arch an eyebrow. "Is that your line?"

He grins. "Would you rather I come up with some cheesy-ass line that you can mock me about?"

"I'd rather you didn't talk to me at all." I'm not usually this mean, but I don't have it in me to deal with small talk tonight, especially not with some cocky cowboy.

"Oof, that was brutal."

I shrug. "Why feed me a line at all? Why not just carry on with your evening and leave me to mine?"

It's his turn to shrug. "I haven't seen you around before so I thought I'd say hello. The concept of someone drinking alone has never really sat right with me." Oh, so he's just super friendly. I wonder if he's been put up to it. It wouldn't surprise me.

"Well, it's not the most fun but it's the easiest way to drown your sorrows. So, here I am."

He looks like he's about to say something, but the bartender places a handful of bottles on the table.

The cowboy collects them, still looking like he wants to say something, but not quite sure what.

"Enjoy your night," I say as I turn back to my drink, leaving him no choice but to carry on with his life. He turns and walks away.

I've barely taken another sip of my drink when he's back.

"Are you a parking ticket? Because you've got fine written all over you."

His voice is deep and smooth in my ear with just a touch of roughness around the edges.

I turn to face him. "Seriously?"

The cowboy grins down me. "Thought I'd try another tack. At the very worst, I figured it would make you laugh."

"At you maybe," I say, forcing my lips to remain in a straight line.

A catcall comes from the corner. "You go, Dallas," a voice shouts across the room. A voice that makes my insides want to curl.

As much as I want him to leave me alone, I can't ignore that. Against my better judgement I open my mouth. "Did he just call you Dallas? Like the Dallas Cowboys football team?"

He indicates the seat, asking if he can sit. I roll my eyes. "Whatever, just answer the question, cowboy."

He slides onto the stool and I definitely don't notice the way the denim of his jeans tightens around his thighs as he props one foot on the bottom rung of the stool. His other foot remains on the floor and he looks so at ease I want to pull his hair out. If I tried to sit like that I would definitely fall off the stool. My feet barely rest on the bottom rung, let alone reach the floor.

And god, those thighs. I press my own together.

"It's a nickname," he says, dragging my attention away from his legs, which is probably for the best. "My name is actually Dean, but all my life I wanted to be a cowboy and the name kind of stuck. I thought I'd left it behind when I moved here, but I was betrayed."

"Betrayed?"

"Yup." He sighs. "By the person closest to me." He places his hand on his heart like he's been mortally wounded.

I roll my eyes and force away another smile. I don't want to find him cute, but I do. I most certainly don't want to find him hella hot. Which I also do.

"So, what brings you to town?" he asks.

"Oh, we aren't doing that are we?"

He shrugs. "We don't have to."

"Good." I take a final swig of my drink and set the glass down, the ice cubes clinking. "Can you keep a secret?" The bad decisions keep on rolling.

He leans in closer, his strong, tanned forearm flexing against the bar. "What kind of secret?"

"One that'll serve you well, if you can keep it."

His eyebrows shoot up. He makes a 'go on' gesture.

"If you can keep your mouth shut and follow the rules we might be able to continue this elsewhere, without the small talk obviously."

"The rules?"

I nod and hold up two fingers. "One is that you tell no one. Not a soul. You don't even talk to people in this town about me, not a single mention."

He eyes me as though I'm crazy, and I probably am for even entertaining this idea. As far as bad ideas go, this is right up there with my worst. An employee at Constellation Station is not the guy I should be going to for scratching an itch.

"I can do that," he says after a pause.

"The other rule is that it's a one-time deal. No repeats, no do-overs, especially no feelings."

"Man, someone did the dirty on you, huh?" It's the sort of line that should make me bristle, but the way he says it I know he doesn't mean to be a jerk.

Besides, he's not wrong.

"Yeah, this hellhole town and cocky-ass cowboys like you."

He leans back and surveys me. His eyes track down my body, taking in my blonde hair falling over my shoulder, the tight white knitted sweater, and jeans that I know hug my ass like they're a match made in heaven.

"I can live by those rules," he says, leaning in to speak into my ear. "I don't have a lot of time for prissy city princesses either, so as good as you look in those jeans, a one-time deal suits me fine."

I place my hand on his shoulder and push him back so I can

look him directly in the eyes. I can't quite tell what colour they are in the dim bar lights but they're fringed with dark lashes.

He stares at me, a cocky smirk curving his lips. I can't wait to feel them on my skin.

"You're toeing the line," I say, warning in my voice but also curiosity about how he's going to play this out.

"You sounded like you wanted a cocky-ass cowboy. I can do that for you, princess."

Oh god. I want to melt at his feet.

"I'm going to the bathroom. Finish your drink ... slowly." I drag out the word. "Maybe I'll see you outside." I stand and slide the strap of my bag over my shoulder, turning for the corridor at the back of the room.

His hand catches my wrist. "What's your name?" His voice is hoarse, eyes bright. He licks his lips. I want him to lick me.

I trail my fingers up his arm and across his shoulder as I lean in to him. I'm almost certain he shivers and I love the rush of power that gives me.

"Maybe if you're real good, you'll find out."

2

———

DALLAS

HOLY FUCKING SHIT.

I am in way over my head right now.

When I saw the blonde sitting at the bar I just thought I'd say hello. But something in the way she reacted to me approaching made me want to go back for more. I'm convinced there was a flash of pain in her eyes, followed by fire. I'm not sure which one drew me in more.

If she'd told me to go away and leave her alone, I would have. I was fully expecting it.

Instead, she propositioned me and now I think I'm heading off to have a one-night stand—with a girl whose name I don't even know.

It's a terrible idea. One of my worst.

But it's been a long, long day and I needed to get out of the house. It's also been a long, long time since I spent any time with a woman that looked at me as if she wanted to eat me—

despite her obvious disdain for me. It shouldn't, but that open scorn makes it even hotter that she wants to take this elsewhere.

She called me a cocky-ass cowboy, which I'm sure isn't an accurate description, but if that's who she needs me to be, I can play the part.

I didn't miss the way the fire flared in her eyes when I called her a prissy city princess either. Again, it shouldn't be such a turn on, but it most definitely is.

I finish my beer and slide the bottle towards Ray, the bartender, shaking my head when he asks if I want another.

On my way out, I stop by the table of local guys who'd adopted me for the night. Despite me telling this girl I'm not into the idea of people drinking alone I'd been planning to do just that, but when I arrived, I found a group of other young farmers taking up a corner table. They insisted I join them.

"I'll catch you guys later," I say.

Max gives me a wolfish grin. "Have a good night." He winks at me and I roll my eyes.

"Don't drive," I tell him. He's put away far too many in the short time we've been here, meanwhile I've only had one. The aim had been to drown my sorrows, but the annoyingly responsible voice in my head kept reminding me I have work tomorrow, and I have to drive home, and that there's a litany of other reasons I can't lose myself in a bottle.

His eyes darken and he scowls. "I wouldn't."

"Good. See you round." I grab my jacket, head for the door and push through into the night. The street is quiet. Just down the block I catch sight of blonde hair highlighted by the streetlight glow.

She's leaning against the brick wall of the farm supply store, one foot propped up behind her. She's got her head tilted back, staring at the star-strewn sky, arms folded tightly across her chest.

I approach slowly, still expecting she'll startle and take off into the night. She doesn't turn to look at me as I prop my shoulder against the wall beside her.

"I forgot how many stars there are out here," she says, voice a little wistful. The fiery girl from inside is gone now.

"You're shivering," I say like a total dumbass. Way to state the obvious.

She rolls her head down to give me a baleful look. "I also misjudged the weather. Sue me."

The fiery girl is back. I grin and hold out my jacket. She scowls. "You're already in, you don't need to be all gentlemanly."

"I'd just rather you didn't freeze to death before we get to see where this is going."

"Fine," she says as she turns and slides her arms into the sleeves. "But only so I don't freeze. Not because you're being all chivalrous or anything. I'm being completely selfish."

"Of course."

She leans her shoulder against the wall, mirroring my own position so we're facing each other. I don't want to think about how damn good she looks wearing my jacket. I cannot get attached. She's made it clear that is not in my best interests. I don't even know if I'll see her again after tonight.

"I know we aren't doing the small talk thing, but can I ask you questions?"

"Sure," she says. Her eyes are tracking over my body, shamelessly checking me out. It's obvious she likes what she sees. "But I can't guarantee I'm going to answer them."

Of course not. She's so exasperating. For a moment, I question my sanity in following this road. "Can I kiss you?"

"I don't know ... can you?" She smirks, then reaches up and swipes her tongue across my bottom lip.

I make an embarrassing noise. I'm twenty-seven, way too old to be this awkward with a woman.

I press forward and capture her mouth with mine. I lean her back into the wall, one arm bracing me above her head, the other hand cupping her cheek. Her skin is so soft under my fingers. Loose strands of her hair tickle my face but it doesn't bother me. I want to feel all of her.

The kiss is hot and heavy. Her hands fist in the front of my shirt, pulling me into her. I comply and my hand trails from her face down her body, moulding to every curve. As I cup her ass, then lift her thigh to wrap her leg around me, she moans. I press my hips against her and she breaks the kiss, tipping her head back as she grinds on me.

My lips drag down her throat. I can feel her pulse racing as her breath comes in short pants. Her hands slip into my hair where she clings tight. I slide my tongue across her collarbone and she twists her fingers. The best kind of pain shoots through my scalp.

I pull away, staring down at her. Her pupils are blown wide and she's breathing hard.

"Next question," I say between my own short breaths. "Want to take this somewhere more comfortable?"

She smirks at me but her voice is a little breathy when she replies. "Thought you'd never ask."

3

———

KATIE

I PULL into the driveway of Wildflower Ridge and come to a stop.

The morning sun is just beginning to line the hills of the farm that used to be my second home. After my vow four years ago, I thought I'd never see this place again and now that I'm here, I'm not sure I can cross the property line.

I don't know why I'm nervous. A few minutes down this driveway and I'll be reunited with my best friend, Olivia, and her mum Violet, who was friends with my grandma.

Olivia and Violet know I'm coming, this isn't a surprise visit and if I delay any longer I'm going to be late for my first day of work at Wildflower Ridge.

Even though I'm working for my best friend—or especially because of that—I don't want to start off on the wrong foot.

I ease off the brakes and my car rolls forward, passing through the wooden gates hand carved with sprays of wildflowers. Olivia once told me her dad, Henry, had made the gates, carvings and all, for Violet when they got married and he named the farm for her.

I used to think I'd find myself love like that.

Now, I'm picking up random guys in bars and taking them home for the best sex of my life.

I let myself have a moment or two, remembering how his body felt tangled with mine, before shoving the thoughts away. He was gone before I woke up this morning, as agreed, and if I'm lucky I won't run into him again.

Constellation Station borders Wildflower Ridge, but the farms are both big enough that the chance of crossing paths out here is slim to none. The farm workers don't usually head into town either, unless it's to the pub or the farm supply store—two places I won't be frequenting.

If I'm really lucky, Dallas is a seasonal hire and he'll be out of here before long. Then I won't ever have to worry about seeing him again.

I let myself have one more lingering thought about how his calloused hands felt on the soft skin of my inner thighs before the farmhouse comes into view, then I lock last night up in a secure box in the far reaches of my memory.

I pull to a stop in front of the house and climb out of the car, staring up at the building. It's just like I remember it, except refreshed. It's been painted sometime recently, but the exact colour it was before—a soft blue-grey that makes the old villa look fresh and inviting.

"Katie!" A voice calls from the side of the house. I turn towards Violet, standing at the corner of her vegetable garden, wide brimmed sunhat and gardening gloves on. She pulls the gloves off as I approach. "It's so good to see you," she says as I reach her and she immediately engulfs me in an enormous hug.

Tears instantly fill my eyes and I never want to let go. I haven't been hugged like this since the last time I was here.

"Let me look at you," she says and pulls back to hold me at arm's length. She catches sight of the emotion in my eyes and pulls me in for another all-consuming hug.

"I'm so sorry I didn't come for the funeral," I say, my face pressed into Violet's shoulder.

"It's okay, my sweet. Henry understood why you left. We all do."

"I should have been here for you all though, like you were for me after Grandma ..." I trail off, the memories of that time too much to process right now.

"You're here now, Katie. That's all that matters."

I nod and wipe at a stray tear that's escaped. "How are you all doing?"

"We miss him very much, but we're doing okay. The shock of it was the worst, but the farm is keeping us all busy."

"Lady Violet?" A small voice calls and we both turn towards a little girl as she skips into the garden. She's wearing a full skirt with her gumboots and has her blonde curls tied up in a messy ponytail.

"Over here," Violet calls to her. "Come meet Olivia's very best friend."

The girl comes to a stop in front of me, eyeing me suspiciously. "I thought I was Olivia's very best friend."

"Hmm," Violet says, clearly trying to think of a way out of

this. "I think you are, but Katie has been Olivia's friend for a very long time, so you're a different kind of very best friend."

The little girl, who must be around four or five-years-old, thinks for a moment. "Okay," she says, then sweeps out her knee-length skirt and drops into a curtsey. "It is a pleasure to meet you, ma'am."

"I'm not sure about the ma'am part," I say with a grin. "You can just call me Katie."

"Lady Katie," she says. "I am Sadie."

"It is a pleasure to meet you, Lady Sadie," I say and bob a clumsy curtsey myself.

She beams at me for playing along with her game.

"Sadie's dad is working for us," Violet says. "I help out with looking after Sadie and she helps me by picking all the strawberries." Sadie giggles and shoots across the garden to the strawberry patch.

"Speaking of work, where's the boss lady?"

"She's down at the barn with the horses. Why don't you go see her? You could take Sadie down for a little bit too if you like?"

"Of course," I say, then call to Sadie. "Lady Sadie, would you like to escort me to the barn?"

She skips back to us. "Can I?" She asks Violet, who gives her a nod. "Can we take the side-by-side?"

I've never driven one before, but I shrug. It can't be too tricky. "Sure thing."

After a quick lesson in driving the farm vehicle, Violet waves us off and Sadie chatters excitedly beside me as we head further down the driveway to the horse barn. She tells me all about her fifth birthday party they had two weeks ago and how she's starting school soon, at the start of next term. She points out all her favourite parts of the farm, like she's giving me a grand tour. She obviously hasn't realised that me being Olivia's long time best friend means I already know all these places.

I pull to a stop outside the yards and grin as I catch sight of the horse Olivia is cantering around the arena.

Scout has aways been my favourite and was always reserved for me to ride whenever I visited, which in my teenage years was at least several times a week. Sometimes I didn't go home and would go to school straight from the Ridge.

Olivia spots us and slows Scout to a walk then leaps from the saddle to engulf me in an enormous hug. "Katie!" She squeals into my ear.

I squeeze her back, just as tightly. It's been way too long since I've seen my best friend. She tried to come and visit me as often as she could, but she's spent the last few years getting a new business off the ground so her time has always been short.

"Oh my god. I can't believe you're actually here," she says.

"Me either," I say with a laugh that's only slightly bitter.

"I got Scout all ready to go for you, and the farm manager will be here soon so he can show you what's on the agenda today. I'm sorry I can't hang out, but I have to get to an appointment in town. I hope you're staying for dinner."

"I sure am. Your mum has already twisted my arm."

"Like you need convincing," she says, grinning. She's right. Eating with Violet and Olivia is a thousand times more appealing than cooking for myself at home. Olivia turns to Sadie. "Morning Sadie. Do you want to wait for your dad with

Katie and have him take you back to the house, or come with me?"

"Can I stay with Katie and Scout?"

"You sure can, just remember—" Her phone rings and she winces at the sound. "I'm so sorry. I have to answer this. I'm so late. I double booked. I should be here to introduce you."

"Liv, it's all good," I say, placing a calming hand on her shoulder. "Go deal with your stuff. I'm capable of meeting your farm manager. Besides, Lady Sadie will be here to formally introduce us. We have all the time in the world to catch up."

Olivia sighs and nods in defeat. "I'll see you at dinner. Later, Sadie."

"Bye, Olivia," Sadie calls as Olivia strides away.

"This is Scout," Sadie says, tentatively reaching up to stroke her muzzle.

I smile. "I know. I remember the day Scout first came to Wildflower Ridge."

Sadie's eyes go wide. "Really? You have been friends with Olivia for a long time then."

"Longer than you've been alive," I say with a smile. "You want to have a ride while we wait for your dad?"

Her eyes go even wider and for a moment I worry they're going to pop out of her head. "Can I?" she breathes.

"Yeah, sure. Scout's a sweetheart."

I help Sadie up into the saddle, then start leading the horse around the arena. Every time I glance up at Sadie she has the hugest grin on her face, like she's going to burst from excitement.

The thrum of a motorbike engine approaches, then cuts off.

"Daddy, look!"

"Sadie, what are you doing?" A man's voice. One I recognise.

I shiver at the memory of the things that voice said to me last night.

"Katie let me ride Scout," Sadie calls back.

I take a deep breath and turn towards where I know he's standing.

He looks even better in the bright light of day. Wearing jeans and a dark green jacket, his boots dusty and worn, Dallas stands in the middle of the open gateway, his arms folded across his chest, emanating disapproval.

Oh, fuck my life. I have screwed up so bad.

4

DALLAS

I'M NOT sure what's more horrifying: seeing Sadie on top of a horse, or seeing last night's hookup standing beside her, shock all over her features as she takes in the sight of me.

I tear my gaze off the woman—Katie, Sadie had called her—and realise I finally know her name. Last night I called her princess, or a bunch of other names that make me cringe in the stark light of day. She never got around to her telling me her name.

How did my five-year-old learn her name before me and I've seen her naked?

I stride across the arena, my boots kicking up dust. "Time to hop down, Sadie girl," I say, hoping my voice doesn't reveal my true feelings. I reach up to pluck Sadie out of the saddle. She gives the horse a pat then wraps her arms around me. I inhale the sweet scent of her and try to figure out what to say to the utterly gorgeous woman standing beside me.

Her long blonde hair is pulled back into a loose braid and

she's wearing a black jacket with jeans that might be even better than the ones she wore last night. Everything is crisp and fresh, like it's brand new for today. Her boots are still pristine.

"Thanks, Katie," Sadie says, in a quiet little voice. It's her shy voice that she uses for people she's smitten with but doesn't know well enough to fully be herself ... and the one she uses when she thinks she's in trouble.

"It was my pleasure, Lady Sadie," Katie says and reaches out a hand to give her a fist bump. Sadie returns it, then squirms until I put her down.

"Daddy, this is Katie. She's Olivia's very best friend," Sadie says. "Katie, this is my daddy. His name is Dean, but nobody ever calls him that."

She raises an eyebrow at me. "Oh yeah, so what do they call him?"

"Dallas," she says with an enormous grin.

Katie's grin matches my daughter's. "Like the Cowboys, huh?" She says to Sadie, then turns her gaze on me. "Hello, Dallas," she says, holding out a hand. She tips up her chin and looks me straight in the eye. It's a challenge.

"Nice to meet you, *Katie*," I say. My voice is sharp, especially on her name. I take her hand. It's so awkward, but I have no idea how else I'm supposed to act in this situation. One-night stands aren't my usual way to spend time and I sure as shit didn't think I'd be seeing this one again, especially at my job.

Katie's eyes widen a fraction, probably also realising I know her name now.

"Sadie, could you go wait for me by the side-by-side. I'll take you back up to Violet."

"Okay, Daddy," she says, then gives the horse a final pat before skipping off.

I watch her go, the bounce in her step tugging at my heart. I turn back to Katie.

"How are you here?" I ask. There's irritation and frustration in my tone. I could barely drag myself out of her bed in the early hours of this morning, could barely tear myself away and have been fighting with myself all morning to erase the memories from my mind.

And now she's standing in front of me looking like a goddamn dream. One that I can't have, and one that I can't afford to be distracting me from this job.

I *need* this job.

Wildflower Ridge is the only place that's accepting of Sadie. Nowhere else would make allowances for me being a single parent. Here, Violet and Olivia help with childcare when they're around the farmhouse, they don't mind if I have to shoot into town to pick up Sadie from kindergarten early and they've helped me come up with a workable plan for when she starts school in a few weeks.

I cannot lose this job. I can't mess it up.

I also refuse to let Violet and Olivia down.

Henry Austin, the owner of Wildflower Ridge and Olivia's dad, took a chance on me six months ago. After his sudden passing only a couple of months later, I've been determined to help out his family any way I can.

Having Katie here ... that's only going to end in disaster. Hopefully she's just stopping by for a fleeting visit.

"You heard Sadie, I'm Olivia's very best friend."

"Alright then. I've got to get Sadie back to the house, then meet a new employee who's starting today."

She crosses her arms and cocks a hip, staring me down. "I'm the new employee, cowboy," she says.

What? No. This can't be right.

"Are you helping Olivia with the event venue?"

"No. I'm working right alongside you."

"But ... but aren't you from the city? Last night you said you're from the city." The memory of her house comes to mind. The house that is clearly hers. I should have bailed when she took me there, not to a motel room like I expected. Because a house means she lives here. I let out a long breath.

"I said no such thing. You made an assumption." She scowls at me, clenching her jaw and straightening her posture and resting her hands on her hips. "Yes, I've been living in a city for the past few years, but I grew up rural. I can guarantee you I know this farm better than you do."

I can't help it. I scoff. Yeah, I've only been here six months, but I've spent hours on this land, learning every inch of it. Every hillside, every area of bush, every stream and drain and contour.

"Look," she says. "I'm no happier about this than you appear to be. Frankly, it's a huge fucking fuck up. But we're stuck working together, because I am not letting Vi and Liv down. You're going to have to suck it up. You remember the rules?"

"Yeah, of course I do," I say with a grumble, because what she's saying, I have to agree with. I'm not letting anyone down either.

"They still stand. We pretend like nothing happened. I met

you here this morning. We get on with this because Vi and Liv deserve that."

I let out a sigh. "Alright, fine. But I've got a tonne of work to get through today, so try not to slow me down."

She visibly bristles and memories of last night assault me again. Moments when that fire took hold of her, when her passion was fuelled by anger and rage. "Go take your daughter back to the house, cowboy. I'll wait for you here."

I scowl at her giving me orders, even though that sass makes her hot as hell, then I turn and walk away.

God, what have I got myself into?

This job was perfect. Steady, reliable, a good house for Sadie, people around to support us.

Now everything feels like it's up in the air. How can I work with Katie when she so obviously can't stand me? And when memories of her body haunt my brain every time I think of her?

I climb into the side-by-side where Sadie is already buckled. She chats away as we head back up the hill towards the house, telling me all about how Violet said she could help make a cake today. I offload her into Violet's care then spin around and head back to the arena where I left Katie and my motorbike.

Katie is mounted on the horse now, looping around the arena. She urges the horse faster, then stands in the stirrups as they increase speed. Her hair streams out behind her and she looks like she was born on a horse.

I may have made a hasty judgement when I told her not to slow me down and when I assumed she was here to help running the function venue in the refurbished old barn on the other side of the property.

Katie sees me coming and slows the horse, but she doesn't head for me.

Instead, she brings the horse to a halt beside a flag set into the arena surface. She gives me a mocking salute, then kicks the horse forward. It leaps into a gallop, flicking up dust with its hooves and speeding toward a barrel.

I've seen Olivia practising her barrel racing in the arena, and even competing in a local race, but she has nothing on Katie right now. Her and the horse move as one, galloping, spinning, racing for the next barrel and once they round the third and final one, they gallop straight back down the line, sliding to a neat stop directly in front of me.

Katie's eyes are sparking with that same energy from last night when I'd called her a prissy city princess, but there's something else there too now. Freedom, or joy, or something I can't quite recognise. Her cheeks are flushed and a grin spreads across her face as she looks down at me.

"Who's slowing who down now, cowboy?"

I grind my teeth. Fuck, she's aggravating.

I've never seen anything hotter.

I'm so truly screwed.

5

———

KATIE

"LET'S GO," Dallas says, barely giving me a glance as I grin down at him from atop Scout.

I want to roll my eyes and tell him to lighten up, but I know I was showing off purely to aggravate him.

I mean, how dare he insinuate I can't do this job? Sure, it's been a long, long time since I've done this kind of work, but I'm sure it'll come back to me. I spent ninety-five percent of my time outside of school here when I was a teenager. I learned everything there was to learn.

Dallas strides to his bike and swings a leg over it, putting a little more aggression into the kick-start than strictly necessary. He speeds off down the farm track, leaving me in his dust.

I grin. Clearly I've got under his skin.

Good, because he got under mine.

I should be nice and act civil, but he's irritating. He was irritating last night, even when we were destroying my carefully made bed.

He's a cocky cowboy—he said so himself—and I have no desire for one of them in my life.

I give Scout a nudge with my heels and she trots along the track. I soak in the sunshine as it burns away the morning's chill. I take in the view and feel like I'm taking my first deep breath in years.

This place feels like home.

Wildflower Ridge always has. It's the rest of the town I have an issue with.

I catch up with Dallas when he stops to open the first gate. It's way easier opening and closing gates from horseback than with a motorbike because you don't have to get on and off all the time.

"Let me get that for you," I say, guiding Scout into position. Dallas grumbles something too quiet for me to hear. I'm having entirely too much fun pissing him off. "What's first on the agenda today? Checking the sheep?" I keep my voice bright and cheery. It probably sounds super fake—which it is—but I figure that'll just annoy Dallas some more.

"Yes," he says, then exhales a long sigh. "We've had a couple lamb already so it's daily lambing beats from now. Then, we'll check the Herefords, make sure they have water and everything's good with them. Those will be your jobs first thing every day. If there's anything wrong: sheep having trouble, water leaks, whatever, you'll need to call me."

"Or, I can fix the issue," I say.

He eyes me sceptically. He opens his mouth as though he's going to respond but I cut him off before he gets the chance.

"Look, I know you don't think much of me, for whatever

reason, but you have to trust me. Liv does, otherwise she wouldn't have given me the job. I know what I'm capable of doing, and I know my limitations. I know when to call for help if I need it. You just need to accept that I'm actually a competent human. If you're hovering over me every second it's hardly making your job easier, is it?"

"You're right," he says, his voice low and heavy. He crosses his arms over the handlebars of the bike and stares out over the next paddock.

I blink at him, stunned. "Excuse me, could you repeat that?"

He glances sidelong at me, then returns to staring straight ahead. "Seeing you here ... it kind of threw me for a loop," he says and I snort.

"Yeah, wasn't exactly on my bingo card."

"I've got a lot riding on this job. I can't screw it up."

I turn Scout, so I can look directly at Dallas. "How long have you been working here?"

"Six months," he answers, but doesn't look my way.

"So long enough to know that Violet and Liv are reasonable, understanding bosses. If you're a solid worker, with the right attitude, they aren't going to kick you out on your ass. Especially not with Sadie."

He sighs and finally turns his head to look at me. "She's why I need this job so badly. It's the only place that acknowledges I have a child. There's no way I can work anywhere else and still be a parent."

"Is her mum around?" For the first time interacting with him, my voice is tentative. It's always a weird thing to ask, but the way he's talking ... it makes me think it's just him and Sadie. I should have waited and asked Olivia later.

He shakes his head. "Long story, but no. It's just the two of us."

"You're lucky to have each other," I say. He doesn't respond. "Now, come on. We've got a tonne of work to do today." I kick Scout forward and she follows the track along the side of the paddock, heading for the next gate just over the brow of the hill.

"Hey, Katie," Dallas calls and I twist in the saddle to face him.

"Yeah?"

"The sheep are that way." He points in the opposite direction to where I'm heading, a huge grin on his face, then he spins the bike and takes off in that direction.

"Ugh," I say to no one in particular. "Come on Scout, why'd you set me up?" The horse doesn't respond, but she willingly turns around and follows Dallas down the track, heading in the right direction.

THE SHEEP ARE two paddocks over. Little white dots that turn into woolly clouds as we get closer. Dallas takes the left side of the paddock, while I head down the right hand side, sweeping through a gully and up over a ridge, keeping an eye out for any sheep struggling in labour, or any lambs who aren't being cared for by their mothers. It's still early in the lambing season, so there aren't too many. In another month this hillside will be dotted with tiny lambs, bouncing their way around the paddock.

I startle a recent arrival and it races for its mother, immediately going in for a feed, its tiny tail wriggling as it latches on. I grin. Lambs will always be adorable.

I crest the ridge and bring Scout to a stop. A fresh spring breeze is blowing straight into my face, winding its way through my hair. I take a deep breath of the clean air and survey the swaying grass sprawling out before me. This place smells like sunshine and I can't believe I managed to stay away for so long. Out here, in the middle of nowhere, surrounded by lambs and fresh air, astride Scout, I wonder how I ever made that vow to never come back.

A small movement in the grass catches my eye and I head towards it. A tiny newborn lamb is sprawled in the grass, trying to get up but failing. I glance around, but there's no mama sheep in the area.

"Hey, it's okay. I got you," I murmur, then scoop it into my arms. Its tiny body trembles as I pull it close. It hasn't even been cleaned properly. Clearly mis-mothered. I wipe the worst of the gunk off, then tuck the tiny lamb into the front of my jacket. Remounting Scout with my new passenger is a little tricky, but I manage without causing harm to any of us.

"Katie?" Dallas calls.

"Over here," I shout back, turning Scout to head in the direction I can hear the motorbike.

"You all good?" He asks as he zooms up the hill, coming to a stop beside me.

"Yep, just found this little one." I pull the front of my jacket aside so he can see the little bundle tucked against my chest.

"Its mother?"

I shake my head. "No idea, nothing nearby."

He looks exceptionally sad for a guy who deals with this kind of thing on a daily basis. "We'd better get her back then," he says. "Everything else is all good."

"The Herefords?" I ask, referencing the herd of red and white cattle.

"We'll get to them later." He seems really determined to get this lamb safely home.

We ride side by side back across the paddock, Scout walking on a loose rein and Dallas continually trying to avoid driving the motorbike into holes.

"You know," I say, "if you rode a horse you wouldn't have to be so careful where you ride it. It's much more relaxing."

"We're supposed to be working. It's not supposed to be relaxing," he says, irritation back in his voice.

"It doesn't have to be misery though," I say and roll my eyes. "On a horse, you can just let it get on with its thing and not worry about going over a cliff because it has a mind of its own."

"Yeah, that's exactly the problem," he mutters.

"Not a horse guy, huh?" I say. I can feel a smile spreading across my face.

"No," he says with a scowl.

I've annoyed him again with my teasing. It makes me grin wider. I think I've found my new favourite hobby.

6

———

DALLAS

KATIE RIDES her horse right up to the farmhouse, loops its rein around a verandah post and strides up the porch steps.

She still has the lamb tucked inside her jacket. She kicks off her boots and walks straight inside the house.

I catch up with her in the front hallway, grabbing her wrist and pulling her to a stop. "What're you doing?" I say, my voice a low rasp.

She turns to look at me, her expression clearly asking what I'm on about.

"You can't just walk on in like you live here."

She rolls her eyes at me—for maybe the fiftieth time today—and turns away, heading back down the hallway. "I virtually do live here," she tosses over her shoulder. "It's like my second home." She pauses when she reaches the door to the kitchen and gives me a 'hurry up' gesture. "Come on, cowboy, this lamb isn't going to feed itself."

She has me there, so I follow her down the hall, hoping

Olivia or Violet aren't going to be weird about me just strolling into their house.

"Lady Sadie!" Katie announces as she spots my daughter sitting at the kitchen table surrounded by felt pens and pieces of paper. "Just the lady I needed to see."

"Hi, Katie," Sadie says, her voice soft and shy. Then she sees me. "Daddy!" She beams, then launches herself across the room into my arms.

"Hey, Sadie girl," I murmur into her hair as I squeeze her tight. She is the sole reason I do anything these days, so as irritating as Katie is, I will persevere with working with her, for Sadie.

Sadie has finally settled in here. She's happy. She's *so* excited to be starting school and she adores both Violet and Olivia. We're not going anywhere.

The only thing she's unhappy about is that I won't let her ride the horses, but she's going to have to come to terms with that, and at some point I'm going to have to deal with what happened this morning when Katie put Sadie on one. She didn't even ask permission. She wouldn't have asked Olivia, because she's fully aware of my boundary and has never once taken Sadie near a horse. Olivia wouldn't have said it was okay, so Katie clearly took it on herself.

From what I've learned of Katie so far, it tracks. Reckless, irritating, knows exactly how to push all my buttons even though she doesn't know me at all.

Sadie untangles her arms from around my neck and slides to the floor. In the time it's taken for me to say hello to Sadie, Katie has stripped off her jacket and is bundling the lamb into an old towel.

Violet is at the sink, already preparing a bottle of milk.

"Do you want to help me feed her?" Katie asks Sadie as she sits cross-legged on the floor, holding the lamb in her lap. The poor thing can barely hold its head up.

"Can I?" Sadie asks, wide-eyed.

"You sure can," I say, really hoping Katie knows what she's doing. She seems to. Aside from being a pain in the ass and relentlessly mocking me, she does seem to know about working on the farm. The basics at least.

"Here you go, Sadie," Violet says, handing over the bottle. Sadie carries it to where Katie is sitting, then watches with rapt attention as Katie tries to get the lamb to drink.

I stoop and pick up Katie's discarded jacket from where she dropped it on the floor, because apparently she couldn't take an extra second to hang it over a chair or something. I'm about to do exactly that, when I realise the lamb wasn't cleaned by its mother before it was abandoned, which means the inside of the jacket is sticky with afterbirth. I take it into the laundry and clean the worst of it off, hoping it'll at least be dried out enough for Katie to wear it for the rest of the day.

There's no way it's warm enough out there for the yellow tank top she has on now. There's also no way I can be around her when she's wearing the yellow tank top, because the amount of skin on show reminds me way too much of last night.

It reminds me of her stretched out across her bed, naked limbs tangled with mine and the contrast of the soft, delicate skin of her breasts, belly and thighs against my rough, calloused hands.

I can't believe my life right now. I throw caution to the wind *one time* and end up working with my one-night stand. The one who made me promise there'd be nothing past that single night. I wanted a repeat so badly, until I saw Katie standing in the arena this morning. Then, I wanted to go back in time and knock some sense into me.

The worst part of the universe's cruel prank is that it didn't even give me enough time between the one-night stand and seeing her again. So, when I see the exposed skin of her arms, all I can think about is the way I ran my hands down them, leaving goosebumps in my wake. Or when the low-cut neckline teases what's below, I have a vivid memory of the moment she pulled her sweater over her head last night, leaving her standing in front of me in killer jeans and an even more killer white lace bra.

I scrub harder at the jacket, trying to clean the memories from my mind. I cannot work with someone who I'm going to constantly have sexy flashbacks about, and because I have to work with her, I have to sort myself out.

By the time I return to the kitchen, with an almost spotlessly clean jacket, the lamb is finished feeding and is curled up in my daughter's lap.

"Look, Daddy," Sadie says, wonderstruck.

"Did she have a good feed?" I ask her, crouching down beside them and stroking first Sadie's head, then the lamb's.

Sadie nods. "She did. Her name is Porridge."

"Porridge?"

"Yes," she says, voice deadly serious. "Katie said I can help look after her, and any other ones that don't have mummies." She looks up at me with her big blue eyes. "Is that okay?" She adds in a whisper.

"Of course, I'm sure we're going to need extra help to look after them. Especially when they're this little because they need feeding lots and lots."

"I can do that," Sadie says, then leans back against the wall, cradling the lamb close to her.

I stand and watch them for a long moment. When I finally turn away it's to find Katie watching them too.

"What's your phone number?" She asks me, out of the blue.

"What?" I ask, caught off guard. She definitely said last night was a one off. Why would she need my number?

"I'll send you some pictures I took." She flashes her phone in my direction, a shot of Sadie and the lamb on the screen.

Oh. The type of thing I always forget to take photos of. I rattle off my number and a few moments later my phone is bleeping as a bunch of messages zing across the kitchen.

Violet feeds us an early lunch before we head back out to check the cattle. Katie finishes hers first and loads her dishes straight into the dishwasher. She's so comfortable in this house and around Violet, who keeps staring at Katie with a look of contentment on her face, like her long-lost child has returned home.

"I'll just clean the lamb goo off my jacket and I'm good to go," Katie says, grabbing the garment off the back of the chair where I'd put it.

"I've done it," I say. "Your jacket. Hopefully it's dry by now."

"Oh," Katie says, flipping it open and running her hand across the clean lining. "Thank you," she says, her voice quiet. "You didn't have to do that."

I shrug. "Seems like the least I could do. You let Sadie help you with the lamb."

"Of course I did." Her expression is puzzled, like she can't figure out what I'm getting at.

"Not everyone would," I say, then push back from the table. "Come on, this work isn't going to do itself."

"Not the actual tonne of it that you have to do, no it won't," Katie says, that sarcastic smirk back on her face.

I grit my teeth so I don't say something I'll regret to her, in front of my boss, and more importantly my daughter.

7

___

KATIE

BY THE TIME Dallas and I are finished with the day's work I'm hot, sweaty, filthy and *exhausted*. My top has gone crusty with lamb afterbirth and I cannot wait to have a scalding hot shower to wash the day's grime off. We just have one more job to do on our way back to the house.

I'm pretty sure I'm being tested. Maybe Dallas is hoping I won't come back tomorrow.

He's wrong. It doesn't matter how much my entire body hurts.

I'll be here, working my ass off to help Olivia.

Henry Austin, Olivia's dad, died suddenly four months ago. It was so shocking—so out-of-the-blue—that I still haven't processed it. He was fit and healthy, still in his prime.

His passing has left a massive hole in both the family, and the running of the farm. A hole Olivia is desperately trying to fill.

When finances became an issue in the city, coming back to

Wildflower Ridge made the most sense for me. I have a house to live in and a job I can rely on.

I didn't come back for Henry's funeral and I regret not being there for my best friend. I had my reasons, but I still have regrets.

I'm determined I'll never let her down again though, so regardless of what Dallas thinks of me, regardless of whatever shit jobs he gives me, I'm not going anywhere.

I don't know what Olivia told Dallas about me, but it can't have been much, which is unlike her. I can tell she's told him next to nothing about me because he picked tasks for today to gauge my competency and show me the property—obviously not realising I already know it like the back of my hand.

A little bit has changed over the years, but not very much. The only thing that's really new to me is the function venue which was once a barely standing old barn.

Now, it's fully refurbished and already has a full booking calendar for this coming summer.

I haven't seen it completed, only in its early stages of the renovation on my last visit back. The visit that caused me to make my now-broken vow.

We've been using the side-by-side this afternoon and I climb out of it as it rolls to a stop in front of the building.

Dallas heads for the toolbox on the back and while I should be finding out what we're doing here and help, all I can do is stare up at my best friend's dream come to life.

The barn is still rustic, showing its original nature, but it's also beautiful. Huge sliding doors seal off the inside that I've only seen in photos. I can imagine this place in the middle of summer, filled with people and fairy lights, joy and love.

A huge wooden sign is mounted above the doors. *Wildflower Ridge* is carved into it in a simple script font. It's almost an exact replica of the one hanging over the farm gate, which was a handmade gift from Henry to Violet on their wedding day.

Tears suddenly blur my eyes, right as Dallas stops beside me. He's probably here to hurry me up and scold me for lagging. But I don't care.

"I'm so proud of her."

"It's pretty amazing," he says, to my surprise. I was expecting a telling off. "She does an incredible job."

"It's always been her dream. When we were sixteen it was all she could talk about. She wanted to get married here herself, like her mum and dad did. We'd talk about it for hours. The flowers we'd choose, the dresses we'd wear, who we'd invite." I let out a bitter little laugh, then left my voice soften. "I can't believe she did all this, but then, it's Liv so *of course* she did it." I turn to Dallas and find him looking down at me, a funny look on his face. "What'd she tell you about me?"

A crease forms between his brows at my abrupt change of subject. "Not much to be honest. Just that someone was starting." He runs a hand through his hair. "It's not like her. Normally I'd get a full run down of experience and often I'd meet the person at the interview, which obviously you didn't have."

"It's not like her at all, you're right," I murmur, turning back to the building. I take a deep breath. "Are they doing okay? Liv and Violet? Are they okay?" I end on a whisper, terrified of his response.

Dallas is quiet for a moment and I appreciate that he's taking time to think about his answer instead of just throwing out the first thing that comes into his head. "I think," he says, voice soft and smooth, "they're okay. They're probably doing better than expected, considering."

Considering.

Considering the love of Violet's life dropped dead from an aneurysm right in front of her.

Considering Olivia got nearly the full responsibility of the farm thrust upon her in a matter of moments, instead of the gradual succession over years, like had been planned.

Considering I refused to come home when it mattered.

Despite all that, they're doing okay. I don't think Dallas would lie to me, especially not about this.

After working with him for a day I can see he's practical and down-to-earth. After seeing him with his daughter and the lamb, I also know he's a bit of a softie. I have photo evidence to prove it.

It makes me wonder how much of his cocky cowboy persona from last night was an act. Or maybe now we're co-workers I'm treated differently to how he acts around women he wants to take to bed.

It's easier to think about Dallas's behaviour than me letting Olivia down, but as I stare up at the sign all I feel is heartbreak and regret.

I clear my throat, sniff and swipe at a tear that's spilled over, hoping Dallas thinks I'm simply shooing away a bug. "Righto, cowboy, what's left to do?" I hope he can't hear the waver in my voice.

IT DOESN'T TAKE LONG to finish the job, repairing some of the railing fence that leads up the driveway, and head back to the farmhouse.

I climb out of the side-by-side. "Guess I'll see ya tomorrow, cowboy," I say over my shoulder as I head for my car to grab the bag of spare clothes I'd brought with me.

Dallas rolls his eyes and it makes me grin.

I kick my boots off at the front door and am barely inside before Olivia accosts me. "Bathroom's all yours. I've just got to catch up with Dallas for a minute, then I'll come find you."

"Sure thing," I say, then head straight up the stairs, turning into the massive bathroom at the top. I love this room. It's all white tile, timber and a massive bath. I don't know what Violet uses in here, but it always smells incredible too.

I stare longingly at the deep bathtub. Another time. Not my first night back.

I twist the shower handles to allow the water to heat, then strip, dumping my clothes in a filthy pile.

I have a quick shower, scouring off the day's sweat and grime and am just pulling on the dress I packed to wear for dinner when the door slams open.

"Geez, Liv! Give a girl some warning." I gasp in shock.

"You put Sadie on a *horse*?" She says horse like it was some monstrous beast, not Scout.

"Just on Scout, for a walk around the arena," I say with a shrug, wiping steam off the mirror so I can attempt to do something my hair.

Olivia closes the door behind her. "Sadie doesn't ride," she says, her voice low.

"Why not? She's plenty old enough to be learning."

"She just doesn't ride, okay?"

"Okay, sorry," I say, holding up my hands, but not really feeling all that sorry. That kid *loved* her five minute ride on Scout. "I didn't know it was a problem. Dallas didn't say anything." I narrow my eyes. "He said something to you, didn't he? Told on me to the boss?" Ugh, this is so typical of him.

"No, he didn't," Olivia says, leaning against the bath and running her fingers through the end of her ponytail. "Sadie told us. Luckily Dallas is okay with it—this time. But please, not again. We need him."

"I won't. I didn't realise it was a thing. But, Liv, she loved it. She's old enough to ride. It doesn't make sense not to let her when she has the opportunity right in front of her."

"Yeah, but it's not my call. If Dallas wants her to ride, one of us will happily teach her, but he doesn't want her too, and as her dad, that's his call."

"Fine," I say, but I still think it's ridiculous. "You're not going to make me apologise to him are you?"

"No," she says with a smile. "I've done it on your behalf this time." Her expression shifts. "Sorry I couldn't introduce you properly, or see you at all since you've got back."

"It's okay, Liv. I understand." I reach out for her and she steps into my arms, leaning her weight onto me.

"I'm so exhausted," she says, her voice a soft whisper in my ear.

"I know, Livvie. But you've got the dream team now. Me and that cowboy will have everything sorted in no time."

She pulls back from our hug and raises her eyebrows at me. "Cowboy?"

"Yup."

"You hate cowboys."

"Yup."

"Oh, god, what have I done?" She groans and drops her head back onto my shoulder. "Be nice to him," she mutters.

"I'm always nice."

I can almost feel her roll her eyes at me. "You are not." Her voice softens. "I need him, Katie."

"Don't worry, Liv. I know exactly how much he can handle."

8

DALLAS

I RACE HOME, have the fastest shower of my life, throw on jeans and a clean shirt and head back to the main farm house in time for dinner.

Sadie and I live in the farm cottage across the paddock from the main house. It's tiny, has draughty windows and I'm convinced it's haunted, but it's the closest thing we've had to a stable home in a long time.

I step through the front door of the main house right as Katie and Olivia are descending the stairs. Olivia's wearing the same jeans, floaty pink blouse and cardigan as when I left, but Katie is like a whole different person.

Her filthy jeans and top are gone and she's wearing a pastel blue dress with wide straps, a square neckline and a full skirt with a cardigan pulled on over it.

It was easier to forget about last night while we were toiling away in the dirt, her dressed like she's spent her life on the farm, but wearing this, it's a solid reminder of the girl I went home with last night. It stops me in my tracks.

Olivia gives me a smile as she walks past and heads for the kitchen, but Katie stops on the last step, so she's closer to my height.

"What are you doing here?" she asks.

I swallow, not sure if she's going to like my answer. "Violet invited us to stay for dinner."

"Oh, yeah, that makes sense. Vi was always big on having lots of people for dinner."

"Sadie helped cook, so she really wanted to stay. I think she might also want to give you an update on Porridge."

Katie grins at that. "That lamb's going to be smothered isn't it? Like, with love."

"Most likely, yes. You might be Sadie's hero now, since you saved that lamb."

"All in a day's work," she says with a grin, then turns away and leaves me standing there staring after her.

She called me cocky, but I think that word suits her better. It looks good on her though, almost as good as that dress.

I step into the kitchen behind Katie. Sadie is setting the table, but she glances up as we come through the door.

"Katie," she says. "I fed Porridge again!" Then her gaze lands on me. "Hey Daddy, are you clean now?"

"I sure am. Do I get my hug now?"

"Yes!" She drops a handful of forks on the table and bounds across the room. I scoop her up into my arms and hold her tight. It's the best feeling in the world.

Sadie kisses my cheek, then wriggles free of my hold and

slides back to the ground. "You should go say hello to Porridge," she says.

DINNER IS DELICIOUS, as it always is when Violet invites us to stay.

Most of the time Sadie and I eat at our place, but sometimes Violet insists. Tonight, with Katie's arrival, they're treating it like a special occasion and I'm not sure if we should have stayed or not.

But when Sadie brings out the cake she helped Violet make, with the proudest grin on her face, I knew I couldn't have deprived her of this moment. Her smile gets even wider when Katie gushes over how gorgeous the cake is, and how delicious it is. Sadie hangs on her every word and it makes something curl in my chest.

I see Sadie with Violet and Olivia all the time, and they're just as caring and generous as Katie is with her.

But, I also know they aren't going anywhere. They're reliable and trustworthy and aren't going to break my daughter's heart. I can't see Katie in the same light yet. It must be something about last night that gives me the feeling she's going to let us all down.

It's not like she was here when Henry passed away, leaving her best friend overwhelmed and grieving. So, as good as she is with my daughter, I can't trust her not to be like the completely self-involved princess I met last night. It doesn't matter how sexy someone is if you can't rely on them.

I tune back into the conversation, refusing to dwell on those thoughts any further, because thinking about Katie's level of sexiness while sitting across the dinner table from her is a terrible idea. I shift in my chair, hoping to ease the pressure in my pants, but it doesn't help much.

"When did you meet Scout?" Sadie asks Katie, gazing up at her in wonder.

"Scout came here about the same time I did," Katie replies. "Her last owner hadn't been very nice to her, so Olivia's dad brought her here."

"Katie looked after her," Olivia adds. "They've been each other's favourites ever since."

Katie shrugs and smiles at her friend. "She helped me through some stuff."

Olivia leans over and drapes her arm around Katie's shoulder, squeezing tight while Katie leans into her for a moment.

"When did you come here?" I asked, surprising myself by joining the conversation.

"When I was sixteen," Katie replies. "My mum had just died and I came to live with my grandma, who was friends with Violet."

"Then she shook up the entire town and left us behind to go take on the world," Olivia says, pride evident on her features.

Katie snorts. "Barely."

"I don't have a mummy either," Sadie announces to the table and a hushed silence drops over us in an instant. "But she's not dead." She turns to me. "Is she?"

My heart might shatter right there and then. My chest

aches. I'm never sure how much Sadie remembers of her mother, or what happened to make me a single father.

"No, she's not dead," I say quietly, willing my voice to remain steady.

I don't know what else to say. I can't say her mum is coming back because it's not something that I even know. And if she did show up again, I have no idea what I'd say to her, or if I'd let her anywhere near Sadie.

Everyone in the room is silent, waiting for me to handle this incredibly awkward moment, but my mind is blank, my heart twisting painfully inside my chest and I don't know how to move back to safer topics.

My eyes lock on Katie across the table and she must sense my desperation because she turns to Sadie.

"Will you help me give Porridge her next bottle?"

I blow out a breath as Sadie excitedly agrees and bounds away from the table. I'm about to open my mouth and remind her to clear her plate when Katie continues. "Hey, hey, Lady Sadie, don't forget your dishes." She says it with a big smile and Sadie happily skips back to the table and clears her plate, coming back for Katie's, then mine.

"Will you come too, Daddy?" Sadie asks, slipping her hand into mine.

"Of course," I say, following along as she leads me and Katie into the laundry room where the lamb is curled up in a cardboard box. She wobbles to her feet when she sees us and emits the tiniest bleat.

Katie prepares the bottle, and to my surprise slides down to sit on the floor, gorgeous dress and all. Sadie plonks down too and pats the floor indicating where I should sit. I fold my legs and sit cross-legged between them.

I realise my mistake the instant my ass hits the floor and I feel the heat of Katie's arm through my shirt.

She reaches forward and scoops the lamb out of its box. I can't believe she's getting lamb all over this dress. The only thing that should be all over that dress are my hands. I blink at the thought, because woah. Co-worker. That was so inappropriate, but I can't help myself. There's a reason I noticed her last night, there's a reason I went home with her and had potentially the greatest night of my life. And that dress ... that dress keeps reminding me of all those reasons. Reasons that cannot matter now.

Because we work together, and because it breaks her very clearly defined rules. I am definitely not brave enough to find out what she'd do if I broke those rules.

But still, she doesn't need to be ruining another outfit because of this lamb.

I'm about to tell her so when she places the lamb in my lap. "Your turn," she says with a challenging grin, a flash of that bratty princess attitude I encountered last night. The one that irritates the fuck out of me ... and makes my blood heat in all the right—or wrong—ways.

9

KATIE

THIS MORNING, Dallas left me to check the sheep and cattle solo.

I can tell it was a big step for him, trusting me with something on my second week on the job.

I tried *really hard* not to roll my eyes when he quizzed me for several long minutes about my capability to do a job I was doing solo when I was seventeen. As if he hasn't seen me capably handling this job every day since we met.

No lamb rescues today but a Hereford cow needed a little assistance with calving. I could tell she wasn't impressed by my presence, but she let me help her without too much stress, for which I'm grateful.

I'm unsaddling Scout when Dallas finds me again.

"All good out there?" he asks, leaning against the stable wall.

"Yep," I say, then give him a run down of the calving. Have to admit, I'm looking forward to his reaction. I'm feeling more than a little smug about it.

"You did *what?*" he asks, voice rising on the final word.

Scout tosses her head. "Woah, chill out," I say to Dallas, while running a soothing hand down Scout's face. This was not the reaction I was expecting and I want to snap at him, but that'll only upset the horse more. "I helped a heifer with her calving. Mother and baby are fine. I'll keep an eye on them in the next few days, but there shouldn't be any issues."

"Uh, no I'm not going to chill out. What were you thinking?"

"That a cow needed help and I was there to give it to her?"

"And what if she hadn't appreciated your help?" He swipes the cap off his head and roughly runs his hand through his hair. I absolutely do not notice how hot he looks when he does that, or remember my own fingers tangled in the thick, sandy-coloured strands. Him touching his hair is always the biggest reminder of what we did and I have to fight back the memories again. Now is not the time to be thinking about his hair. "What if you'd been hurt? You'd still be lying out there in that paddock."

"But I'm not. I'm fine. Not a scratch on me."

Dallas takes a deep breath and exhales slowly. "You cannot do shit like this. Trying to calve a cow, alone."

"It's fine. I'm fine." I do snap this time. I step away from Scout, closer to Dallas. His height pisses me off because I'd really like to be glaring down at him in this moment.

"It only takes one tiny moment for that to be completely different, princess. One tiny moment and you could have been killed."

My blood goes hot in an instant when he calls me princess. I was wrong about the hair. The word princess is the biggest trigger for me remembering that night. I roll my eyes, hoping the heat I'm feeling inside isn't evident on my face. "I'm *fine*."

"This time, maybe," he says, not backing down as I stalk closer. "Next time, maybe not. You can't do reckless shit like that. What if you got hurt?" His voice drops with the final five words and there's something in his eyes that pulls me up short. Something that looks a lot like fear.

"I wasn't reckless," I say, my voice lowering. "I do know when I need help. This wasn't one of those times. If I had been hurt—*if* I was—you knew where I was. You would have come to find me."

Dallas nods, somewhat reluctantly. "Yeah," he says, his voice raspy and god, if it isn't the sexiest thing I've ever heard. One simple word. It could be that he's agreeing with me, but I think mostly it's him in general. I startle when fingertips brush against my neck, just below my ear. It sends a shiver, and some-thing else, straight through me. "I couldn't stand it," he says in that same low, raspy voice.

My breath catches.

This is not how things are supposed to go.

I was supposed to share one simple night with this hot as hell guy, then never see him again, or, worst case scenario, see him in passing on the odd occasion I go into town.

I was not supposed to see him every day. I was not supposed to stand a hands-width away from him in the stables with his fingers trailing down my throat. "You?" I whisper, because I'm fucked already so why not make this worse than it already is?

He blinks, clears his throat, steps away and drops his hand.

"Me ... Olivia, Violet, Sadie." His voice returns to its normal level and reality hits like a brick to the face.

I spin around to face Scout. "I'll be careful," I say, focusing on detangling the mare's mane.

"Good," Dallas says. "Thank you. Are you free now?" he asks, as though he doesn't know he sets my work for me.

"Um, yes. You haven't given me anything else to do yet."

"Right, yeah, okay. I'm going into town to grab some stuff. I need you to come with me."

"You don't have anything that needs doing here?" I ask, turning back to him. I really don't want to go into town. Like, I *really*, really don't. I may love Wildflower Ridge, but that does not mean I love the town it's a part of.

I left Kauri Creek the last time for a reason. A reason that I can guarantee hasn't magically evaporated in the intervening years.

"We need to pick up the farm ute, so I really need you to come with me," Dallas says, running a hand through his hair, then sliding the cap back into place. Covering that hair is probably for the best.

Working with Dallas is fine. It's nothing. It's whatever. But every so often, there's a flash of that first night that almost makes me dizzy with longing.

My first day working here, when I came down the stairs and found him in the front doorway staring up at me was one of those moments. Wearing dark jeans, a dark shirt and smelling like he did at the bar, I almost dragged him straight up the stairs for a repeat. I'm sure it was the smell. It had lingered in my house for days, even after I'd washed my sheets.

Then, there was two minutes ago, right here.

I sigh. "Fine. I'll be five more minutes with Scout. I'll meet you at the house?"

"You know, I'm not asking you to pull out your own teeth or anything. It's the easiest job ever. I figured you'd appreciate a little break from all the physical stuff. It must be a bit of an adjustment for you."

And the arrogant bastard comes back out and reminds me why I set my very clear rules around sleeping with him. Because cocky cowboys can't be trusted.

"It's fine, cowboy. Give me five minutes to finish here."

He nods and strides away without another word, leaving me to finish grooming my horse, muttering under my breath.

DALLAS PULLS into a parking space outside the farm supply store.

"This isn't the mechanic," I say.

"It's not, no," he replies.

"Or the tyre place. Where exactly are we picking the ute up from?"

He snickers and it makes me want to punch him. I'm still irritated by what he said back in the stable, and more than a little thrown by what happened during the heated conversation.

But right now, mostly irritated that he implied I can't handle the work. That I'm just a prissy city girl. He's wrong, but he's also right in that I really could do with a break from some of the physical work. My ass and legs are aching from spending time in the saddle again and my hands are already blistering from manual labour. I know they'll harden up soon enough, but for now, it's not much fun, and sitting in a vehicle for a drive to town is a nice break. Apart from the town part, obviously.

"It's at the mechanic's," he says, exasperated. "But we need some stuff here too. We'll only be five minutes, then we're grabbing lunch."

"Whatever," I grumble like a petulant teenager, but climb out of his ute when he gestures for me to go with him.

Dallas quickly falls into conversation with the guy at the counter, ordering feed and minerals for the animals and probably some fence posts or something equally as exciting. I wander the aisles and quickly find myself in the horse supplies section. The smell of fresh leather bridles centres me and I run my fingers over the stitching in a stunning saddle. It's far too nice to be sold in this hell-hole town.

"Holy shit," a voice says and I freeze. I know that voice. It's the same one that called out to Dallas in the pub. The one that turned me reckless. "Look who came crawling back to town."

I turn slowly, hoping that I'm wrong, hoping that this isn't the person I think it is. The person I *know* it is.

"Max Sheridan," I say. "A fucking delight, as usual."

"Come back to fuck everything up again?" he asks, crossing his arms across his chest and glaring down at me. God, those eyes. They're way too familiar. The memories assault me.

I spin on my heel and stride for the front counter, where Dallas is still engaged in conversation with the store person. Yep, fenceposts.

"Time to go," I say.

"Hang on, I'm not done yet."

"Don't care," I say. "I'm out." I'm about to head for the door when Dallas reaches out and grabs hold of my sleeve.

"Hold up," he says, giving me a puzzled look.

"Oh, I see," Max's voice follows me. "Of course. I should have known. You've come crawling back to your bestie. I noticed you weren't here when she needed you, but that's not surprising, is it?" Max appears beside us. He's got his typical smug smirk on his face. "You probably don't know this yet," he says to Dallas, "but you've got to watch out for this one. If you're not careful she'll screw you up and fuck you over all in one go. Ain't that right, darlin'?"

"Fuck off, Max," I say, a snarl in my voice. I turn to Dallas who's standing there, dumbstruck, his gaze bouncing between me and Max. "I'll walk down and get the ute. See you back at the Ridge."

Then I turn and stride from the building, definitely preferring to walk to the other side of town than be near Max Sheridan for one second longer.

10

DALLAS

I HAVE no idea what just happened.

Katie told Max to fuck off, then stormed out of the building.

I don't know the guy well, but he's not *that* bad is he? Obviously they have some kind of history.

Maybe it's something that goes back to their teen years.

Maybe they dated in high school.

Though their interaction seems like it was something bigger than a high school romance. Maybe there was real heartbreak on one or both sides.

It does something weird in my stomach when I think of Katie having a romance with someone else, even a hypothetical one that happened years ago. I've really got to keep a lid on that shit. Much like I've got to keep a lid on the shit that happened earlier in the stables.

I still don't know what the fuck I was thinking. Worrying about her being hurt is one thing. Reacting like an overprotective asshole that thinks she can't handle herself—when she's proven time and time again that she can—is a whole other level.

And touching her …

That was so far beyond every line there is. The ones she drew around the night we spent together and the ones set by the law.

She could go straight to Olivia and get me fired on the spot. And rightly so. I need to deal with that, apologise to her. It might save my job, even though I don't deserve it.

God, what would happen to Sadie if I get fired for harassment? I wouldn't be able to find another job without a reference from Olivia.

Though, Katie doesn't strike me as the kind of person who wouldn't handle it herself. She's shown me repeatedly she can handle herself *and* my bullshit. I like that about her.

As much as the thought of Katie reporting that moment stresses me out, a tiny, optimistic part of my brain recalls the moment she almost leaned into the touch, when she asked what I meant by me saying I couldn't handle her getting hurt.

I *really* liked the look in her eye then and I have to extinguish the spark of hope that flares every time I think of those brief seconds.

I watch Katie go, then turn to Max, who's standing there with his hands in his pockets, smirking like a class-A asshole.

"What the hell was that about?" I manage to say, trying to keep my voice casual and not like I want to throttle him for being an ass and scaring her off.

He pats me on the shoulder. "Like I said, watch out for that one. She's a pain in the ass, total trouble maker. Screws up everything and then bails, leaving total destruction in her wake." What he's saying should sound like a joke, but he's got a dark look in his eye that makes me think he's deadly serious about this. "Olivia will never turn her away, so I guess she's come back crying victim again. Just be careful, especially with Sadie. You don't want her getting hurt."

~

BY THE TIME I get back to the farm, Katie has returned the ute, but she's nowhere in sight. Violet tells me she's at the function venue when I call into the main house to say hello to Sadie and drop off the lunch I bought in town for them.

I skid my motorbike to a stop outside the refurbished barn and stride inside.

I've been simmering on what Max said the whole way home, going around and around in circles. His warning about watching out for Katie and protecting Sadie from her, doesn't sit right, not after seeing Katie interact with Sadie, Olivia and Violet over the past two weeks. How she interacts with me is another story, because I'm pretty sure the night we met, I leaned into a persona she actually can't stand, and now I've been permanently branded with that.

Occasionally the memory of brushing my fingers against her skin in the barn earlier pops up. It pays not to think about it, but the feel of her skin isn't so easy to ignore. The memory of it makes me simmer in a whole different way.

What the fuck was I thinking?

I hadn't been. That's the whole problem.

I was freaking out that she could have gotten seriously hurt, and then she got all feisty and up in my space. I couldn't resist it.

Then I really stuck my foot in it when I said I wouldn't be able to bear her being hurt. She questioned me with a mixture of scepticism and something I'm refusing to believe was hope, but looked a lot like it, in her face.

It was seeing that emotion that snapped me out of it. Because Katie isn't hoping for more. She's probably hoping I fall into a hole and she never has to see me again.

She definitely isn't hoping for me to touch her, or care about her, or want her more than I've ever wanted anything.

She doesn't need to hope for that anyway. Me wanting her more than anything I've ever wanted in my life is a foregone conclusion.

Katie's inside the function centre building, unstacking and arranging chairs and tables. She barely glances up as I approach.

"Want to tell me what the hell happened in town?" I ask. I don't mean for it to come out as harsh as it does, but once the words are out, it's too late. I should be trying to apologise to her, not having another go at her.

"Not really," she says, then reaches for another chair.

I grab hold of it, stopping her from sliding it into its correct position. I take a breath and force my voice to soften. "Why's he warning me to watch out for you, especially when it comes to Sadie?"

"That fucking *bastard*," she mutters under her breath. Then to me she says, "It's nothing you need to worry about."

"When it comes to Sadie, all I do is worry. So please tell me what happened?"

She turns on me, eyes blazing. "All you need to be concerned about, *cowboy*," she says, slinging the nickname like a slur, "is how well I do my job. You don't need to know a single thing about my personal life."

The way she speaks to me, with that fire in her voice, takes me straight back to night one. "Oh, come on, princess, what'd he do? Break your heart? Or did you break his?" I can't help it, but I love the way she flares up when I call her princess. It's so dumb, and it's one hundred percent a dick move, but when her eyes flash and she takes a deep breath, standing taller with her hands fisting on her hips, it's such a turn on.

"Neither, you asshole. If you must know, I dated his brother," she snaps.

"His brother?" I didn't know Max had a brother. A younger sister, yes, but I've never heard mention of a brother.

Katie nods, face grim and eyes dark. "His twin."

Woah, okay. I try and put pieces of the puzzle together, but I'm missing too many, and Katie is glaring at me like she'd like to kill me with her eyes.

"I didn't know he had a brother, let alone a twin," I say eventually, hoping she'll indulge me with an explanation.

Multiple emotions flicker across her face. Pain, confusion, regret and sadness, something like wistfulness. "I guess he doesn't anymore. He's dead."

11

————

KATIE

I HATE Max Sheridan more than anyone else on this earth.

The feeling is mutual so I don't even feel bad about it.

I don't know what caused it, but when I moved to Kauri Creek he took an instant dislike to me.

Him and Olivia being friends before my arrival and no longer friends after it probably didn't endear him to me.

Neither did me dating his brother.

Max and Toby were alike in so many ways. Being identical twins they had the same dark hair and eyes, but Max has a more severe look to him. Or maybe it's just his expression hardening every time he looks my way.

They were both gorgeous and charming, but Max leaned towards arrogant and cocky where as Toby was gentler, more subtle.

It was that subtlety that ruined me in the end. Maybe if he'd been more like Max the truth wouldn't have hit me so hard. The truth I didn't learn until the day he was killed in a car accident.

I hate Toby now too, as much as I loved him, which is an interesting feeling to have.

But right now, my rage is directed firmly at Max. For the way he spoke to me, for what he said to Dallas, for making me remember Toby.

I stormed out of the function room moments after shocking Dallas into silence with the reveal that my ex is my ex because he's no longer alive. I behaved like a bratty kid, spinning on my heel and stomping off, slamming the back door behind me.

Dallas, to his credit, didn't follow me.

A huge relief since I don't want him to see me like this, my face red and blotchy and unstoppable tears spilling down my cheeks.

I've done a lot of crying over Toby and our relationship. Tears of grief and pain, tears of anger and hatred. But none of them have hit quite as hard as these ones.

Being back at Wildflower Ridge, the place where it all started, has brought all the memories rushing back.

Coming face-to-face with Max and being reminded of how much he hates me was something I thought I was prepared for, but I don't think I could have ever been fully ready for that moment, for seeing the anger and grief in his own expression.

He blames me for taking his brother and best friend away from him. I can understand that. But he doesn't know the full story and I don't think either of us will ever be in a place where we can have that conversation.

I haven't been paying attention to where I'm walking, just knowing I need to get as far away from Dallas as possible right now, but when I reach the lake I manage to release a full breath.

It's a bit fancier than the last time I was here. Obviously they've done some work to it so it can be used for wedding ceremonies and photo locations. I skirt around the gazebo on the water's edge and slip into the shade of a massive Totara tree. The bark is rough under my fingertips as I trail them across the trunk. I glance up into the branches and falter.

Not this tree. This is the tree in which Toby and I hid during a game of spotlight. He was already in the tree when I started climbing it, unaware of his presence. When I realised he was there I tried to climb down again, but he grabbed my hand. Electric shocks had zoomed up my arm as he whispered, "stay."

Until that point I assumed he disliked me as much as Max did, but after that night ... I knew different.

I continue around the lake until I find a different tree with a solid trunk. I slide down and sit with my back against the bark, pulling my knees up to my chest.

In the peaceful quiet, I release the rest of my tears.

I HAVE no idea how much time has passed when someone sits down beside me. Since my tears ran out I've sat here and stared into nothingness, my emotions exhausted and numb.

At first I worry Dallas has followed me, but this person isn't big enough to be him, and when their arm brushes against my own it's a soft warmth, not the blazing heat I've come to expect from Dallas's touch.

Olivia tilts her head and rests it on my shoulder, not saying a word, but being there for me when I'm ready to speak.

"I shouldn't have come back," I whisper eventually, my voice scratchy and hoarse.

"I'm happy you're here," she says back, her voice soft, the love in it evident. Love for me. Love I don't deserve.

"I'm so sorry, Liv." My voice cracks. "I ruin everything."

"Shush," she scolds. "You do not. Max is a jerk."

"How do you know about Max?"

"Dallas told me. He was worried about you. Said you saw Max in town and that you were upset, but he didn't think you'd appreciate his presence right now."

I snort. "He's right about that." I sigh and press my eyes into my knees. "Max told him to watch out for me. Told him he needs to protect Sadie from me." My voice breaks properly this time and I'm sobbing again.

Olivia hisses through her teeth. "I'm going to kill that bastard," she declares. "That *fucking asshole!*" She takes a deep breath and refocuses with a shake of her head. "He's wrong, okay? You know that, don't you?"

I shrug helplessly. "I can't stay here, Livvie, not with him here."

"Katie," she says, her voice serious. She takes my face in her hands and forces me to look her in the eye. "We do *not* let Max *fucking-bastard* Sheridan dictate what we do. Do we?"

I shrug again but Olivia stares me down until I admit defeat. "No, we do not let Max *fucking-bastard* Sheridan dictate what we do."

"Good," she says, releasing my face after giving my cheek a gentle pat. "Why did you come home?"

"Because you needed my help," I say, pulling out my line.

She scoffs. "Yeah, right. I know you love me, but you know we'd cope even if you weren't here. That's not saying I'm not happy you are here, but I know that isn't your real reason."

I sigh. I knew I couldn't keep this under wraps for long, not with Olivia anyway. "I lost my job and ran out of money. I had nowhere else to go. Grandma's house was my only option, at least until I'm allowed to sell it. Renting it was helpful, but it doesn't bring in the kind of money I need to live in the city."

"You lost your job?" She's incredulous. I should have also known that I couldn't slip that one past her.

"I filed a complaint that a manager was harassing a girl in my department."

"You know they can't fire you for that right?"

"Yeah, they didn't fire me. They conveniently 'restructured' and my position was 'no longer viable'."

"Fucking bastards," she mutters.

"I know, but there was nothing I could do. I needed a job and I needed somewhere to live. This was my only option."

"But you don't want to stay?" She looks disappointed.

"I want to stay, but only for Wildflower Ridge. I can't stay, because of Kauri Creek. You know that, Livvie. This is a short-term fix, for both of us."

"I know, I just wish you could stay. This place is your home. You could be happy here."

I wish it were true. I really do. But this place isn't my home, not anymore, and I'm not sure I'm capable of being happy anywhere. I don't answer her, just lean my head against hers as we sit and stare out at the sunlight dappling the water of the lake.

Her phone buzzes and she pulls it out of her pocket, checking her messages.

"Everything okay?" I ask.

"Yeah, it's just Dallas checking in. Making sure you're okay."

"Dallas?" I ask, my voice sceptical.

"Yeah," she says, smiling down at her phone as she taps out her reply.

"I feel like we know different versions of the same man."

She looks up then, confused. "What do you mean?"

I shake my head. "I can't even explain it. Everyone seems to think he's God's gift to man, but none of you are seeing that he thinks that too, about himself. He's so arrogant and frustrating and ... irritating."

"You're right. You're seeing a totally different side to him. Arrogant is not a word I'd *ever* use to describe him. He's totally down to earth, cares about nothing except doing a good job and looking after Sadie. He's great at his job and an even better dad." She's not looking at me as she speaks, but out across the water, a funny smile on her face.

"Liv," I say, not sure I want to ask the question I'm about to, but I have to know. "Are you into Dallas?"

She blinks—once, twice, three times—and turns to face me. "No," she says, but I'm not sure it's the actual truth or she's in denial. "He's a great guy and an excellent farm manager and I absolutely am not interested in him in any form other than professionally."

"Sounds like you're protesting a little much," I say, teasing. But underneath I'm panicking.

I haven't told her about my one-night stand with a random stranger who turned out to be my boss. I haven't told her about it at all, let alone that the guy was Dallas. If she's into him, I'm going to have to come clean, but that could mess everything up for them before they even have the chance to start something.

"It's okay, Katie," Olivia says, standing and reaching out to take my hand. I let her pull me to my feet. "I promise I'm not into him."

"Why are you promising me?"

She shrugs. "I don't want you thinking I'm into him and it getting in your way."

"In my way?" I splutter. What the hell is she talking about? Does she *know*? Oh, my god. If he *told* her, I'm going to throttle him.

She gives me a coy smile and turns away, making her way back around the edge of the lake, leaving me standing, dumbstruck under a tree.

"All I'm saying," she calls back over her shoulder, "is maybe there's a reason you find him so ... *irritating*." She giggles and sprints away as I chase after her.

"No, no, no, no," I say when I catch up to her, grabbing her around the waist. "Absolutely fucking not."

She pinches my cheek. "Who's protesting too much now?"

Ah, shit.

12

DALLAS

I'M PACING.

Which is weird, because I should not be this concerned about a woman that clearly hates me.

But Katie dropped the bombshell about her ex—Max's twin—dying, then ran from the building. I tried to follow her once my brain caught up with the situation, but she'd already disappeared.

Then I realised she probably wouldn't want me to find her anyway, so I called Olivia.

It was the weirdest conversation of my life, but I couldn't leave Katie upset like that. If she's mad at me for telling Olivia then I'll deal with that later. It's not like she could hate me more than she already does.

I'm at the barn, waiting for Flynn, one of the farm hands, to arrive with a new horse. He's been away for a couple of weeks visiting friends up north and Olivia arranged for him to pick up the horse on his way back to the farm. We weren't expecting him back for another two days, but I'm glad his arrival is providing a distraction from the rest of today.

Flynn and Olivia go way back, having known each other most of their lives like everyone else who's grown up in this town. From the stories I've heard, their parents were best friends.

Flynn's been working here longer than I have. From what I've gathered he started here full-time right after he left school, and was working here during holidays and weekends before then.

I can't understand why he didn't get the manager job I ended up with.

Flynn is hardworking and motivated and knows this farm inside out. But for some reason Henry wanted someone older, more experienced. I never had the chance to ask him why Flynn wasn't the perfect choice for the job. It can't just be his age, because Olivia is now running this place and she's the same age as Flynn.

When I called Olivia, she asked me to come down to the barn and meet him while she went searching for Katie.

I wish I'd just found Katie myself and faced her wrath because this waiting is giving me too much time to think.

I'm pacing back and forth on the gravel beside the arena. I'm not sure why I need to be here. Flynn is perfectly capable. I'm sure he can unload a horse and put it in the paddock without too much drama.

His ute comes over the brow of the hill, pulling the horse float. He pulls up beside me. "Hey, Dallas," he grins. "Didn't expect to see you here."

I grunt. "Olivia had something come up," I mutter.

He grins at me, the cheeky little shit. He knows how much I hate horses. Well, it's not actually that I hate them. I think they're amazing animals. But they're also terrifying and I cannot get past that detail to actually go near them anymore.

"Well, I don't think you'll have to get to close to this one," Flynn says. "But, can you open up that yard gate? I'll back right up to it."

I raise an eyebrow, but do as he asked. We usually just unload horses in the middle of the driveway, where he's currently parked.

Well, I don't, but other people do.

Flynn backs the float right up to the gate, so there's barely a space between the float and the gateposts. When he climbs out he joins me at the gate. "She's not tied up in there, and I'd say she's going to be pretty keen to get out of there. So we'll drop the ramp and when I open the bar, stay right out of her way."

"What the hell kind of horse is this?" I ask, anxiety creeping into my muscles.

"One that's not had a very good time of it," Flynn says, his normally smiling face turning grim. "It's not her fault though, and Olivia will turn her around."

I nod and we lower the ramp of the float, then I move well out of the way as Flynn prepares to open the bar that contains the horse in the float, so she can't barrel out while the ramp is being dropped and squash someone.

"That's a good girl," Flynn murmurs in his soothing horse voice. All horse people seem to have one. I haven't found mine yet, but I suspect it's not far off the one I use when Sadie's upset.

Flynn releases the bar and the horse shoots backwards, rattling down the ramp until her hooves hit dirt. She spins, kicking out her back legs as she charges around the yard, keeping her distance from us.

She's a sorry looking creature, with a light-coloured, matted mane and tail, a dull brown coat sprinkled with white hair, and ribs sticking out. Even I can tell her feet need a trim and she has a look in her eye that's far more terrified than angry.

Flynn and I lift the ramp again and I pull the ute forward while he closes the gate. By the time I'm out of the ute, he's standing on the fence looking down at the horse.

"She's going to be a beauty," he says, grinning at me again as I climb up beside him. "All that white hair mixed in with the chestnut makes her a strawberry roan. I don't think I've seen one before, but I can imagine how gorgeous she'll be once she's all cleaned up."

I look at the mare sceptically. "Yeah, sure," I say, hoping I don't sound as doubtful as I feel.

I don't know what Olivia is thinking, bringing another horse here, especially one that clearly needs this much work. She has no time to work with it, neither does Flynn and no one else has much affinity with horses, especially not me.

Then I remember Katie and her confident way in the saddle. I know who this horse is for, and I suspect I know why it's arrived now too. It's another thing to keep Katie here, like Olivia is worried she'll leave.

I think about that myself. I can't figure out why she's here. She clearly hates the town. I'm not sure even her evident love for Olivia and Wildflower Ridge can be enough to counteract

Max Sheridan's attitude. I wonder if other people around here have the same reaction to her.

I realise I'm standing next to someone who probably has all the details right now. I clear my throat and Flynn looks up at me.

"This horse is for Katie, isn't it?"

I didn't know it was possible for Flynn's face to smile bigger, but it does as soon as I mention Katie.

He nods. "I can't wait to see her," he says. "It's been way too long."

"She had an ... ah ... encounter with Max Sheridan today," I say.

Flynn's grin disappears and he visibly flinches. "Oof," he says. "Did she punch him in the face?"

"No."

Flynn looks disappointed.

"But she did tell him to fuck off," I add.

His expression immediately shifts back to his usual grin. "Atta girl," he says.

"I thought you were friends with Max?"

He shrugs. "Look, living in a town like this, you have to suck it up and just get along sometimes. But it's never really sat right with me the way Max treated Katie. He's never liked her, and no one's ever been able to figure out why." He pauses and rubs his jaw, thinking. "I don't know. But the last time she was back, he was a complete asshole to her."

"What about other people in town? Are they the same?"

"Some," he says. He looks like he's about to say more when

Olivia's ute crests the hill. It pulls to a stop beside Flynn's. Olivia and Katie climb out.

"Katie!" Flynn jumps off the fence and rushes towards her.

I study her face, while hanging well back. It's a bit pale and her eyes look a little red, like she's been crying, but it's hard to tell from this distance. She looks wary as Flynn gets closer, but when he grabs her around the waist, picks her up and spins her around, she tilts her head back and laughs.

Flynn sets her back on the ground and Katie wraps her arms around his shoulders. "It's so good to see you," they both say at the same time, then burst into giggles.

"Come see the new horse," Flynn says, leading the two women towards the yards. I'm leaning on the fence trying to look casual.

I catch Olivia's gaze and she gives me a smile and nod. Katie's okay then. I try to meet her eyes, but she won't look my way.

The four of us climb up on the fence and look down at the mare, still cowering on the opposite side of the yard.

"Oh, the poor thing," Katie breathes. Her arm brushes against mine and electricity shoots through me. I force my attention back to the horse instead of the way Katie immediately moves away from me, but the feeling of her skin against mine doesn't leave.

"Feel like working with her for a while?" Olivia asks.

"Of course," Katie says, swinging a leg over the top of the fence and gently dropping to the ground inside the yard. She looks up at Flynn. "What's her name?"

"She didn't come with one," Flynn says. "But I was thinking

Aurora. She's the Roman goddess of the dawn and new beginnings. It felt right for her."

Katie stops, staring up at us lined up on the fence.

"Aurora," she says softly. "It's perfect." She turns towards the mare, approaching with slow, careful steps.

The horse watches her getting ever closer. Flynn holds his breath beside me and Olivia's nails are digging into the wooden railing.

Katie's fingertips reach out. "Aurora," she says again, voice soft and soothing.

The horse sniffs at her hand and presses her muzzle into it for just a second before snorting, tossing her head and wheeling away.

I catch my breath as the horse spins around. I'm expecting her to buck and kick out at Katie, but she only races to the other side of the yard.

I'm also expecting Katie to be disappointed, but she relaxes against the fence where she's standing, staring after the horse with a smile on her face.

She looks calm, relaxed, and most importantly, she looks happy.

13

———

KATIE

"HOW COME you didn't take the manager job?" I ask Flynn as we sit side by side on the yard railings watching the new horse get used to her surroundings, and hopefully us at the same time.

Flynn glances at me sideways, his dark auburn hair falls into his eyes. "I didn't want it," he says, and takes an enormous bite of his sandwich.

"Why not?"

Flynn finishes his mouthful, then answers. "Because if I had that job, do you think I could take off surfing for two weeks at a time? Plus, I'd have to manage the staff and while some might not be too bad, there's this new girl ..." He laughs as I scowl at him, but after a moment, I'm laughing too. The job was too much responsibility for Flynn. I should have known.

I haven't stayed in touch with Flynn, other than the occasional like or comment on each other's social media posts, and I regret it. What happened wasn't his fault and when I left Kauri Creek, I didn't want to leave him, or Olivia.

But I let too much time go past as we both got caught up in our own lives and it felt like too big of a gulf to reach out to him. I should have known better, because being with him now is like I've never been away. It makes the regret even worse.

But there's no use whinging about something I can't change, and that I brought upon myself.

"But if you'd taken the job I wouldn't have to deal with him," I mutter, gesturing towards where Dallas is deep in conversation with Olivia.

"Who? Dallas?" Flynn looks confused. "What's wrong with him? He's a great boss and a nice guy."

I really, really wish people would stop telling me what a great guy he is. It's hard to keep hating him, especially when he backs up their comments by genuinely being nice, even if it is only on the odd occasion around me.

"Well, mostly to me he's been a condescending jerk, who doesn't think I can do the job and am only here because Olivia loves me."

"I mean, that is the reason you're here, isn't it?" Flynn grins at me again. The little smart-ass.

I narrow my eyes at him and he backtracks. "We all know you can do the job, Katie Kat. But he doesn't know you from a bar of soap. Give him a chance." He looks thoughtful for a moment. "He was asking me about you before. He mentioned you saw Max today."

Immediately my mood darkens. I hate that man.

Before I can quiz Flynn further about what the heck Dallas was asking about, Flynn climbs down the fence. "Better skedaddle," he says. "Don't want the boss on my case, especially considering I only just got back." He grins up at me. He's being a smart-ass again, mocking me for my dislike of Dallas. It's his default setting, I shouldn't be surprised. I roll my eyes. "We should catch up later," Flynn continues. "We can go into town, grab a drink and celebrate your long-awaited homecoming."

"Yeah, sure," I say, absolutely not meaning it. As much as I'd love to hang out with Flynn over a couple of drinks, I do not want to be doing it in Kauri Creek. I sigh. I guess this is my life now. At least I'll have plenty of time to catch up with Flynn when we're working together.

He walks backwards away from me. "I mean it," he says. "I'm sure Hunter would love to see you too."

I laugh at that. "I don't think Hunter loves to see anyone."

Hunter is Flynn's older brother. He's moody and unimpressed by everyone and everything, especially when it has to do with his irresponsible little brother and his friends.

In Hunter's defence, from what I've heard, the guy hasn't had it easy and when their parents died when Hunter was eighteen, he had to stay at home and look after Flynn instead of adventuring off into the big wide world with his best friend, Olivia's older sister, Willow.

"Only Willow," he says, with a wink and I burst out laughing, drawing the attention of Dallas and Olivia. "Catch you later, Katie Kat," he calls to me, then turns to Dallas and Olivia. "We're going out tonight. No is not an acceptable response." Before either of them have a chance to answer, he's already asking what they need him to do this afternoon.

The three of them appear ready to walk away and leave me here, so I assume I'm just working with the horse this afternoon.

Olivia had told me about her on the short drive over from the function venue after my meltdown. A young mare that was picked up by a welfare organisation and was looking for a home that would be able to rehabilitate her. Olivia reached out immediately and arranged for Flynn to pick up the horse on his way back from his surf break.

She wasn't sure what condition the horse would be in, and it's not a pretty sight. But I know with a little time and attention, this horse is going to be stunning. Hopefully she has a personality to match.

Olivia waves at me and Flynn shoots me some finger guns, before they turn and head back to their utes. My eyes land on Dallas, who's already watching me, then he turns and begins to walk away too.

"Hey, cowboy," I call out and am gratified when he raises his head and looks back at me. I gesture for him to come closer. He lets out a sigh big enough that I can see it from this distance, but turns and strides back towards me.

"You're free to work with the horse this afternoon," he says, as he reaches me. "Olivia wants you to spend time with her every day if you can. It's part of the job."

"Yeah, I wasn't confused about that."

"What, then?" He looks wary, like he's not sure what I'm going to come out with next. He's probably worried I'm going to bring up my dead boyfriend or him pushing me way too far about what happened with Max.

"What was rule number one?" I ask, my voice so low and he has to lean in to hear me properly.

"Rule number one?"

I raise my eyebrows at him. He can't have forgotten. Or maybe he has, and it's just me that lies awake at night, replaying the feeling of his hands trailing across my skin, my hair tangled in his fingers, the press of his mouth on mine, and in other places.

His eyes darken and I know. I absolutely, one hundred percent know. He hasn't forgotten. His posture shifts and he leans even closer. "Tell no one," he breathes into my ear.

"And?" My voice wavers on that one simple, tiny word and I fight to retain control of my body, that just wants to lean back into him and feel his touch again. I shouldn't want that. I'm trying to tell the guy off, not get back into bed with him.

"Don't talk to people about you," he murmurs. "I only mentioned to Olivia that I was worried about you," he says, the look in his eye something very similar to the one he gets when he's talking about Sadie. One that looks an awful lot like he cares about more than how good my jeans fit my ass. "Because I was."

"I wasn't talking about Olivia," I snap, fighting all my instincts to lean in. "You asked Flynn about me and Max."

His breath catches, and his eyes widen. He knows he's been busted. He runs a hand through his hair. "It wasn't like that," he says.

I roll my eyes and step back, creating the distance I need to break the spell he has on me. "Whatever. I'm not your topic of conversation, alright? You want to know something, ask me. If I want you to know, then I'll answer it. If I don't want you to know, then, well," I shrug. "You'll have to suck it up and get over it, won't you?"

"Apparently so," he says dryly. "For what it's worth, I'm sorry. I didn't mean to cross a line ..." He trails off and after a beat continues. "I feel like I've crossed a lot of lines that I shouldn't have, and I'm sorry."

He looks truly regretful and I wonder what other lines he means. Does he mean sleeping with me in the first place? He can't have known who I was. His shock at seeing me on the farm the morning after was clear enough.

I dismiss the thoughts and wave off Dallas's apology. "It's fine, we can just move on and continue pretending like nothing happened." I fix him with a look. "But, stay out of my business."

He nods. "Alright." He gestures towards the mare eyeing us through the yard railings. "You okay here?"

I appreciate his change of subject. "Yeah, of course. We're just getting used to each other for a while."

"Okay. Let me know if you need anything."

I grin at him. "You're going to help me with a horse?"

I could be imagining it, but I swear his cheeks turn pink. "Ah, probably not. Let me know if you need anything that doesn't involve me going near that thing, okay?"

"That *thing* is called Aurora. And don't worry. I'm sure I'll have you two being besties in no time."

Aurora is the perfect name for her. Flynn did a great job. The goddess of new beginnings. It's exactly what she needs. She's not the only one.

Dallas laughs, but it doesn't sound like there's much humour in it. "Yeah, sure. Whatever you say." He pushes away from the railing where he's been leaning. "You'd better get to it. Especially if you plan on heading out with Flynn later."

"That's not actually going to happen," I say, one foot already on the railings, ready to climb over.

"Why not?"

"Because, as you saw earlier, me going into town isn't exactly a stellar experience for anyone involved. I'm better off just going home to bed."

His eyes flash and something low in my belly twists at the sight of it. God, this man. Why does he have to be so damn sexy and such a terrible idea, all rolled into one?

"You can't live like that," he says. "You can't spend your life worried about Max's opinion of you."

"Who says I'm worried about Max's opinion of me?"

He crosses his arms and looks down at me. He doesn't need any words. I know exactly what he's saying.

"Shut up," I say. "It's none of your business."

"I didn't say anything," he says, then chuckles as I grumble curses at him and scale the fence.

"See ya later, Katie," he calls softly as my boots hit the dirt inside the round yard.

I ignore Dallas, but look up and meet the deep brown eyes of my new friend Aurora. "Hey, pretty girl," I say. "Who needs annoying men anyway?"

She blinks and at and huffs a breath, but doesn't back away as I take a step towards her.

I let out a breath and all of the drama that's happened over the past few hours, and focus on one thing and one thing only: this poor, broken horse.

14

DALLAS

I HEAR the music before I even set foot on the porch. It's so loud I'm sure the whole house is vibrating.

I kick off my boots and step into the front hallway. I don't normally enter Violet's house unannounced, but there's no way anyone is going to hear me knocking.

Shrieking echoes down the hall from the kitchen and my body goes on immediate alert. Then I realise it's joyful shrieking and my daughter isn't in peril. It's such a visceral response I need to take a moment to calm myself again before I head down the hall.

It's like that now. The slightest hint of fear in Sadie sends me into over-protective mode. I'm never not going to be worried about her. I don't think it used to be this bad, but who's really to know if it's to do with the events of her life, or if the growing anxiety I have is normal in all parents. I don't exactly have a lot of parent friends to ask.

I shake off that fear now, especially when I reach the

kitchen. I lean against the doorframe and take in the utter chaos before me.

Sadie is clinging to Katie's back, as she piggybacks her around the room, alternating skips for bad dance moves. Both of them are giggling hysterically. They aren't even half the chaos though.

The rest of it is Flynn, who's piggybacking Olivia.

"Joust!" Flynn yells as he reaches the other side of the room to Katie and Sadie. The two with feet on the floor spin to face each other and paw at the ground like bulls about to charge.

"Giddy up," Sadie squeals and Katie charges across the room at the same time Flynn launches in their direction.

Sadie and Olivia have their arms held out, like jousting poles and at the last moment, as Katie and Flynn slide past each other, they reach out and slap a high five. Olivia flinches like she's been taken out and Flynn stumbles to a stop while Katie and Sadie celebrate their 'victory'.

"Welcome to the mad house," Violet says beside me, her voice indulgent as she watches the three adults behaving like bigger children than my daughter.

I laugh softly but continue watching as Katie swings Sadie down from her back and begins to twirl her around the room.

I should be watching Sadie and enjoying this moment of pure happiness for her. But my gaze keeps drawing back to Katie. She's like a magnet.

Her hair is tied in it's usual braid, but half of it has pulled loose around her face. She's wearing jeans and a ratty old t-shirt, like she does pretty much every day on the farm. What I'm seeing isn't anything out of the ordinary, and yet, I can't help but feeling that something here is remarkable.

I can't believe no one has noticed me standing here yet. Clearly they're having way too much fun.

I try to remember the last time Sadie and I danced in the kitchen. When the memories don't come, I realise it's been way too long. Emotion hits me square in the chest. I should be doing better.

"Heya, cowboy," Katie calls across the room, finally catching sight of me and snapping me out of my moment of melancholy before I have a chance to really wallow in it. "Come to join us?"

"Daddy!" Sadie shrieks when she spots me. She sprints across the room and leaps straight into my arms. Her confidence in my ability to catch her unwavering. I squeeze her to my chest. "Hey, Sadie girl," I murmur into her hair.

She kisses me on the cheek. "Did you have a good day? Flynn said there's a new horse. He brought it back with him."

"That's right. There is a new horse. Her name is Aurora," I say and feel a flutter I most definitely shouldn't when Katie shoots me a sly smile.

She's started dancing around the kitchen with Olivia, while Flynn begs Violet to join them. Eventually Violet drops the potato she's been peeling and lets Flynn lead her into the middle of the room where he begins to waltz.

"This is not the right music for waltzing," Violet says through a laugh.

"Shh," Flynn scolds. "You'll mess up my counting."

Sadie wriggles down and goes back to join Olivia while Katie leans on the wall beside me.

"I feel like I've missed something," I say.

"What do you mean?" She's looking up at me with those stunning grey eyes, confusion evident on her face.

I gesture at the room. "All this chaos. I feel like I missed the memo."

"But … isn't this normal?"

"Nooo," I say, regretting it as soon as I see the confusion turn to concern. "I mean, maybe. But I haven't witnessed it before."

"It used to always be like this," Katie whispers, her voice so low I'm not sure I'm supposed to hear it.

"I probably just miss it. They probably do it when I'm home with Sadie."

"Yeah, maybe," she says, but she doesn't sound convinced.

After two songs, Violet escapes Flynn and he joins us by the wall. Olivia turns the music down and Sadie collapses into a chair, her smile huge and relaxed.

I love this job. This place. This family.

"You're coming out with us, right Dallas?" Flynn asks after catching his breath.

"Ah, nah, not tonight," I say.

"Aw, come on," Olivia whines. "Live a little."

"I've got Sadie," I say, gesturing to where she's now helping Violet peel the potatoes.

"Don't worry about Sadie. She can stay with me," Violet calls over her shoulder.

"But—"

"No buts," Violet says. "We'll have a great time. Won't we, Sadie?"

Sadie grins up at her and nods vigorously. She doesn't even need to open her mouth to argue the point before I concede, because now the offer of a sleepover with Violet has been made, I'm not getting out of it.

"Alright, as long as that's okay with you, Violet."

"Of course it is. You deserve a bit of a break. And we're apparently celebrating the reunion of the three musketeers."

"Which means," Flynn says, his smile turning wicked, "we just need Katie Kat to agree."

She shakes her head firmly. "No."

"But Katie Kat—"

"I said no, Flynn. I'm happy to see you, truly. But I don't want to go into town."

"Max won't be there," Olivia says, her voice quiet. "It's Tilly's birthday. They're having dinner at home. Please come."

Katie lets out a huge breath. She's about to admit defeat.

"Yeah, come on," I say. "If the boring old guy can go, then you can. Plus, the rest of the world really needs to lay eyes on those killer dances moves of yours."

My comment has the desired effect and her eyes flash before she snaps, "Fine, but we're stopping at my place to get outfits for me and Livvie."

"Done," Flynn crows. He slings an arm around each of the girls' shoulders and squeezes them tight.

TWO HOURS later and I'm pulling into Katie's driveway, after pretending I don't know exactly where she lives. We ate dinner with Violet and Sadie, then cleaned ourselves up after a day on the farm.

We all piled into my ute for the drive into town, because apparently mine has the best stereo. We'll leave the ute at Katie's place, the girls will get changed and then we'll walk to the pub. The plan is to stagger back here at some point later tonight and crash, then head back to the farm in the morning.

All in all, it's a terrible plan on so many levels, mostly to do with me setting foot inside Katie's house again.

It's hard enough keeping the memories of that night at bay as it is. Revisiting the scene isn't going to help. I didn't really have a choice though and my only comfort is the feeling that Katie isn't super keen on this adventure either.

I wish she didn't feel that way, but her reluctance makes tonight easier for me. I can worry about her having a good time instead of thinking about how I should be at home, spending more time dancing in the kitchen with Sadie, even though she's asleep right now and it's all irrelevant anyway.

Flynn leaps out of the ute with the girls, herding them to Katie's front door. He's ushering them along, trying to get them to hurry up.

I always knew the guy had more energy than a Labrador puppy, but seeing him with Olivia and Katie is another level altogether. He waves for me to join them and I reluctantly slide out of the ute.

Katie's house isn't much different from the last time I saw it, except there's a few less boxes lying around. It's still a barely furnished cottage. There's furniture: a couch, a dining room table, a bed that I know about from experience, but there isn't much of a personal touch, except for the bookshelves in one corner of the lounge.

"Geez," Flynn says, taking it in. "Do you even live here?"

"Shut up, I've been busy," Katie snaps, then drags Olivia down the hall where they disappear into the bedroom.

Twenty minutes later, they appear again.

Flynn groans. "No. I can't take you out like that."

Katie snorts and rolls her eyes. "Really not concerned about your opinion, Flynnigan."

"I know, but you're going to break half the population of Kauri Creek."

He's not wrong. This town has probably never seen anything like it.

Olivia, who've I've seen pretty much permanently in jeans and a worn out hoodie since the day I met her, is wearing a dress. A dress that shows off all of her legs. It's navy, with little sparkles all over. Loose through the top, it dips low in the back and hugs around her hips, ending barely halfway down her thighs. She looks incredible.

But it's hard to acknowledge when Katie is standing next to her.

She's entirely in black. A leather jacket. A super short skirt too, this one not even reaching her mid-thigh, but it doesn't show off her legs. Because she's wearing thigh high black suede boots.

I suppress a groan. This girl is *killing* me.

Then, she slips the jacket down her shoulders and twirls in front of Flynn. That's when I catch sight of the bare strip of skin around her middle. Coupled with the thin straps of the tight black tank top and a peek of her bra strap, it might make me explode.

"Damn girl," Flynn says, then reaches for Olivia's hand and twirls her too. She giggles, clearly more hesitant about her outfit than Katie. "You too," Flynn says. He turns to me. "They look smokin', right boss?"

"Yep, let's get this over with," I mutter, unable to control my voice and what was supposed to be a sort-of joke, just comes out with me sounding like an asshole. I mean, it's an accurate representation. The thoughts going through my head are asshole level right now. I don't want to go to the pub, I want to take Katie into her room and strip that fucking gorgeous outfit right off her body.

Thankfully no one seems to notice my snarky tone.

Olivia and Flynn tumble out into the rapidly cooling night and I do everything I can to avoid staring at Katie's cleavage, or the stretch of her torso laid bare, or the glimpse of her thighs between the boots and skirt.

I'm not concerned about the population of Kauri Creek anymore. Only me, and it's already too late for me.

"You alright there, cowboy?"

"Spectacular." I refuse to look at her. I already know what I'm going to find. Smudgy dark eye makeup, vampy red lips, probably curled into a wicked grin at my obvious discomfort. Lips I'm going to want to kiss and probably never let go.

I thought I was screwed before, the first day I saw her standing in the arena at Wildflower Ridge, but this ... this is so much worse than I first realised.

15

———

KATIE

DALLAS CAN'T EVEN LOOK at me.

I don't know why that makes me so happy, but it does. I'm practically gleeful.

I'm still furious with him for everything that's happened today. I'm also completely exhausted from it all. Seeing Max, arguing with Dallas and even letting the memories of Toby rise to the surface. My massive cry by the lake and talking things over with Olivia. The new horse, seeing Flynn, jousting matches in the kitchen with Sadie, and Dallas's revelation that it doesn't happen as regularly as the sun rising anymore.

The last thing I want to be doing right now is going into a bar full of people who probably hate me. Max has had years to poison their thinking about me. He's always blamed me for taking his brother away and because he hated me before I even started dating Toby, I've never felt like I could explain to him what actually happened.

I don't even understand why he hates me so much. I sort of

get this thing where he thinks I took his brother away from him, then got him killed—which is absolutely not what happened. But the vendetta against me from *before* Toby. That's the part I don't understand.

The first time I met Max he dismissed me. Olivia and he had been friends back then. I couldn't understand it, until she told me he acted differently around me than he had anyone in his whole life. She would know. She's known him almost that long. The only part of Max's life that Olivia wasn't there for was the time when she wasn't born yet.

She didn't have a choice but to be friends with him. Their parents were friends, they were neighbours. There weren't a lot of options.

So it was Olivia and Max and Toby and Flynn. Until I arrived and somehow took Max's place without even trying.

I'd feel worse about it, except he's such a massive jerk that even Olivia and Flynn distanced themselves. Toby never said Max was a reason for leaving town, but he didn't have any issues leaving his twin behind.

I turn all of this over in my head, for the millionth time, and I'm still no closer to an answer or explanation than I have been over the past six years.

Some tiny part of me had hoped Max would soften over time, but he clearly hasn't.

So, Dallas has to bear the brunt of my frustration. My frustration about tonight, about Max, about being stuck back in this tiny town when I worked so hard to break away from it, despite loving so much about living here.

If I have to endure tonight, then I get to have a little fun with it.

I'm not sure he really minds, though the fact he hasn't been able to look at me properly once since I changed my clothes might mean I'm causing him more drama than even I intended.

I just wanted to feel desired, to have someone admire me. It doesn't count when it's Flynn who's been like my brother since we were sixteen, and Dallas makes an easy mark.

I wanted that admiration from a man I know finds me attractive. I just didn't realise how effective it would be.

Dallas is slouched over a corner table now, staring into his beer like he wants to murder it. Olivia is chatting to a girl who seems vaguely familiar. She could be someone who was at school as the same time as us, though I'm sure she wasn't in our year.

"You coming to dance with me, cowboy?" I reach over and nudge Dallas's shoulder.

He grunts, and looks up, but not directly at me. It's like he tries but just can't do it. His gaze focuses just over my shoulder. "I'm good."

"I thought the whole reason you came was to watch me show off my dance moves." I lean in close, so no one can overhear. My knee presses into his thigh. "But you can't even look at me."

He sucks in a breath and his eyes finally meet mine for the briefest second. "I'm sure Flynn will dance with you." His voice is tight and he presses his leg right back into mine.

"Yeah, of course I will," Flynn says from my other side. "Come on, Katie Kat."

I grit my teeth. I love Flynn to pieces. But his timing right now couldn't be worse. I'm finally making progress. Progress towards what, I'm not exactly sure. Making myself feel better by tormenting Dallas?

I let Flynn take my hand as I slide out of the booth, using the movement to hide my sigh of disappointment.

Flynn twirls me onto the patch of worn flooring at the side of the room we call a dance floor, then grabs my waist and pulls me in. He's an exceptional dancer when he's not attempting to ballroom dance, and I follow his lead, getting lost in the beat. Songs pass in a blur. For a moment I forget where I am and just enjoy being reunited with my friend.

A slower song comes on and without hesitation Flynn pulls me close. I wrap my arms around his shoulders and rest my forehead against his neck.

"What'd you do to the boss?" Flynn asks in his typical teasing tone.

"Dallas? Nothing." I give a half-hearted shrug.

I can practically feel him roll his eyes at me. "Sure, sure. So why can't he stop watching you, but only when he doesn't know I'm looking? Whenever I catch him out, he looks like I've walked in on him in the middle of a murder or something."

It's my turn to roll my eyes now. "You exaggerate, but also, have you seen these boots? The sole reason they exist is to bring men to their knees."

He releases me from his tight hold and takes a step back, assessing me. "You're right. They're fucking excellent boots. But, I think this is more than the boots, Katie." He pauses and rubs at the back of his neck. He's going to say something awkward next. "Maybe you should give him a chance. He's not a bad guy."

"A chance? A chance for what? We work together, there isn't anything else to this, Flynn."

He shrugs as he pulls me back into dance position. "I just think you'd be a good match for him."

I gape at him. Do they know? Between Flynn and Olivia dropping hints about me and Dallas, I feel like they know. But they can't, unless Dallas told them. If that's the case …

Before I'm able to respond to Flynn's wild claim that has zero relevance to *anything*, there's a tap on his shoulder. We both turn to find the subject of our conversation standing beside us. Dallas shoves both hands into his pockets and still refuses to look at me as he mutters something.

"I can't hear you," I say, despite being pretty confident I know what he said.

"I said, can I cut in?"

Flynn grins down at me. "Sure thing, boss." He turns away and is back by our table before I have a chance to process he's gone.

I turn back to Dallas. His hands are still in his pockets, his shoulders are hunched and he's chewing his lip, like he's nervous. His gaze hovers somewhere around my knees and off to the side. He finally lifts his eyes and looks directly into mine. He puts out a hand, palm up, and waits. He's not going to force this. He's still giving me the choice.

I put my hand in his and feel a ripple of heat pass through me as he gently closes his calloused fingers around it. I step closer and he slides an arm around my waist.

"Warning you," he says against my ear. "I cannot dance like Flynn can."

I want to laugh, but I don't want to give him the satisfaction of knowing he made me laugh, so I keep it in. Instead, I focus on the way he holds me against him, our bodies not exactly pressing together, but touching all the way up.

This is a terrible idea.

It reminds me far too much of the first night and what his hands felt like on my waist then, when he lifted me so I was straddling his lap.

It reminds me of the way those calloused hands roamed over my skin, from my waist to my breasts and down to the curve of my ass. The way he fitted his hand against the side of my neck and brushed his thumb across my mouth.

It reminds me of how he kissed me against the wall, trapping me with his hot hard body as he pressed it into mine.

A wave of lust and desire crashes over me and after a quick scan of the room to check Flynn and Olivia aren't paying us any attention, I grab Dallas's hand and pull him into the darkened space between the end of the bar and the jukebox. There's a short hallway that leads to a storeroom and probably an office or two.

I don't know what my plan is, and as far as terrible ideas go, this one blows everything else out of the water.

"What're you—" Dallas starts to say, before I yank him into me and he cuts himself off. I press my back against the wall and his arm comes to rest beside my head as his body crowds mine. It's so reminiscent of the first night we met that my knees go weak for a moment.

Dallas is finally looking at me.

I press my hands against his chest, slide one higher to curl around his neck and catch in the soft strands of hair at the nape of his neck.

His free hand comes to rest on my side. He licks his lips and looks at me like he wants to devour me.

I lean forward, push up on my toes and reach towards him.

My mouth is an inch from his. His grip tightens on my hip.

"Katie," he breathes. "No."

16

DALLAS

MY TWO SIMPLE words break the spell like a hammer shattering glass.

I know what Katie wants and I want part of it too, but on different terms. I'm certain of it.

I want to be clear before we do yet another thing that's going to mess with everything else.

Katie goes rigid under my hands. She recoils from me and immediately tries to duck under my arm to get back to the main room.

"Katie," I say.

"Sorry, just forget tonight ever happened," she says.

"Katie, wait." I don't know what I'm going to say or why I so desperately need her to stay, but I know that her walking away from me right now isn't the right thing. I need to make this okay before I let her out of my sight.

She sighs and leans against the wall. I haven't been able to look at her all night, but now it seems like the roles are reversed.

She stares at the toes of our boots: hers, an incredible pair of thigh high ones with towering heels; mine, a clean replica of the boots I wear on the farm every day.

Two pairs of boots, two completely different lives.

"We had a deal," I say. "One time. No repeats, no do-overs." I don't say the last part out loud.

Especially no feelings. We don't need to look too closely at that part of the rule, especially when I'm on the verge of breaking it.

"I know," she says.

"I don't think it's in our best interests to break that arrangement."

"I'm offering you zero-strings attached sex," she says, crossing her arms and glaring up at me for a moment before dropping her gaze again. I take a millisecond to appreciate the way her crossed arms and that tiny cropped tank top accentuate her chest, then tear my gaze away.

"We have to work together," I counter.

"We do alright."

"I'd like to think we could do better," I admit.

"Seriously, you want to turn this into a review of my job performance?" She sounds incredulous. No wonder, if that's what I've just implied.

"That's not what I meant. Not at all." I rub at my forehead. I have a headache brewing. "This is the worst place for a conversation."

She laughs at that. "Most people aren't here to converse, cowboy."

"I am aware that this appears to be a pick up bar, which is so weird considering how small this town is. Surely everyone already knows everyone."

She shrugs. "You'd be surprised at the strangers you can find in a place like this." The fiery spark is coming back to her. The one that dragged me into this corridor in the first place. The one that had me taking her home the first night we met.

"What I was trying to say before," I say, trying to get back to the point before my mind goes on a trip down sexy memory lane.

But a commotion in the main room interrupts me.

"The party has *arrived*," a voice booms, somehow over the music.

"Oh, fucking hell." Katie is frozen beside me. Somehow her fingers have found their way around my wrist, where she has me in a death grip.

"What is it?" I recognise the voice, but I'm too caught up in the last few minutes with Katie to place it, to understand what is happening.

"Max."

Oh, shit. "I thought Olivia said he would be at Tilly's birthday dinner."

"Yeah, well, I guess she was wrong."

"You want to go?"

She nods, as I expected she would. "My stuff is all over there though." She gestures towards the table where her jacket is tossed over the back of the booth and her handbag is on the seat beside Olivia and the girl she's still chatting with. To get to it she has to cross the entire room, going straight past Max.

"You get out. I'll get your things and meet you outside."

She nods again. Her confidence from a moment ago has vanished and her movements are shaky and unsure.

I step away and her grip slips from my wrist. I immediately miss the strength and heat of it, which is ridiculous.

It wasn't a romantic gesture, it wasn't sexy or sensual. It wasn't even friendly.

It was her clinging to a life line.

It shouldn't make me feel as good as it does that she was clinging to me like that, but here we are.

I skirt around the edge of the dance floor, keeping my head down and hoping Max doesn't notice me.

Or maybe I should draw his attention so he's less likely to notice Katie trying to slip out.

I glance over my shoulder and spot him waiting at the bar. There's enough people around him. He shouldn't notice either of us.

Olivia is alone when I reach our table. She has Katie's jacket in hand, scrunching it in clenched fists.

"Max is here," I say.

"I know. I told her he wouldn't be." Her eyes are wide and glassy in the coloured bar lights.

"It's okay, she's okay," I say to reassure Olivia, but mostly it's for myself.

"Where's Flynn? We need to find him before we go."

"I haven't seen him for a while. But you stay, have some fun, Olivia. I told Katie I'll get her things and meet her outside. We'll see you back at her place later."

Olivia starts to protest, but I shake my head, trying to figure out how to tell her I need to be alone with Katie without telling her that.

Olivia studies my face, then she closes her mouth, releasing the jacket when I reach for it.

"Just ... look after her, okay?" she says, eyes boring into mine.

It feels more significant than five simple words. It feels more significant than just tonight.

"I will."

IT'S LIKE DÉJÀ VU.

Katie is waiting for me in the exact same spot as the last time we left this bar.

She's leaning against the brick wall in a spill of light, one foot propped against the wall. She doesn't turn her head as I approach, just keeps staring up at the stars.

It's a perfect spring night with clear skies and that fresh chill in the air that makes everything feel clean and new. Katie is entirely underdressed for the temperature, but it doesn't seem to bother her.

"Seriously?" I say, leaning against the wall beside her. "Here?"

She laughs and I feel the sound in my soul. "We could recreate that night. The offer's still on the table." She's looking at me now, up through her lashes, a coy smile curving her lips.

I groan and tip my head back until it's pressing into the brick. "Katie ... we can't."

"We actually can. You just won't." She shrugs. "I thought we both had a good time, but if it wasn't for you ... I'll get over it. My ego might take a hit for a while though."

I push off the wall and spin to face her. My palm finds the wall to brace myself, to hold me back from stepping into her and sweeping her up into my arms, or worse, pressing her back into this wall with my body.

"Your ego," I say, my voice coming out low and rough, "has *nothing* to worry about."

She blinks up at me, eyes wide as though I've startled her with my sudden movement. She licks her bottom lip and I trace the entire movement with my gaze.

"That night ... fuck, princess. That was one of the best nights of my entire life."

"So, why don't you want to go again?" Her voice is barely a whisper, more like a breath. It's full of uncertainty and I wonder if it's her ego she's really worried about. I don't dare to hope and smother the little spark of it I feel.

"Because, it's already hard enough working with you every day and not think about that night *constantly*. I'm trying really, really hard not to be the gross pervy guy at work."

She giggles. Her head is resting back against the wall and she's staring up at me. "You're not pervy at work. But you could be tonight. You even got rid of our friends for a while."

"That," I say, raising a finger to emphasis my point, "was not so we could do that." Putting my hand anywhere near her was a terrible, terrible mistake. My fingers burn with the need to touch her.

She takes hold of my wrist and places my palm flat against

her waist. My fingers curl around the curve of her without my conscious thought, fingertips brushing the exposed skin on her back.

We're so close. I can feel her chest moving as she breathes. Short, rapid breaths. My fingers trace patterns across her bare skin and she shivers.

"You're cold," I say.

"I'm fine. Tell me why." Her voice is soft, and she lifts her hand to trail her fingers lightly down the side of my face.

Tell her why? I've completely lost track of the conversation. At this point I'll tell her whatever she wants me to. I'm completely under her spell. Why ... why won't I take her home again? My brain clicks back into gear.

"We'd have to renegotiate the terms," I murmur as her palm connects softly with the edge of my jaw. I turn my face into the feeling.

"What's wrong with the terms?" A fingertip traces along my eyebrow and I close my eyes. I hadn't meant to tell her why. I was supposed to just keep denying this could ever happen. "Hey, cowboy, tell me."

The way she says 'cowboy' is what does it.

Usually when she's calling me that there's sarcasm and threads of disdain woven into it. It's sassy and mocking. This time there's none of that, just a gentle softness like she really wants to know, and isn't going to use it against me later.

"I'm not a one-night kind of guy," I say after a steadying breath. I open my eyes and meet hers head on. Ready for her spark of defiance. But all I see there is confusion.

"You were before."

I shake my head. "No, princess, I wasn't."

"But, that's exactly what we did. One-night. We weren't even supposed to see each other again."

I laugh softly. "Yeah, that probably would have been easier for us both."

My hand is still on her body and I know I need to move it, but it's like it's magnetised there. I can't pull it away. Her hand is still on my face and I also know I should pull back so it falls away. But the sensation is too good and I can't quite bear to end this moment.

"Why did you do it? If you don't usually?"

I sigh. This conversation is so far outside of my control. "Let's start walking," I say. "That way when you freeze solid I don't have to carry you as far."

Katie snorts, but drops her fingers from my face. The movement feels reluctant, like mine is when I finally pry my hand away from her side.

She takes her jacket from the hand I've been bracing against the wall this whole time. She slides her arms into it and wraps it tight against her body. "Happy now?"

"Better, but come on." I head down the street, towards the little house Katie lives in on the edge of town.

Katie falls into step beside me. She reaches out and slips her hand into mine. I startle, but try to cover my reaction. This is entirely unexpected. "Talk, cowboy." She squeezes gently.

I sigh. I've effectively cornered myself into having this conversation. "I was having an epically shit day." I shrug, but Katie doesn't comment. She's clearly waiting for me to elaborate. "I was meant to just go drown my sorrows a little. But you were there. And honestly, you looked *sad*. I wanted you to look less sad. I wasn't expecting you to be pissed at me."

"To be clear, I wasn't actually pissed at you. Just this place." She circles her hand in the air, encompassing the town as a whole. "I was pissed about being back here. You just bore the brunt of my frustration. But, please," she shoots me a small smile, "continue."

I take a deep breath. I really want to get into this some more. Dive into what she just said. But she's urging me to carry on, so I do. We can come back to her story later.

"So, I wasn't expecting the feistiness, or for you to proposition me. I figured since nothing else has ever worked for me, maybe I should embrace that persona you put on me."

"But you're not a cocky cowboy are you?" Her voice is gentle, a soft whisper in the fresh spring night.

"Not really, no ... well, maybe." I shrug. "I guess that's for you to decide. I try not to be an ass anyway."

She watches me as we walk for a few long silent moments, the only sounds are our boots hitting the concrete footpath. I avoid meeting her gaze.

"No," she says eventually. "You're not a cocky-ass cowboy." Another long pause. "I'm still going to call you cowboy though."

I glance down at her and she's grinning up at me. That smirk that means she knows she's pushing my buttons. "Whatever you want, princess."

Her eyes flash at the nickname and she bites her lip. I jerk my gaze away, unwilling to stare at her teeth catching the soft flesh, trying not to remember her doing the same thing to *my* bottom lip.

"So, you're not willing to try again? I could call you a cocky cowboy again, be sad or angry or whatever, if it'll help?"

I stay silent. I can't answer her.

I want to go again. God, who wouldn't want another night with her? I want to pick her up right now, wrap her legs around my waist and feel her hot, strong body pressed against mine.

But, more than that. I want to be able to wrap her up in my arms afterwards and keep her there.

I'm completely screwed.

"No," she says quietly before I can answer. A thread of disappointment laces her voice. "Not without redefining the terms." She's quiet again, another long pause stretched out between us.

We reach her house and she unlatches the front gate, leading me up the path without ever releasing my fingers. When we reach the door, she finally slips them free, so she can dig in her purse for the keys. She finds them, but instead of inserting them into the lock, she props a shoulder against the door and stares up at me.

"You want the whole thing don't you? The long term commitment, the white picket fence, siblings for Sadie."

I nod, unable to form words as she spells it out for me. The thing I've never actually been able to solidify. But she's nailed it.

Mostly I need security for Sadie, that's the one thing I've always focussed on, and one-night flings aren't going to find us that.

As much as that night with Katie was hot as hell, casual is not in my nature. I want exactly what she just said.

She's assessing me. Her eyes tracing the outline of my face, trailing down my arms, the length of my body, then back to my face.

"I can't give you that," she says, her voice impossibly soft. So soft I can barely hear her.

I exhale sharply. It's exactly what I was expecting her to say, but it still hits me hard. I knew she wasn't going to tell me that it's all she's ever wanted and that she wants to make something work between us. I knew that wasn't on the cards, but I wasn't expecting her to be so raw and honest.

"I wish I could, Dallas. But I can't be that person. I understand though, and I'll leave you alone."

She turns and unlocks the door. She's inside before my brain catches up, still tripping over her use of my name, or at least the name everyone calls me. I stride into the house and catch hold of her wrist as she's setting her keys down on the hall table.

"Maybe not completely alone," I say, my voice raspy. "Perhaps we could be friends?" I sound like such an idiot, but the words are out before I can stop them.

Katie smiles up at me. It's timid and maybe even a little shy. "Okay, that sounds really good. I quite like Sadie and hanging out with her will be easier if I'm not in your bad books."

The timidness flees and the familiar spark of fire is back.

I roll my eyes. "Fine. I'll let you use me to get to my daughter. But only because she needs more bad ass women like you in her life."

She grins at me, the compliment clearly hitting it's mark.

"We've got a deal, cowboy."

17

____

KATIE

MY HOUSE IS TOO quiet and far, far too small with a man like Dallas standing in the lounge.

Thankfully he's not looking at me as I frantically search the kitchen for something to offer him to drink. Instead, he's studying the bookshelf along the wall that's crammed with a bunch of my grandma's old paperbacks and a few framed photos.

I'm pretty sure Olivia or Violet put them all back out after the last tenants vacated, but I've never asked them. I'm just happy to have the familiarity of my teenage years and my grandmother's comfort surrounding me these days.

"I'm sorry," I say, leaning on the doorframe joining the kitchen to the lounge. "I can offer you water. I have nothing else to drink. I do have a bag of popcorn though, if you'd like some?"

Dallas turns. "It's all good," he says. "I'm fine."

I barely hear the words because I'm staring at the photo in his hands. Between the spill of the streetlight coming in the window and the glow of the kitchen light behind me, I can recognise the frame from across the room. The metallic gold. I forgot that one was up there. He's picked it up and is studying it closely.

My feet carry me across the room and I gently take the frame from his hands, staring down at the girl I used to be.

"Your school ball?" Dallas asks and I nod.

"One of the best nights of my life," I say, my voice a soft rasp. It was at the time. That night was incredible and if it could have just been about the three of us in the photo—me, Olivia and Flynn, howling with laughter while wrapped up in each other's arms—maybe I could still remember it that way.

But like all of my memories of my time in Kauri Creek, Toby and therefore Max, are woven so tightly into it, it's hard to remember the joy.

"It's quite a dress."

I snort. "It was quite the discussion piece. I don't think this town had ever seen so much skin."

He chuckles. "I get the feeling sixteen-year-old you would have shaken this town up quite a bit."

I laugh, but it feels hollow. I sure did shake the place up, just not in a good way.

I place the picture back on the shelf, then collapse onto the couch. "Sorry I don't have a drink to offer you," I say.

"It's okay, Katie. I'm a solo dad. It doesn't really go with heavy drinker."

I sigh and tip my head back against the cushions, closing my eyes when they suddenly feel hot. "I'm also sorry I ruined your night out. You didn't have to be a single dad tonight, you were supposed to have a good time. You could always go back. I'm fine here."

The couch dips and I can instantly feel the heat from Dallas's body as he sits beside me. I want to lean into him. I want to feel his arms around me again, his palm pressed against my skin.

As much as I know I shouldn't be, I keep replaying all our near-misses tonight. The dancing, me dragging him into that hallway and how close I was to having his mouth on mine.

Choosing to wait for him in the same place as I did the first night we met was no accident. It sent a little thrill through me when he found me there and commented on it.

I so desperately wanted him to bring me home and wipe all the stress and anxiety of today away with his body.

But, I should have known he'd never go for it, regardless of how good the first time was. It shouldn't have come as a surprise for him to say he's not a one-night type of guy. And once he said that, it all clicked into place.

He has a child in his care. He's all she has. He's not interested in random flings. He wants to settle down. He wants a family for Sadie. Stability, security, a home.

"You could head back to the farm, be with Sadie. You haven't drunk much."

"Are you trying to get rid of me?" Dallas asks. There's a thread of something in his voice that makes me think he might be offended.

"No," I say with a sigh.

"Do you want to be alone?"

I tilt my head to the side and crack my eyes open. He's right there beside me, blue eyes gazing softly down at me.

"Not really, no," I say. "I'm really tired of being alone." My eyes burn again at my confession.

It's the raw truth though, one I've been desperately trying to avoid. But since Toby died, and even before he did, I've been alone. It's part of the reason I came back to Kauri Creek.

I knew it wouldn't all be roses, but I thought being with Olivia again, my best friend in the world, would help.

And it does. Being with Olivia and Violet, Dallas and Sadie, and now with Flynn's return, it's like being part of a family again.

If I could spend all my time at the farm, with the only people I truly care about in the world, I'd be happy. But the farm is here, in this tiny town where seeing people I don't want to see is unavoidable.

Maybe I could handle Max if it was just Max hating me for some unknown reason.

But it isn't just Max's hatred I have to deal with. I've seen him three times since I've been home and every time it's like my heart is shattering over and over.

He's too much like Toby. The way his hair falls over his forehead, the dark eyes I always found utterly sexy, even the tone of his voice is too similar to the guy I once thought was the love of my life.

Until he left me heartbroken, then took whatever was left of me and completely shattered it.

I can't stay in this town. I can't live here, surrounded by the pain of the past, seeing Max all the time and remembering the heartbreak and devastation his brother left in his wake, all while enduring Max's wrath.

So as much as I want to tell Dallas I can stay, as much as I want to tell him we can have a shot at something more, I can't.

Because as soon as I have some money saved and I'm back on my feet, I'm out of here and this time, I won't be ever coming back to Kauri Creek.

"Want to watch a movie or something then?" Dallas's voice pulls me back from the spiral of painful memories.

"Yeah, that would be good," I say, hoping my voice doesn't sound as shaky to him as it does to me.

I pass Dallas the TV remote and slip off my boots. Dallas watches me, the remote clutched in his hand and a little thrill goes through me. He may not want to act on it, but he's clearly fighting some internal battle over it. He has been all night. I flash back over the moments of this evening when he's been far too close for colleagues, or even friends.

It's not as good as taking him into my bedroom and sliding onto his lap, or having his weight press me down into the bed as he fits himself between my legs, but the little glow of knowing he can't help but stare at the length of my thigh as I slide my boots off helps soothe the sting of his rejection.

I drop the boots on the floor and drag my favourite fleecy blanket off the end of the couch, draping it over our laps. The comfort is instant. Dallas is flicking through the movie options now.

"Rom-com?" he asks.

"Really? Thought you'd be an action guy."

He shrugs. "I'm not particularly fussy, but you look like you need a rom-com. Or something to cry over so you can pretend you're crying over the movie and not whatever else has happened today."

"Well, that's ... hit the nail on the head."

"So, crying movie it is." He flicks through a few more options before settling on one I haven't seen. "This is the best one. For crying."

"You sound well educated in crying movies."

He shrugs again. "You're not the only one who needs them sometimes, you know."

I study him as he stares at the TV screen. Between the streetlight and the TV, the room is a soft wash of colours, striking Dallas on all the sharp lines and soft curves of his face, neck and shoulders.

He finally turns to face me, as if wondering why I haven't responded to his comment. I haven't said anything because I don't know what to say.

"You've had a big day." His voice is soft and he reaches out to brush hair out of my eyes and gently tuck it behind my ear. "It's okay to be upset over it." He hesitates, then lifts his arm.

It's an invitation, for me to curl into his side, to have him wrap his arm around me and hold me close.

This doesn't feel friendly and at some stage we'll need to define some boundaries, because we've already blurred them so epically, I don't know where we stand.

I've been staring at the space beside him for too long.

"It's okay," he says, beginning to lower his arm.

Before I lose my chance, I slide across the couch to him and slip myself under his arm. It comes to rest across my shoulders and he gently pulls me into him, my head resting against his chest and somehow my legs hooked over his.

"Is this what friends do?" I whisper into the semi-darkness.

"Probably not," he says, "but tonight, it's okay."

"Okay," I whisper back.

"We'll sort the rest out tomorrow."

"Okay," I say again.

"I'm going to start the movie now."

I never find out if it's the best crying movie. I fall asleep long before we make it to the sad parts, wrapped up in Dallas's body.

It's better than any blanket.

18

———

DALLAS

FALLING asleep wrapped up in Katie was probably a terrible idea.

Scratch that. It was definitely a terrible idea.

Not only am I supposed to be creating distance between us, but Olivia and Flynn stumbled into the house sometime in the early hours of the morning and saw us tangled together on the couch.

They must have, because when I woke up again at 3 a.m. and carried Katie to bed, with her snuggling into my chest in a way that made me not want to let her go, Olivia was already there.

I tucked Katie in beside her best friend and since Flynn had claimed the spare bed, I returned to the couch and stretched out, trying to ease the crick in my neck from curling around Katie for several hours.

Later that morning, when everyone finally emerged, with Flynn and Olivia rather worse for wear, and Katie looking bright-eyed and refreshed, our sleeping arrangements weren't mentioned.

No one has said a thing in the week since that night.

I should be glad for it. I should appreciate that Flynn has kept his mouth shut and not brought it up. I fully expected him to joke about it, to tease us, to expect a complete update on our current relationship status.

But he hasn't said a word and I'm desperate to talk to *somebody* about that night.

The first night I spent with her, I'm happy to keep to myself. But the second one ... so many things came up that I want to know more about. I want to dig deeper and uncover her.

I keep wondering why she said she can't give me long term. She said she wants to be able to, and there's something in the way. Something that's stopping her.

She's kept her distance over the past week, going about her farm duties and spending time with the horse Flynn brought back with him.

When we cross paths, she doesn't mention anything that happened that night either. She treats me like she always has, but she's softened. Her outright mocking is now just gentle teasing. Not that it happens often. She seems to be using Flynn and Olivia as a pretty effective buffer between us.

The school bell rings and startles me out of my thoughts. I'm leaning against a tree outside of Sadie's new classroom, waiting for her to finish her first week of school.

She's taken to school like a duck to water, though she's absolutely exhausted. Every afternoon she excitedly tells me about everything they did that day in class, then passes out half way through eating dinner. We haven't even been eating at the main house with Violet and Olivia because Sadie can't stay awake that long.

Violet tells me it's normal. At first I was hesitant to believe her, and fretted about there being something wrong, some illness I needed to take her to the doctor for.

"Daddy!" Sadie yells in my face as she runs up to me, flinging herself into my arms.

"Heya, Sadie girl." I wrap her up and feel her immediately snuggle into me. It's the best feeling in the world.

"She's had a great week," Sadie's teacher says, following the herd of children out of the classroom, making sure they each find their parent.

Miss Hayes, is young for a teacher. I think this is her first year teaching. Her dark hair is pulled up into a ponytail and she smiles at me. "She's settled in really well and is getting used to the routines. She's a great kid, always trying to help. She's been telling us all about the farm."

I grin. "Yeah, I bet you know far more about Porridge than you ever wanted to. The lamb I mean, not the breakfast."

She laughs. "I always had lambs as a kid, I remember what it's like." She pauses. "Sadie mentioned Katie, someone who works on the farm. I'm assuming she means Katie Barton?"

"Yeah, she does." Apprehension fills me as the teacher absorbs my words. Katie seems to think everyone in Kauri Creek hates her and this feels like a test.

"Oh, I didn't know she was back. Can you tell her I said hi and that I'd love to catch up with her?"

"Uh, yeah, sure." I must look as confused as I feel because she continues.

"Katie and I were at school together, though she's a bit older." She hesitates. "She might not remember me, but I always thought she was super cool, and nice."

I smile, filled with a warmth I wasn't expecting.

"She is the coolest," Sadie says, agreeing with her teacher. "I love her."

"I'll let her know," I say. "Thanks. Sadie's had a great week."

Miss Hayes smiles. "We'll see you again Monday. Bye, Sadie."

"Bye, Miss Hayes," Sadie calls. She doesn't even pause for breath before she continues. "Daddy, can we get ice cream?"

I laugh. "Sure, Sadie girl. Let's go."

WE EAT our ice cream at the park and Sadie plays for a few minutes before we head back to the farm. Her eyes are already starting to droop by the time we park outside the main house.

Violet meets us on the porch, taking Sadie from my arms. "Come help me make dinner, sweetie," she murmurs to Sadie, who I'm pretty sure is going to be doing more napping than helping.

I don't really want her to sleep so close to bedtime, because she'll want to be awake half the night, but I'm pretty exhausted myself and just appreciate Violet taking Sadie for a few hours while I finish some jobs. "Join us tonight, Dallas," she says to me. "You look like you need a break too."

I rub at my jaw and feel the rasp of stubble. She's right. "That'd be good. Thanks Violet. I'll just go finish up."

I climb back into the ute and continue down the driveway, pulling up outside the storage shed on the opposite side of the yards to the barn and stable. I have a tray load of fencing supplies and native trees for planting, which I somehow have to fit into the schedule over the next week or so, before the plants all die.

"Hey, cowboy," Katie calls from the yards. I hadn't even noticed her as I drove down the driveway. She's with the new horse, standing in the middle of the yard. The horse is wearing a halter, the rope held loosely in Katie's hand as she runs a brush over the horse's coat. Olivia and Flynn tell me she's making good progress, but I haven't witnessed any of it myself until now.

Katie wanders over to the railing, and the horse trails along behind her. Clearly she's built some trust there.

"How was Sadie's first week?"

"It was good. She's probably asleep already."

Katie laughs as she unclips the lead rope and climbs over the railing. She leans on it beside me. "It must be such a huge adjustment for a little person."

"Massive," I agree. "Also, her teacher, Leah Hayes, asked me to say hi and if you remember her she'd like to catch up sometime."

"Leah is Sadie's teacher?"

I nod and lean against the fence too. Immediately I feel the hot breath of the horse puffing against my neck.

"Stay still," Katie says, her voice low. "She's not been near anyone else yet."

I freeze. I was about to push away, but Katie looks so excited to see the horse near another person. I shove down my own feelings about being this close to a horse. At least there's a solid railing fence between us.

"That's super cool that Leah is her teacher. I didn't know she'd come back."

"Yep," I say, trying hard not to throw myself away from the horse.

"She was sweet."

"Still is as far as I can tell. Sadie adores her already."

Some emotion crosses Katie's face, but it's gone in a flash and I'm left wondering if I imagined it. I'm probably wishful thinking but it looked like jealousy.

"I'll bet," she says and I can tell she's fighting to cover up the emotion, whatever it is.

"She adores you too, just so you know. She told Leah that she loves you."

"I love her, too." Her voice is so quiet I can barely make out the words over the huffing of the horse breathing down my neck. "I'm going to miss her. Probably more than anyone."

"You'll miss her?" My brain stops functioning. My heart freezes. The only way she'll be able to miss Sadie is if one of them isn't here, and Sadie isn't going anywhere. "You're leaving." It's not a question and we both know it.

"Eventually. Not yet. I need to save some money first."

I finally step away from the horse, throwing a hand up to grip the back of my neck as my stomach plummets. The horse tosses her head at my sudden movement and skitters across the yard away from us. I don't have it in me to care.

"What happened to you being so determined to prove yourself? To show you belonged here? That you wouldn't let Olivia down?" I spin back to face Katie, my desperation turning to frustration. "What happened to all that, princess? Was it all just talk?"

The shock on her face at my outburst quickly settles into the hard lines of anger.

"I wish I could stay. If I could just live out here on the farm and pretend it isn't a part of Kauri Creek then I would, but I can't. I'm trapped here. I need a place I can put down roots and actually grow. I'm never going to get that here. It's all caught up in the past and I refuse to live in a place where people hate me for something I didn't even do. I don't want to be here because it makes me remember. And I don't want to remember." Her voice finally gives up and breaks. "You don't get the right to accuse me of anything, cowboy. I already told you I can't be what you want, because I know I can't stay. I can't get involved. I won't do it to Sadie and I won't do it to you."

A tear spills over and streaks down her cheek. She's breathing hard, her face flushed and fists clenched at her sides.

"Princess," I say, my voice soft as the frustration evaporates at the sight of her pain. I step close.

She raises a balled fist and presses it to my chest, right above my heart. It's not a gentle caress. It's a warning.

I ignore it.

"Princess." I say again, reaching up to swipe away the tears that continue to fall. "You know the good thing about memories? You're always making new ones."

"I'm aware of that," she grumbles, still holding me at arm's length with the fist against my heart. Symbolic really.

"So, if you don't want to go, make new ones. Make new ones here, with Olivia and Flynn and Sadie ... and me."

"It's not that easy. And who says I don't want to go? Maybe I do want to go. Maybe I can't wait to get out of this place."

"You just said if you would stay you could. God, you're so stubborn it's infuriating."

"See, you don't even want me here. You said the other day that it would be easier if we never saw each other again."

"Fuck's sake, princess, that was after the first night. Not after the rest of it. Not after I got to know you and you kept calling me cowboy like it didn't drive me insane, or maybe you called me that because you know it does, which now that I know you is probably more your style. You're fucking gorgeous and sassy and incredible. Of course I want you to stay."

I'm breathing hard now too, staring down at this infuriating woman who I do not want to let go. She's looking straight back at me, tear stained cheeks and fury in her gaze.

Fuck it.

I throw caution to the wind and put it all on the line as I bend down and press my lips to hers.

19

———

KATIE

DALLAS'S MOUTH comes crashing down on mine and it wipes every thought from my head.

I'm not sure if we're arguing and mad at each other, or not.

Right now, with his lips pressed against mine and his hand cupping my jaw to tilt my chin just the right way, it seems irrelevant.

His tongue brushes against my lips and I open for him. Any resolve I had before is gone. I virtually melt into him as he kisses me.

He's gentle, but also completely in control. He knows exactly what he's doing and he's not afraid to prove it, exactly the way I remember.

My fingers clutch at his shirt. The hand that held onto his chest to keep him away, now pulling him closer and helping to hold me on my feet as my knees wobble, threatening to give out completely.

He pulls away, but only for a breath before he presses

another kiss to my cheek and breathes into my ear. "We don't want you to go, princess. Give us a chance. A chance to make new, better memories."

Reality comes crashing back in and I shove Dallas away.

"I can't," I say. "I'm leaving, hopefully by winter. It's probably best if we just forget about the friend thing."

I spin around and climb back over the railings, leaving Dallas staring after me. I don't care. I need to keep the distance. I've managed to avoid him most of this week, I should be able to manage it for another few months.

Even if all I really want to do is crawl back into his arms.

I am not being that girl again. I'm not just going along with everything because a gorgeous man convinces me he loves me. Not that Dallas is anywhere close to loving me, but I still can't change my plans for him. I can't.

Aurora wanders over to me once I'm far enough away from Dallas. I hear him sigh, then the crunch of gravel under his boots as he strides back across to the storage shed where he begins unloading the ute.

AFTER YESTERDAY'S argument with Dallas that had him kissing me before I stormed off like a petulant teenager, I didn't see him again for the rest of the afternoon.

It's not unusual. I was already trying hard to stay out of his way.

We've blurred so many lines that creating distance between us seems like the best course of action.

When I propositioned Dallas last week I'd been exhausted from the emotional upheaval of seeing Max, of seeing Flynn, and from bawling my eyes out over Toby.

That's why I'd tried to kiss Dallas. Nothing else. I just lost my marbles for a bit there.

So I've stayed away from him all week. Now though, I don't know what he's asking of me, especially after what happened in that moment yesterday when he his lips came down on mine.

When I arrived at the main farm house for dinner last night, I realised my luck in avoiding him had run out when I saw his boots by the door.

We survived the meal without drama though, and Dallas left early when Sadie started to droop, her first week of school obviously catching up with her.

I spent the evening sitting on the back porch of the house with Olivia, a bottle of wine between us.

It was the perfect night.

This morning is not so great.

I slept in Willow's room, not wanting to drive back to town after drinking, and when I enter the kitchen, I find Violet standing over the sink filling lamb bottles. Sadie is on the porch, pulling her boots on. I've clearly overslept.

"Oh, hey Katie," Violet says when I step up beside her.

I can tell immediately that something is off. I take her in, the rough ponytail, the rumpled clothes, the red eyes that are far too glassy.

"Here," I say, taking the milk jug from her. "Sadie and I will take care of the lambs, then I'll take her with me for a couple of hours."

"Oh, no, Katie, it's fine." Her voice wobbles though and I know it's not okay. I wrack my brain for the date and try to remember if it has any special significance. I can't recall anything, but I know from my own experience that the grief plays on its own schedule.

"Vi, it's okay. You deserve a little break. I don't mind hanging out with Lady Sadie. Don't worry about it."

She smiles at me, one that reminds me so much of my grandma. It tugs at my heart. "Thank you, Katie. We're so lucky you're home."

That statement tugs at my heart too, but in a totally different way.

I turn back to the lamb bottles as Violet makes herself a coffee, then I head outside where Sadie is waiting, surrounded by a small flock of orphaned lambs. She loves feeding them every day and she's named every one of them. We had to spend a significant amount of time convincing her we are capable of taking over feeding duties while she's at school.

Once the lambs are taken care of, Sadie and I head down the driveway. She reaches up and wraps her small fingers around mine.

My heart isn't ready for it. Not today.

With being confronted by Violet's grief and Sadie's joy, my own emotions are all over the place.

"Can I trust you to stay right here while I work with Aurora?" I ask Sadie, leading her up onto a platform that overlooks the yard where Aurora is.

Sadie nods solemnly. "I promise," she says. "And I'll be super quiet and not move so I don't scare her."

I reach out and tug at one of her pigtails. "Good job."

I climb over the railings and drop lightly to the dirt. Aurora is on the other of the yard, munching on the hay Olivia must have given her this morning. When she sees me she nickers and immediately heads in my direction.

I grin. The joy of seeing the horse beginning to trust me overriding the already emotional morning I've had.

I clip the lead rope onto her halter and give her neck a solid rub. Aurora nuzzles into me. We walk a few laps of the yard, with Aurora keeping pace beside me. It feels like she'd follow me anywhere. On our third lap I glance up and see Sadie staring at us over the top rail, her eyes wide with awe. I stop beside where she's watching.

"Would you like to meet her?"

Sadie's eyes widen further. She nods, then stops. "Can I?" she whispers, and I can't tell if she's worried about scaring the horse or if voicing the question is going to stop her being able to.

"Of course. Come here."

Sadie climbs over the top railing, moving nice and slowly. She's so aware of Aurora and any time the horse fidgets, Sadie pauses, waiting for her to settle again. I reach out and grab Sadie from the railings, holding her in my arms. Aurora is standing back, her lead rope stretched long between us, while she eyes up the new addition to our team.

"Hey, pretty girl," I croon to the horse. "This is Lady Sadie and she'd like to meet you. Think that's a good idea?"

The horse puffs out a breath, and takes a tentative step forward.

"Hello, Aurora," Sadie says quietly, copying my soothing tone. "It's so nice to meet you."

The horse takes another step and as Sadie reaches out her hand, Aurora stretches her nose towards her.

"Sadie?" The voice behind us comes out sharp, and both little girl and horse pull back, moments before making contact. "What're you doing?" Dallas asks.

I close my eyes and let out a breath as Sadie curls into me, the hand she had reached out for the horse wrapping itself tightly around my neck. "He's going to be mad at me," she whispers.

That has my eyes flying open again. "Why?"

"Because I'm not supposed to go near the horses."

"He won't be mad at you, Lady Sadie," I say softly into her hair as she clings to me.

"I don't want him to be mad at you either," she says as I reach the railings and balance her feet on them.

"Don't you worry about me. I can handle it." I give her a smile and she scrambles over the top of the fence, landing back on the viewing platform beside her father.

"What're you doing down here?" He asks her. "I thought you were with Violet."

"Violet needed a moment," I say, climbing the railings to put me on a better height with Dallas. I don't need him literally talking down at me while he's telling me off. Because I know it's coming.

Yeah, I know Sadie isn't allowed to ride. I didn't know she wasn't allowed near the horses at all.

"So, you brought Sadie to the horses?"

I look pointedly at Sadie while he talks, then jerk my head off to the side. I'm sure Sadie knows what's going on when Dallas asks her to stay where she is, but at least she doesn't have to hear it.

"You're upsetting her," I whisper shout at him when we're far enough away that Sadie doesn't have to hear us arguing. "She's absolutely fine."

"You had her in the yard with a half wild horse," he snaps.

"She's not half wild and I was holding Sadie. I would have kept her safe."

Dallas is breathing hard, glaring down at me. "I'll take her back to Violet."

"No, you won't." I straighten. There's no way I'm going to even get close to his height but I'm not going to let him bulldoze all over me. "Violet needs some time to herself."

"She's fine to have Sadie. She has her every day. She's never said she needs a break." He doesn't sound certain though, it's like he's trying to convince himself.

"She's not going to ask you for one when she's having a bad day. She probably just wants to shove all the grief down and carry on anyway. But she needs a morning off. I told her I'd take care of Sadie, and I *will*."

Dallas's eyes soften a little when I talk about Violet. "I don't want her near the horses," he says, his voice low and stern.

"She loves them," I say. "And she's good with them. Why can't you give her a chance? Keeping her away from them isn't going to do you any favours later. She's surrounded by them every day."

"She's not going near the horses. She can be with me while

you finish with Aurora." He turns and strides away, back to where Sadie is leaning over the railings, cooing down at Aurora, who's watching her carefully, but taking slow steps forward. Dallas pauses as he takes in the sight, then shakes his head, as though he's removing the image from his memory, before going over and lifting Sadie down from the platform, talking with her in voices too low for me to hear.

I sigh. Whatever. I let myself back into the yard and approach the horse. She nickers at me again, and gently butts me with her head.

"Come on, sweet girl. Who needs him anyway?"

20

DALLAS

DAMN IT ALL TO HELL. This woman is going to be the death of me.

Yesterday I was kissing her and nearly begging her to let me help her make new memories, ones worth sticking around for.

Today, I'm snapping at her and telling her off.

I can't help myself when it comes to Sadie and those horses. I saw her there in the yard, so close to that horse and my brain shut down. My heart rate spiked, adrenaline shot through me and all I could see were broken bones and bruises and my life imploding.

No doubt Katie's back to thinking I'm a raging asshole.

First for leaving Sadie with Violet today, when she's struggling with her grief, then for losing my shit over Sadie being near a horse.

I know Katie would never intentionally put Sadie in danger, and would do everything to protect her if something went wrong. I know she loves her and doesn't want any harm to come to her. But sometimes, all the love in the world isn't enough to stop someone getting hurt.

And I can't go through that kind of terror and pain again.

Even with the image of Sadie leaning on the railing, talking down to the mare in a soft, calming voice, just like the one Katie uses, playing in a loop in my mind.

I'm banging around in the shed, getting organised for planting all the native trees and shrubs on Monday while Sadie sits on the tailgate of the ute watching me.

"I'm sorry, Daddy," she says, as I toss a spade onto the trailer, making it crash against the steel side. She flinches at the noise and I hate myself a little more, but she reaches out one of her tiny hands for me, so I step in closer. "Please don't be angry at Katie."

I sigh as she wraps her arms around my waist and rests her head against my chest. "I'm not angry with Katie, or you," I say. "I'm sorry I reacted like that. I got scared."

"Why?" she asks, bright blue eyes identical to my own peering up at me.

"Because sometimes horses can be scary or dangerous," I say.

"Flynn said Aurora is more scared of us than we are of her."

"He's probably right about everyone but me. I'm probably more scared of her than she is of anyone else here."

"Katie could teach you how not to be scared, like she's teaching Aurora." Sadie says the words, then nestles her face back into my chest, hugging me tightly.

Images assault my brain.

Ones of Katie teaching me not to be scared of horses, of her gentle hands tracing over my skin, her voice soft in my ear.

Then visions of me teaching Katie not to be scared of the life she could have here. A life she could have with me.

But for that to ever become a possibility, I need to learn some things too, and one of them is going to have to be to let go a little.

"You can watch Katie from the platform," I say, my voice gruff. "Don't go in the yard, and be careful you don't spook the horse."

Sadie breaks away from our hug and looks up at me, excitement already in her eyes. "I can?"

"You can." I nod.

"Thank you, Daddy." She gives me another tight squeeze before leaping off the ute tailgate and bounding from the shed.

"I'll apologise to Katie after she's done," I murmur, but Sadie is long gone. I can see her across the driveway, slowly climbing back onto the platform, watching carefully that she isn't spooking the horse.

Once she's safely up, I turn back to my work, studying what I've already loaded onto the trailer and trying to remember what else we need to take out with us.

As I load more supplies, I think about all the things Katie has told me in the time I've known her.

I think about how much she loves Olivia and Violet and Flynn and this farm, how much she loves my daughter, and how good she is at her job. I think about the contentment that radiates from her when she's out on the land, or rescuing orphaned lambs, or working with terrified horses.

Katie belongs here, with the people she loves, and the ones who love her in return.

I'm going to make it my mission to show her that, whether I get to be one of the people she loves or not.

By the time I've finished loading the trailer, I have a vague plan outlined in my head. Sadie is still on the platform, gazing raptly down into the yard, so I assume Katie is still there, working with Aurora.

Sadie spots me when I reach the edge of the platform and reach up to pull myself up. She presses her finger to her lips, eyes wide with awe, then points into the yard.

Katie is beside the horse, whose coat now shines instead of appearing fuzzy and dull, like it did when she arrived. Katie's wearing a helmet, and has the lead rope looped over the horse's neck. There's a wooden box is on the ground next to where they stand.

Katie steps onto the box, all the while talking to Aurora in her usual low tone. She leans across the horse and when she doesn't skitter, she leans further across.

Soon she's draped over the horse's back and all Aurora does is turn her head to sniff at Katie's legs.

Katie slides back down onto the box, rewarding Aurora with a hearty rub along her neck.

The next time Katie tries, she slips a leg over the horse's back and in a flash, is sitting astride her.

I suck in a breath, anxiety clawing at my throat. This horse was virtually wild when she arrived here mere weeks ago and now Katie's sitting on her with no saddle or bridle in sight.

But she's absolutely beaming, giving the horse more pats and encouragement.

Sadie squeezes my hand. I glance down at her and realise she's trying so hard to contain her excitement over this huge milestone. "She did it," Sadie breathes, the awe and admiration in her voice unmissable.

Aurora is totally relaxed, standing in the middle of the yard, Katie on her back.

Until a bird swoops past her head.

The horse tosses its head and skitters sideways. Katie grabs for her mane, trying not to slip off the spooked horse. The rope slides across Aurora's neck, the trailing end loosely wrapping around her foreleg and that's all it takes for her to lose any cool she had. She spins violently and Katie doesn't stand a chance.

"Katie!" Sadie yelps as Katie goes flying through the air.

"Stay here," I tell Sadie, wrenching my hand free from her terrified grip. I jump the railings and land on the packed dirt of the yard.

Aurora has shot to the far side, the rope already untangled from her leg. She stands against the railing, head down, panting hard, but no longer freaking out.

I turn for Katie, who's lying in the dirt. Unmoving.

"Katie," I race towards her, falling to my knees at her side.

She groans. "Mother fucker," she mutters. "This ground is too hard." She rolls over so she's flat on her back, a grimace on her face as she stares up at me. "That's going to fucking hurt."

"Are you okay?" I gasp the words out between panicked breaths. "Katie, are you okay?" My hands are hovering in the air over her body. I want to touch her, to feel every inch of her and make sure she's okay, but at the same time, I'm too scared to touch her in case I make it worse.

"I'm fine," she says with a groan.

"Where does it hurt? Is anything broken? Can you get up?"

"Hey, cowboy," she says, reaching up with one hand to rest it against my cheek. "I'm fine. Nothing's broken, just a little bruised."

"Are you sure?" The feel of her palm against my face is calming my breathing, but it's still coming in short, sharp pants.

She reaches for my hand with her free arm, wincing slightly as she uses it to pull herself to sitting. We end up way too close together, her mouth mere inches from mine and I have to fight everything in me to stop myself eliminating that gap and pressing my lips to hers. I ease back instead and her hand slips from my face.

"I'm fine, I promise. Not my first fall, won't be my last."

"That doesn't help," I say as I grit my teeth and try to force my breath to steady.

She gives me a half-hearted smile and a shrug, which causes another wince. "Is Aurora okay?"

I nod. "Yeah, I think so. I was more worried about you."

She raises an eyebrow at that. "Really?"

"Yes, really."

"And here I was thinking you were going to bollock me for being reckless or something."

"Oh, that's definitely coming. What the hell were you thinking?"

"I was thinking I was doing my job. I was thinking Aurora was doing fabulously and was ready for the next step."

"What about having someone here to keep an eye on you?" I remove my cap and run my hand through my hair

"You're right here," she snaps, gesturing between us. "I can't have a spotter every time I work with an animal, but I'm also not stupid. I wouldn't have done it if you weren't here."

I exhale heavily and push up to my feet. I extend a hand and help to pull her up too. Another flicker of pain crosses her features but I manage to not ask if she's okay, again.

"I'm sorry," I say instead.

She blinks at me, then raises a hand and presses it against my forehead. "You feeling okay? Or am I hearing things?"

I roll my eyes and she grins. "I overreacted, okay? About Sadie and about you just now." I scuff a boot in the dirt. "I couldn't handle it if either of you got hurt."

Katie reaches out and wraps her fingers around my forearm. "Thank you. I appreciate the apology. I promise I'm not being reckless, especially with Sadie."

"I know you're not. Thank you for looking after her."

She shoots me a smile. "I'll hang out with your kid any time, cowboy. She's awesome." She tilts her head towards the horse. "Better get back to this one and make sure she's okay."

"Alright. I'm pretty much done around here, so I can get Sadie out of your hair for the afternoon."

"Do you mind hanging around for another ten minutes or so?"

"Yeah, no worries. Why?"

"Because I need a spotter." She turns towards the horse and shoots me a cheeky grin over her shoulder. "The boss keeps accusing me of being reckless and I want to prove him wrong."

I shake my head and laugh, then scale the railings to stand next to Sadie.

"Is she okay?" Sadie asks, her expression filled with concern.

"She's absolutely fine," I reassure her.

A few minutes later, Katie is back astride Aurora, her grin wide and confident as she glances over at us.

Sadie waves. I can't because I'm too busy gripping the fence rail, digging my fingernails into the wood.

But as Katie slides off the horse, on purpose this time, I relax and the hope that's been smothered by panic and fear while watching her work with the horse revives itself.

The hope that maybe one day she'll think I'm as awesome as she thinks my daughter is.

21

KATIE

GOD, my ass hurts.

There's a huge bruise across my hip from where I hit the dirt coming off Aurora on Saturday, but it could have been a whole lot worse, so I'm not complaining. Much.

I adjust myself in Scout's saddle but it doesn't really help. It's just going to hurt like a bitch for a while.

Despite the agony in my backside, every time I think about sitting on Aurora I grin. She's making such great progress and has come such a long way from the terrified animal that arrived a few weeks ago.

I can't wait to get back to working with her this afternoon, but first I have to check the cattle, then spend the day planting trees. Olivia is already stressing out about them dying before we get them in the ground, even though Dallas only picked them up on Saturday so we're having a team effort today to get it done.

When Scout reaches the top of the next hill I draw her to a halt and spend a moment just taking in the sight laid before me. From this spot I have the perfect view of the farm; from the main house, to Dallas's cottage, the barn and woodshed, right around to the Wildflower Ridge Function Centre and further out, to where the creek this town is named after spills from the hills.

I can make out the farm ute from here, heading slowly along a farm track to where we'll be planting soon. Once I'm done with the cattle I'll head straight to where they are. The ute pulls into the paddock it's heading for and I smile as I see Olivia and Flynn's tiny figures climb out.

I haven't seen Dallas this morning, but I expected him to be with them. I shrug, he obviously got busy doing something else and will head out when he can. I turn Scout to continue on our way.

I check on the cattle, making sure everyone's happy and healthy, has access to water, and that the fences haven't been breached.

By the time I'm done, the sun is starting to bear down, burning off the last of the morning chill. I strip off my heavy jacket and loop it around my waist. It's going to be a stunning day.

I'm about to head for the planting spot when my phone rings. I wince at my bruises as I lean to be able to slide it free from my pocket.

Olivia.

"Hey," I say. "What's up?"

"When you're done with the cattle, can you head to the pine tree paddock and check on Dallas?"

"Isn't he with you?"

"Well, he should be," she says and I notice the concern in her voice. "He went out to fix a water leak and was supposed to meet us back here. But he hasn't shown up and it's been ages since he left." A cold feeling settles in my stomach. "He should have been back by now, and since you're closest ..."

"Of course. I'm heading that way now. I'll update you."

I turn Scout in the opposite direction, urging her into a canter as we follow the farm track through this paddock and over the hill to the pine tree paddock, creatively named for the single pine tree that stands on the top of the hill.

I peer down into the gully. If Dallas is fixing a water leak he'll be near a water line, which run along the bottom of this paddock if I recall correctly.

I nudge Scout forward and lean back as she descends the steep hill. As we round the curve of the hillside I spot him. Well, his motorbike.

"Dallas!" I shout.

"Here," he calls back immediately. There's something wrong in his voice. He hasn't just been delayed. I urge Scout faster and pull her to a stop when my eyes finally land on Dallas.

He's on his knees behind the bike, his right hand wrapped firmly around his left forearm. But it's not doing much to prevent the blood running down his arm.

I throw myself from Scout's saddle and fall to the ground in front of Dallas.

"I can't get my phone out of my pocket without the bleeding starting again," he says through gritted teeth. His face is a little pale underneath his tan, the few freckles across his nose standing out a little more than usual.

"Wouldn't have helped anyway," I say. "There's no service here."

I take his wrist and gently unwrap his fingers. A jagged red line up the inside of his arm immediately wells with blood.

"Shit," he murmurs. "I can't get the bleeding to stop."

I pull my shirt over my head without hesitation, but a moment before I go to press it to the wound, I pause.

"What is it?" He asks, eyes not quite focussing as he peers up at me.

I shove the fabric against his skin, wrapping it as tightly as possible and placing his hand back over it to hold it in place. "Nothing. It's just my favourite shirt. But we either sacrifice it or you. And I don't want to have to tell Sadie I let you bleed out because I liked my shirt."

He chuckles in a vague, not all there kind of way. "It's a good shirt," he says, his eyes drifting down over my body.

I'm wearing a sports bra today, like most days when I'm on farm. It's not sexy in the slightest, just a plain navy blue bra that keeps the girls in check while I'm riding.

But the way Dallas's eyes are lingering you'd think I was wearing skimpy lingerie. His tongue slips out and swipes across his bottom lip. The sight, and the memories is stirs, makes me shiver.

"Righto, cowboy," I say, pulling us both out of the moment. "Let's get you up."

I pull him to his feet and he sways a little. His paleness and the swaying concerns me. So does the way he's apparently struggling to focus.

"We need to get you onto Scout," I say, leading him towards the horse and grateful she hasn't wandered away since I abandoned her in panic.

"No," he gasps, stumbling backwards a step. "Not the horse."

"Yes, the horse. How else am I going to get you back?"

"Bike," he mutters, trying to pull away from me but staggering.

"You can't ride the bike with your arm like that. And I can't leave Scout out here alone. You need to get on the horse."

He turns his wide blue eyes on me. I've seen a lot of emotions in those eyes—frustration, anger, concern, lust—but not this one. Not pure, unfiltered terror. "Can't," he whispers, his voice rough as he flicks his gaze away.

"You can, cowboy." I place both my hands on his face, forcing eye contact. "You have to. We have to get you to the hospital." He tries to pull away but I hold him still, the rasp of his stubble grazing my fingertips. "Gotta get you back to Lady Sadie."

A small smile tugs at his mouth. "She loves that you call her that."

"I love to call her that." I stroke a thumb over his cheek. "I'm going to get up on Scout and we're going to get you up behind me, okay? I'll make sure you're okay. I promise."

Dallas glances down at his arm, the blood already starting to seep through my lilac coloured shirt. Then he looks at me, over my shoulder at Scout and fixes his gaze on my face again. "I don't think I can."

"Can you try for me?" I don't understand. This man is so sure, so capable, and he is truly terrified to get on Scout. I knew he had a fear of horses, but I assumed it was just that he wasn't used to being around them. This is so much more than that. "I don't know how else to get you back."

He must pick up on the thread of desperation in my voice because he gives a shaky nod and I exhale in relief.

I need to get him back to the house and into a vehicle so I can get him into the hospital. The quick glance I got of the wound in his arm tells me he's going to need it cleaned out, stitches and probably a hefty dose of antibiotics. He's in no state to ride the motorbike back, even if he could take the pressure off his arm.

"You'll have to help me," he says in a shaky voice.

"I'll help you," I say, smoothing my fingers across his tense brow and cupping his cheek again. "I promise. I've got you."

I turn away and swing myself into Scout's saddle, then reach down for Dallas's good arm. I grip it tight and he uses the stirrup to boost himself up while I pull. It's awkward and clumsy but we get him on board. It's a blessing Scout is such a steady mount.

Dallas slides into place behind the saddle, wrapping his fingers around his injured arm again.

"Put your arms around me and hold on in front of me. It'll help you stay on."

He hesitates, then does as I said. I shiver as I feel his arms slide against the bare skin of my waist. He reapplies pressure to his wound and presses his face into my shoulder.

I place my hand over his and squeeze gently. "I've got you," I murmur as I urge Scout forward.

Dallas tenses as she moves, but after a few strides he settles again.

"Talk to me," I say, desperate for the distraction from both the memory of the injury, and the feel of his arms around me. The mixture of bare skin and firm grip has me flashing back to the night we met again, but now just doesn't seem like the time.

"Sadie had a riding accident," he mutters into the crook of my neck. I can feel his breath ghosting over my shoulder and I close my eyes in a moment of bliss at the sensation. "She was on a horse with Abi and they got thrown."

"Abi?"

"Her mum. Abigail." Dallas draws a shaky breath. "I thought we were going to lose Sadie."

With the hand not on the reins, I reach up and run my fingers through his hair, gently holding his head against my shoulder. "She's okay now though, right?"

"Yeah, but that accident still screwed everything up. It's the reason we lost Abi." Another shaky breath is exhaled against my bare shoulder.

"What happened?" I whisper.

"She blamed herself and after she healed enough to be able to look after Sadie again ... she just couldn't. She had panic attacks every time she was left alone with her. Sadie was only two. In the end Abi couldn't be around us anymore. She wanted to get herself sorted out, and I haven't seen her since. I send her emails, giving her updates on Sadie. But she obviously isn't ready to come back to her yet."

I thread the fingers of my free hand through his hair again, caressing his scalp. "I'm so sorry."

"It's not Abi's fault. And our relationship was struggling already. In the end, we were together because of Sadie. But it's still a kicker."

"And you've not gotten over the horse fear?"

He shakes his head. "I could ride before. I wasn't good at it like you. I didn't love it like you do. But I could get on a horse if I had to."

"You're on one now," I whisper, resting my hand back over his.

"Don't remind me," he groans.

"You're doing great," I say, a smile tinging my words. He snorts and my smile turns into a laugh. "When you're feeling better we'll go on a proper ride."

"This one's actually pretty amazing," he says, brushing his cheek against my shoulder in a movement that almost feels like a soft kiss. I shiver. "You're cold."

"I'm fine. I meant I'll take you on a ride you can enjoy without worrying about bleeding out. Trust me, it'll be more fun."

I can feel his cheek curve against my back and I think he's smiling.

"I might hold you to that," he murmurs. "Can I ask another favour too?"

"Course you can, cowboy. But I can't promise I'll agree."

He snorts. "Typical. I hope you'll agree to this one though." He takes a deep breath. "Will you teach Sadie?"

"Teach Sadie ..." I repeat, hoping I'm understanding his meaning, because there's nothing I'd like more than what I think he's asking me.

"Yeah, will you teach her to ride?"

22

DALLAS

MY ARM IS THROBBING. I can feel it everywhere. Somehow I can hear it.

I wrap it tighter around Katie's middle and press my uninjured hand to the shirt she's sacrificed.

I rest my cheek against her bare shoulder and close my eyes again. It's somehow easier to forget I'm on a horse if they're squeezed shut, even though the rolling gait of the animal is a dead giveaway.

In a total dick move, I'm using Katie as a distraction, and she's proving to be an excellent one, from both the throbbing in my arm and the fact I'm on a horse.

If I think about my arm too much, I start feeling woozy.

If I think about the horse thing, the panic starts clawing at me.

But Katie smells like hay and flowers and something sweet, like caramel maybe. Her skin is smooth and warm where I'm resting my head against it. I shouldn't be. I should be keeping distance between us.

It seems impossible for Katie and I to be on the same page. Every time things are going well I stick my huge foot in it.

And things are going well now, so I definitely don't want to screw it up ... again.

"Are you sure?" Katie asks, her voice quiet.

It takes me a moment to bring my mind back around to what I'd said.

I asked her to teach Sadie to ride.

"Yes," I murmur, feeling my lips brush against her skin and refusing to move my head to prevent it. The sensation is too good. The throbbing vanishes in that brief moment, overwhelmed by the feeling of desire shooting down my spine and coiling in my belly.

"I'm going to check with you again when you aren't experiencing blood loss."

"I'm fine." I tuck my face into the crook of her neck. At this point she doesn't even flinch because I've been all over her like a rash since she managed to get me on Scout.

At first it was just me trying to ignore the fact I was on a horse, but then she started running her fingers through my hair, like she wanted my head resting against her shoulder, my face pressed into her skin.

Now, I never want to stop touching her. I never did. Not after our first night—as much as she tried to play into the prissy city girl persona to piss me off—and not since.

"Whatever you say, cowboy." She pats my cheek. Her

thumb rubs across my jaw and I have to purposefully think about me riding a horse right now so I don't think about Katie riding me.

Maybe the blood loss is worse than I thought.

"You're right," I say. "She needs to learn." I lift my head and glance around. A wave of nausea hits me.

"We'll talk about it later, okay? Just hold on for now. We're almost back, then Vi can take you into town."

"Violet's not there." I squeeze my eyes shut and drop my head again. "She took Sadie to school and was getting a few things while she was in town."

"Shit," Katie mutters.

"I'll be fine," I say. I don't want to acknowledge what's going on with my arm under Katie's shirt.

I was cutting a piece of alkathene water pipe with my knife, because somehow I'd forgotten the proper tool when I headed out this morning.

The blade slipped and sliced up my forearm.

I barely had the chance to glance at it, let alone inspect it, before the blood came. I slammed my hand over the wound, pressing down to slow the bleeding, but every time I tried to release the pressure so I could reach for my phone, the flow started again.

I don't want to remove the shirt and have to actually deal with the consequences of my stupidity. I can still move all my fingers, so I'm hoping everything inside my arm is okay and it's just a shallow wound.

"You're absolutely not fine," Katie says and I know she's rolling her eyes at me.

When we reach the main farm track leading back to the barn, Katie fishes her phone out of her pocket with her free hand. She's ridden the entire way back one handed, totally relaxed like she doesn't have a care in the world. Her free hand has ranged from resting atop my own, still keeping pressure on my injured arm, to running through my hair, and—my favourite —gently resting against my face.

Katie has a quick phone call with Olivia, letting her know I'm alright, and when we reach the driveway, she draws Scout to a stop next to the house.

"Time to get you down, cowboy."

I freeze. Getting up here felt impossible, and I'm all for getting off the horse, but it also means releasing Katie. It means this moment we've shared, without pissing the other off, is over. I don't want to let that go.

My arms tighten involuntarily around her waist. I press my forehead into her shoulder again, with a little more pressure than earlier. I allow myself one, two seconds like that, then slowly relax and lift my head.

"Thank you, Katie," I murmur against her neck.

She shivers again, goosebumps rippling across her skin. "Hop down, get in the ute. I'll drive you to the hospital." Her tone is almost neutral. Almost. There's a slight tremor there, like she's not shivering because it's a chilly morning and she's only wearing a bra with her jeans.

I release my arms, letting my good hand trail across her stomach as I draw it back, then I slip my leg over the horse's rump and slide to the ground.

I stumble as my boots hit the dirt and Katie scrambles down

after me, steadying me. "I'm good," I mumble, a burn of embarrassment heating my cheeks.

I've barely made it to the ute by the time Katie has stripped Scout of her tack and released her into the small paddock beside the house. Her gaze lingers on the sweat staining the horse's back and I know she's regretting not being able to give Scout the grooming she deserves.

"I'll help you with Scout later," I say as Katie climbs into the driver's seat of my ute. She looks at me sideways as she twists the key to start the ignition. "What? I need to get over it. You're right."

She gives me that eye roll again. "Sure, cowboy. We'll come back to this when you're not bleeding everywhere."

It's like she's refusing to believe that I can get over this fear. That I want to get over the fear.

I still can't believe I told her about Abi. About the accident that changed everything.

I was there when it happened. Abi was sitting on the horse, Sadie on the saddle in front of her. Sadie's two year old face was filled with so much glee and joy. I snapped a picture as they walked past where I was standing.

Then the horse tripped.

It stumbled, falling to its knees with Abi and Sadie tumbling off. Abi fell clear, but Sadie was still too close when the horse pushed back to its hooves. The screaming—from Sadie, from Abi, from me—startled the horse and ever since, that's all I've been able to see when I go near a horse. That placid pony's wild eyes and flared nostrils, its head tossed back in panic, and its massive hooves connecting with my daughter's tiny body.

Sadie made a full recovery. She doesn't even seem to remember the fall. Physically she's perfect.

But Abi never got over that day, and neither did I.

Even Aurora sniffing me through the yard railings is enough to set my heart racing and shorten my breathing. I've never told anyone here why I don't go near horses, why I don't want Sadie riding, and they've never questioned me, never pushed the issue.

But the smile Sadie had on her face the very first day Katie arrived here, when she unknowingly broke my biggest rule, has stuck with me.

It reminded me of the expression on her face on the day of the accident. The joy, the glee, the happiness. As much as I never want Sadie to go near another horse again in her life, my life dictates she'll always be around them in some capacity.

So, Katie will teach Sadie to ride, if she wants to, because there's no one else I trust more with my daughter.

The drive to town is quiet, and I wonder if it's because Katie thinks I'm talking nonsense every time I open my mouth. Yeah, I don't feel spectacular, but I'm not completely away with the fairies right now.

I'm present enough to be fully aware Katie still hasn't found a shirt.

She pulls into a park outside the hospital. It's only a small hospital: a few nondescript low buildings, with a couple of emergency doctors and a single ward for minor stays. Anything more serious gets transported to the big hospital three hours away.

"Come on," Katie says, unbuckling her seat belt and moving to climb out of the ute.

"Shirt," I say like a fool.

Katie glances down at herself, shrugs and gets out of the ute anyway. She rounds the front of the vehicle and meets me at my door, helping me out like I'm an invalid.

"You'll be cold," I mutter as my boots hit the asphalt of the carpark.

"I'm more concerned about your arm right now," she replies, slipping an arm around my waist. "People see more of me in a bikini."

I close my eyes at the visual my imagination conjures at the word bikini. Unfortunately, because it's inside my head, closing my eyes doesn't help in the slightest.

She leads me into the emergency waiting room and sits me down on the first available seat before approaching the check-in desk.

A moment later, she's sitting down beside me with a clipboard in hand. I go to take the pen from her to fill in the paperwork, but she bats my hand away, then starts interrogating me as she fills out my information. When she's finished and after she returns the form to the front desk, Katie returns to my side.

"It's okay, you don't have to wait," I say. She gives me a sideways look so I continue. "I'm sure you have other things to do today."

"Ah, not really. My boss isn't on farm today so he won't be busting my ass about it."

I huff a tiny laugh. "Sounds like your boss is a jerk."

She shrugs. "He has his moments, but I think I mostly misjudged him. There's a little more to him than I first realised."

With that, she slides her hand around my arm, tucking it in against my bicep, then rests her head on my shoulder.

I tilt my head and rest it against hers, hesitantly at first, but when she exhales a soft sigh and nestles even closer, I relax.

"Thank you, Katie," I whisper.

Then, we wait.

23

____

KATIE

I DON'T KNOW how long we sit side by side, resting our heads together, on the hard plastic chairs of the waiting room. One of my hands is resting over the top of Dallas's on his injured arm, the other one has slipped inside the sleeve of his shirt and is tucked against the soft skin of the inside of his bicep.

Usually this kind of wait time would frustrate me, but Dallas's presence has me calm and grounded. I'm not even bouncing my foot in agitation because I don't want to leave this moment.

Dallas readjusts his grip on my shirt, still wrapped around his injury, and lets out a hiss. The sound instantly has me on alert.

As much as I'm enjoying just sitting here with him, the man is injured and bleeding.

I push to my feet, reluctantly letting my fingers slide free of their position on his arm.

"Where are you going?" Dallas asks, his voice low and soft, just a question, not a demand.

"To find out how long it'll be," I say, peering down at him to check how he's doing. He's still far too pale for my liking.

He reaches up with his uninjured arm and wraps his fingers softly around my wrist, holding me in place. "Don't, it takes as long as it takes. It's not their fault it's slow." His fingers slide down and twist with mine.

I stare down at him. My heart is hammering in my chest and I don't understand why. We've been more intimate than this.

"Stay with me," Dallas whispers and I feel like the words mean more than just sitting down now.

My breath catches in my throat. I have no idea what to say, but I move to sit down again.

"Dean McLeod," a woman's voice calls from across the room.

Instead of me sitting, Dallas now stands. He sways a little and I reach out to steady him.

It's alarming.

How much blood can a person lose? He hasn't been bleeding that much since I got to him. My shirt's sacrifice has been worth it to stop the bleeding. Maybe it's the pain that's making him unsteady on his feet.

"You alright there?" The woman's voice asks, from right behind us. The relief of knowing there's someone else here to take over is immense.

Dallas looks past me at the nurse, but his gaze immediately shoots to mine, his eyes wide.

I spin around, wanting to know what caused his reaction.

"Katie?" The nurse takes in my appearance: dirty jeans and sports bra, Dallas's blood somehow streaked along my arm.

My chest tightens and my eyes immediately start to burn.

Clarissa Sheridan is standing in front of me.

Toby and Max's mother.

The woman who could have been my mother-in-law.

The last time I saw her was when I came home for Toby's funeral, but those few days were a blur of chaos, grief and heartbreak.

I don't remember much of them, except that I barely spoke to anyone.

I couldn't bring myself to speak to Clarissa. She has a way of making you want to talk, to open up and share everything and I didn't want to slip and accidentally tell her what had really happened between Toby and I.

Clarissa is exactly how I remember her. Tall like Toby and Max, dark hair pulled back in a French braid, dark eyes like her sons', except hers are traced with soft lines that I know are from smiling.

I struggle to suck down a breath, until I feel Dallas pressing his fingers into my back. He's not pushing me forward, he's simply lending his support.

"Clarissa," I croak out.

I have no idea how she's going to react to seeing me. It's been years.

One son is dead, the other blames me for his death. I don't know where Clarissa stands on that. I don't know if she believes the same things as Max, if she feels the same way.

We were fairly close when I lived here before and she

always seemed to approve of my relationship with Toby, but that was before we left, before he died.

"Oh, Katie. I'd heard you were back in town," she says, then reaches forward and wraps her arms around me, pulling me in for a tight hug.

My arms automatically come around her and I find myself clinging on, tears welling despite me trying to push them down.

The relief that she doesn't hate me too is overwhelming. I want to curl into her and let her hold me forever.

Eventually Clarissa releases her hold and steps back. She wipes at her cheek and it takes me a moment to process that she's wiping away tears.

She clears her throat. "Alright, sorry Dallas, let's get this arm looked at." She reaches out and rubs my arm. "It's good to see you, Katie. I hope you're doing okay. Are you cold? Do you want me to find you something to wear?"

I shake my head. "I'm fine. Just look after him." I gesture towards Dallas, who's watched our whole interaction silently.

He must know Clarissa is Toby and Max's mum. His reaction to seeing her tells me he does. Why else would he look at me like I was going to bolt right out of the hospital?

I almost did. If she hadn't surprised me with that hug, I'd be long gone by now. I always assumed Max had convinced his parents of his side of the story, whatever it is, because Clarissa never reached out to me after the funeral. Any communication I had with them was through their lawyer when it came time to handle Toby's possessions after his death.

But that hug ... maybe she doesn't hate me as much as I thought.

"Come on through," Clarissa says to Dallas, heading for the examination rooms.

I watch her go, then turn to resume my position on the hard plastic waiting room chair. "I'll wait for you here," I say.

Dallas cradles his injured arm against his chest and reaches out his good hand. "Come with me," he says, voice impossibly soft. "Please."

"You don't need me," I say.

"You'd be surprised," he says. He reaches out and slips his fingers back into mine. "Please," he repeats and the plea in his tone has me following him soundlessly.

DALLAS HAS HIS INJURY INSPECTED, poked and prodded, cleaned out and stitched closed. I stay right by his side for the entire process, for much of it with his good hand in mine.

The doctor is certain there isn't any major damage inside his arm, which is a huge relief. Tendon damage would mean surgery and Dallas wants none of that. When the doctor tells us all the injury needs is a thorough clean and stitches, Dallas wilts against me, muttering something along the lines of 'thank fuck'.

Clarissa talks him through caring for the injury, when he needs to come back to have the stitches out, then releases us back into the world.

Aside from her initial show of emotion when she hugged me, Clarissa was entirely professional during our visit. She spoke to Dallas, but largely ignored my presence, except for a long moment when she took in the sight of our hands linked together.

She treated him with care and respect and wished him well with his recovery, saying she'd see him again in a week to check the wound.

I blink rapidly at the bright sunlight as we step outside.

"What time is it?" Dallas asks while I readjust to the outside world. Being in a hospital is such a weirdly disconcerting feeling, with no sense of time or place.

I check my phone. "One-thirty."

He sighs. "By the time we get back to the Ridge, it'll be time for me to come back in to get Sadie. What a waste of a day." He scowls over his shoulder at the hospital like it's personally wronged him.

"First of all, you're not driving anywhere right now, let alone with Lady Sadie in the car. Did you see the painkillers they gave you?"

Dallas scowls at me this time. "My daughter needs picking up. What else do you suggest I do? Leave her at school?"

"No," I say, folding my arms across my chest. "Stop being a jerk, it's not my fault you hurt yourself. If you gave me a second I'd tell you that we can wait in town and head back after we pick her up."

Dallas blinks at me. "Don't you have things to do?"

I peer at him. "You're the boss, you tell me."

He cracks a small smile at that. "You've wasted a whole day babysitting me because of my own stupidity. I don't want to waste more of your time."

"I get the afternoon off, what part of that doesn't sound great to you?"

He laughs properly this time. "Okay. What did you have in mind for us to do with this time off?"

"Well, first we need to feed you, because you shouldn't be on painkillers like that without decent food in you. And also, I'm hungry. Then we can do whatever, but I suggest hanging out at my place, because then I can have a nap. You can watch TV or whatever."

"Do I get a nap too?" His gaze connects with mine and it causes my heart to do that weird hitching thing I've been feeling way too often around him. His eyes are dark and intent on mine.

I clear the block from my throat and shrug. "Sure, if you want."

"Alright, sounds good," he says, his voice rough and low.

Goosebumps skitter over my skin and I turn away, pulling the keys from my pocket.

"Hey, princess," Dallas says, reaching out and snagging my wrist. I twist back to face him and try to ignore the way he's tracing his thumb across my pulse point, sending more shivers my way. "Thank you," he says.

I shrug him off, trying to pretend I'm not affected by him in the slightest. The real truth is, I am. Constantly. He's always on my mind and I can't seem to stop touching him.

I want his hands on me again, rough but gentle. I want his mouth on mine and his scent filling my nose. I want to feel him shiver as I trail my fingers across his skin. I want to relive every moment of our night together, and more.

But I shouldn't want that. And we definitely shouldn't go there again.

We climb into the ute and I drive to the centre of town. We grab filled rolls and danishes from Sugar, the best cafe in town, then head back to my place to eat them.

I let us into the house and immediately regret suggesting we come here.

So far, having Dallas in my house has only led to bad decisions and awkwardness.

It confuses the boundaries that are already so blurred they're virtually non-existent. I don't know where we stand anymore and bringing him here, into my own space, with no one else around to be a buffer is asking for trouble.

We eat in silence but the moment I swallow my last mouthful I know I have to deal with the fact Dallas is in my house ... again.

"Do you want a shower?" I ask, my voice coming out hoarse.

Dallas shakes his head. "Nah, I'm good. I'll just maybe have a sit on your couch."

"You can lie down in the bedroom if you want," I say and when he raises an eyebrow I can tell he's thinking about my bed and the last time he was in it. "The spare room has a good bed," I choke out. "I'm going to shower."

I flee to the bathroom, wanting to shower off the sweat from this morning's work, and the stench of hospital that's still clinging to my skin. I only waited until after lunch because I was starting to think I'd pass out if I didn't eat immediately.

I enjoy the heat of the water sliding down my body, easing

away the tension of the morning and the anxiety over Dallas's wellbeing.

But, I can't stay in here for the next hour. I need to be able to be around Dallas—even in my house without a chaperone. We're definitely friends at this point. I should be able to be near him, have a conversation with him.

I shut off the water, dry myself off, and pull on a pair of leggings and a worn t-shirt.

Towel drying my hair as I walk, I head towards my room at the front of the house. The door to the guest room is wide open, as usual. I assume Dallas hasn't made it to lying down yet, until I glance in and stop in my tracks.

Dallas is stretched out on the bed, his injured arm resting on his chest, the white bandage a stark reminder of his injury.

He's shed his shirt, which was filthy from his morning's work and covered in his own blood. His jeans are also tossed on the floor beside the bed, but thankfully he's covered his lower half with the throw that usually lies across the end of the bed.

I trace the lines of his torso with my eyes, admiring what I see. Smooth skin, hard muscle, a body perfectly shaped by physical work.

"Stop staring, princess," he says, startling me. His eyes are still closed. I don't know how he even knows I'm here, quite obviously perving on him.

"I—I didn't know you were awake," I mutter.

"Clearly," he says, humour clear in his voice. "Come here."

I take a few hesitant steps forward. "What do you need?"

His eyes crack open, the clear blue guileless and earnest. "You," he whispers, reaching out and sliding his fingers into mine for what feels like the millionth time today. It's happened so often it almost feels natural. The fireworks it sets off in my body is anything but though.

"Me?"

"Yeah, will you stay for a bit?" He drops my hand and runs his fingers through his hair, staring at the ceiling. He glances back at me, his expression the tiniest bit sheepish. "Please?"

"You know this is a terrible idea," I murmur.

"Yeah, but what's new where we're concerned?" He lifts the side of his mouth into his cocky smile and the sight of it makes my stomach swoop. I don't see a lot of that smile, he's always too serious at work. "Don't run away, princess. I'll think you're scared of me."

I laugh at that one. "Yeah, right, cowboy. As if." I toss my towel down beside his pile of clothes, and climb onto the bed with him.

24

———

DALLAS

I DIDN'T ACTUALLY EXPECT her to stay.

I thought she'd laugh in my face, give me her reasons for why this is the very last thing we should be doing and leave me to my own devices.

She's not wrong about this being a terrible idea.

I'm currently lying on a bed, with the most gorgeous woman to ever exist beside me and I'm not wearing any pants.

Ditching the jeans was not smart.

As she settles beside me, I readjust my position on the bed, rolling onto my side to hide my reaction to her proximity.

"How's the arm?" she asks, reaching out to trace a finger along the crisp white bandage Clarissa Sheridan applied before we left the hospital. Her touch tickles and is electric, sending both sparks and shivers through my body.

"Hurts like a bitch," I say.

"I can imagine."

I trap her fingers under mine before she can run them down the bandage again. "How are you doing?"

"I'm fine." She glances up at me, then quickly away. "Why wouldn't I be?"

"Clarissa. I'm assuming you weren't expecting to see her today?"

Katie lets out a long breath and rolls onto her back, away from me. "No, I wasn't. I haven't seen her since Toby's funeral."

I watch her carefully. She's blinking rapidly as she stares at the ceiling. "She seemed happy to see you," I say.

Katie shrugs, then covers her face with her hands. "I thought she'd hate me too," she says, her voice muffled behind her hands.

I don't know if I should ask the question sitting on the tip of my tongue. It could see Katie break down some of her walls, or it could cause her to build them back up.

I throw caution to the wind, because I need to know everything possible about this woman, and the words slide free. "Why would she hate you?"

Katie's hands fall back to the mattress and I reach over to entwine my fingers with hers. The movement just happens now, without my conscious thought, but the feeling of her hand in mine hasn't lost its novelty yet. It probably never will, no matter how often I'm allowed to do it.

"Max blames me for making Toby leave town. He thinks it was my idea, but it wasn't. I didn't want to go. I *loved* it here." She takes a shaky breath. "I hadn't felt like I ever had a home before. When I was with my mum we moved around all the time and nothing was ever stable. Moving here to live with my grandma ... I hated it at first, but I made friends and I was happy here. It was home. I didn't want to leave." She rubs her hand over her face again.

"Toby decided he wanted to go and I didn't feel like I had a choice but to go with him —" She breaks off.

"You don't seem like the kind of girl to just go along with what a guy says," I say, wary that I might be throwing gas on the fire.

She snorts. "I'm not. I wasn't then either." She takes a steadying breath and rolls back onto her side. Her grey eyes meet mine and I can clearly see the tears shining there. "I was pregnant," she whispers. "I thought we'd be a family. I didn't realise eventually I'd lose everything. The baby, Toby, my job. Everything."

My breath catches at her admission, and my heart breaks for her. I couldn't imagine losing a baby. As much of a surprise that Sadie was, I wanted her from the second I knew about her.

A tear spills over and rolls down Katie's cheek. "I didn't think I'd end up here again, especially not after Max screamed at me after the funeral. That's when I decided I'd never come back."

I reach out and wipe away her tears with my thumb. She lets out another shuddering breath and presses her face into my hand. "But you did come back," I say, voice quiet in the mid-afternoon hush.

"Yeah. I lost my job. I was running out of money and Livvie needed the help. My grandma left me the house after she passed, but I'm not allowed to sell it until I turn twenty-five, so coming back here seemed like the best option. I thought I could do it. Maybe try and make my life here again ... but Max has had years to convince people to hate me. I can't live in a town where everyone does."

"Princess," I say, my fingers sliding down to caress her neck. "The only person in this town who has the slightest problem with you is Max. Every other person you've seen has loved you. Max doesn't deserve that power. Don't give it to him."

She's silent for long moments, just lying there staring at me as my fingers stray further and further. They brush against her throat, trail along her jaw, trace the gentle curve of her cheek. When she doesn't move, doesn't stop me, my fingers continue exploring: the arch of her brow, the line of her nose, the full, luscious swoop of her lips.

"I'm scared of giving anyone any power over me anymore," she whispers as my palm finally comes to rest, cupping her face.

"I can understand that," I say, thinking about the horse she got me on this morning. "But maybe today is a good day for getting past some of our biggest fears."

Her eyes widen and she grins. It's a complete shift in her demeanour. "You rode a *horse* today, cowboy."

"I did, yes."

She reaches out, her hand coming to rest against my face, mirroring my own position. "I'm so proud of you," she says, sincerity in her eyes. None of the cheeky mocking she's usually giving me.

"I meant what I said too. I want you to teach Sadie."

"I'd love to." Her voice is husky and I'm hit with a wave of longing so strong I can barely give her a chance to get her next words out. "But I understand if you want to put a hold on it for now."

"Absolutely not. I want you—"

Then I cut myself off, and close the minimal gap between us.

I press my mouth to hers, feeling her tiny gasp of surprise. My hand slides into her hair as her fingers find their way to the back of my neck. After a second of shock passes between us, Katie opens her mouth and shifts closer to me.

A rough sound comes from the back of my throat as I angle my head to deepen the kiss. Katie's tongue runs along my bottom lip, then slips inside my mouth, brushing against my own. I make that noise again and roll, attempting to push her back into the mattress.

I come up short though, when I crush my injured arm underneath me.

"Fuuuuck," I grit out, breaking off the kiss.

Katie is on her back, staring up at me with eyes wide, cheeks flushed, damp hair spread across the pillow, looking a little stunned at the abrupt end to the kiss. "I'm sorry," she whispers.

"What? Why?" I readjust my position, so my injured arm is clear of any colliding bodies.

"I shouldn't have done that."

"Princess, I started it."

She blinks up at me again, opening her mouth as if to argue. I lean in and cover it with my own again. This time I'm gentle when I taste her.

When I pull back, I gently disengage, then smooth a stray

lock of hair back from her face. "And I don't regret it for a second."

"I thought you didn't want this," she whispers, her fingers tracing over my face. My stomach swoops and a pulsing need shoots through me.

"Oh, I want this, princess."

Her eyes flutter closed at the stupid name. "Even if I can't commit to anything?"

I stroke my fingers through her hair, wondering how to answer that. Because I've already told her I don't want a once off. She opens her eyes and peers up at me, uncertainty written across her face.

I press my lips against hers again. A brief moment of bliss. "Will you give me a chance to change your mind?" Another kiss. Her fingers trail down my neck, tracing the shape of my collarbone. "Give me a chance to replace the old memories with new ones?" I swipe my tongue across her bottom lip and she groans. I want to devour the sound. Devour her. "Let me prove to you that you can be happy here."

I kiss her once more, then pull back and stare down at her. Her eyes are glassy and cheeks flushed. I prop myself on the elbow of my injured arm, ignore the throbbing pain and trail my fingers through her hair. "Can you do that?" I whisper.

Her eyes close as my fingers stroke across her scalp, then slowly open again. "Yes," she says, her voice hoarse. "Okay. I can try."

"That's all I need," I say, then fit my hand against her neck and capture my mouth with hers.

It's a solid kiss, sure and slow. Then her hand runs down my bare chest, along my side, and slides around my waist.

I groan and press myself into her, like I've wanted to since I first kissed her. One of my legs is over hers and the feel of her thigh between mine makes my eyes blur and the world spin.

The sound I make, and the pressure against her leg switches something in her. She makes a hoarse gasping noise and pushes her hips into me. One moment, she's underneath me, the next, she's rolled us so I'm flat on my back, her leg hooked over my body.

"Holy shit," I say, dazed. I blink a few times as I readjust to the new position.

Katie laughs and pushes off the bed. Next thing I know, she's straddling me. She swirls her hips in the most sensual way, grinding down on my cock. It's been hard since she lay down beside me but now it's rock solid and aching.

"God, I've missed this feeling," she murmurs, looking down on me.

My hands land on her hips, helping to guide her motion. I'm incapable of words, but another breathy sound escapes me.

She laughs again, the sound light and breezy. "I've been thinking about it since the night we met." She stops circling and thrusts her hips forward in a sharp motion.

"Fuck." The word leaves me riding another guttural cry and Katie grins down at me, all of her caution and wariness gone. "Come here," I say as I snake one hand up her body and grasp the nape of her neck, pulling her down into another searing kiss. "You're going to kill me."

"You can take it," she says, smiling against my mouth. "I

however, might not be able to take it much longer if you don't touch me."

"I am touching you." I press a kiss to her jaw, then trail a line of open mouthed kisses down her neck. She shivers and shudders against me.

"Properly," she hisses, then follows up the word with another thrust of her hips. She's only wearing leggings and I'm only in my underwear so I can feel *everything*. "Touch me," she utters the command on a moan, which takes away some of the authority but not my desire to do as she says.

I trace my fingers across her hips, holding her lightly, then gently sweeping my hands higher. Katie growls and yanks the worn t-shirt off over her head.

She's wearing another sports bra, this time bright pink. It pushes her breasts together, a soft swell spilling over the top of the low-cut neckline as she heaves in a deep breath. I just about lose my head right then and there.

Her shirt removal tactic did exactly what she wanted it to. I push myself to sitting, remembering not to use my injured arm at the last second, then reverently run my hands over the pink fabric. I cup her tits in my hands and run my thumbs across the velvety smooth skin. I lower my head and press a kiss to the exposed skin, then trail my tongue along the edge of the bra.

"This is so fucking hot," I murmur, unable to lift my mouth from her flesh.

"Hotter than the first time?" She asks, her voice teasing as she threads her fingers into my hair, holding my face against her chest.

The memory slams into me. The one of Katie pushing me

down onto her bed, then stepping back and staring down at me for a long moment. I propped myself up on my elbows and watched as she trailed her gaze over my body, pausing when she reached the fly of my jeans and slowly licked her bottom lip.

She pulled her sweater off and dropped it to the floor, then tugged her silky tank top over her head and tossed it onto my chest. She popped the button and lowered the zipper of her jeans, letting me see enough to know that her underwear matched the skimpy white lace bra she was wearing.

She watched me take in the sight, then stepped forward and popped the button of my own jeans as she dropped to her knees between my thighs.

Katie's fingers tug at my hair, bringing me back to this moment. I lick across her breast again, then press my open mouth over the cup of the bra. She arches back, pushing her hips into mine and her chest forward. Her hair spills down her back and I tangle my hand in it, holding her in that position.

"Yeah," I mutter. "Hotter than the last time." She utters an unintelligible sound. "I know who you are now." I use my free hand to tug down the front of the bra. It's too rigid to move far, but I catch a glimpse of the dusky edge of her nipple. I press my mouth as close as I can to it and suck her skin into my mouth, rolling it between my lips and tongue.

Katie arches back even further with a hiss of pleasure. The sound shoots straight to my groin where my throbbing cock is still pressed against her. "You like putting in the work, huh, cowboy?"

"Only if it's worth it." I tug her hair to expose her neck further, so I can tease the skin there with my mouth. I slide my other hand down and grip her ass, admiring the gorgeous curve and how well it fits into my palm.

"Oh, I'll make sure it's worth it." Another groan and a flurry of shivers ripples through her. She pushes her ass back into my hand, trying to change the angle so my fingers brush the inside of her thighs. I'm just beginning to slide them forward when a sharp sound cuts through the room.

Katie's head jerks up as I slam my eyes closed and press my face into the curve where her neck meets her shoulder. "What's that?" she asks.

"My alarm," I say into her neck as I settle both my hands on her waist. She's stopped grinding down on me and we sit with her across my lap, her fingers in my hair as we pant together. "I set it before in case I fell asleep. I didn't want to sleep through school pick up."

"Well, it's probably a good thing you set it, because we would definitely have missed pick up otherwise."

I huff a laugh and lift my head, reaching for my phone on the mattress beside me to shut off the alarm.

Katie threads her fingers into my hair and stares at me, her gaze soft as it meets mine. Her confidence from a moment ago seems to have evaporated.

I close the tiny space between us and press my lips against hers in a sweet, chaste kiss. "We'll resume this another time," I whisper in the quiet between us.

She nods. "We should probably discuss what all this means at some point too." She chews her lip, looking nervous and uncertain.

I kiss her again. "We will. Soon. I promise. But, for now, can we be careful around Sadie? I don't want to confuse her."

"Of course," Katie says. She pushes back and slowly climbs off my lap. "Come on, cowboy." She reaches for my hand and helps pull me off the bed. "Let's go get your girl."

I reach for my jeans and laugh as she eyes what's going on in my underwear. "Your fault, princess."

She smirks and looks far too pleased with herself.

I LOVE Sadie with all my heart, but does she have to finish school *right now*?

Dallas was so close—*so close*—to running his fingers along the centre seam of my leggings when that cursed alarm went off.

I grab my t-shirt off the floor and pull it over my head. When I can see again, I catch sight of Dallas. He has his jeans on now, hiding the impressive sight of his hard length pressing against his dark boxer briefs.

I shiver at the feeling still lingering between my legs, the one caused by spending the last however long grinding my pussy against that dick with only a few layers of thin fabric between us.

Dallas taps at his phone screen a few times, then slides it into his back pocket. He's still shirtless and the sight of the muscles in his back flexing as he moves nearly sends me to my knees.

It wouldn't be a bad position to be in right now.

I shake that thought from my head. I have to get it together. We have to pick up Sadie in a few minutes and then I have to go back to work and pretend like I don't want to climb her dad every chance I get.

Dallas turns and catches me ogling him. "You can't look at me like that," he says, his voice raspy. "I'll never get anything done."

"Well, maybe you shouldn't look like that." I gesture at his shirtless body. "I mean, fuck, I knew what you looked like without your shirt on, but god damn, now I know I get to do that again ..." I trail off and bite my lip.

Dallas's eyes flare with heat as he steps closer. "You get to do it again, and more, princess. Soon." He presses his hot body against me and leans down to ghost his mouth over mine.

"Stop," I groan, as a twist of lust lances through my pelvis. I push him away. "You have to not touch me right now or we're never going to make it to pick up Sadie." He sighs and runs a hand through his hair. "And please, put your shirt on or I can't be held responsible for my actions."

He tips his head back and laughs, then picks up his blood-covered shirt and studies it. "Hopefully I have a clean one in the ute," he says. "You ready to go?"

"Just give me a second to put some jeans on."

"But ... those leggings." He eyes them, that dark look back in his eye.

"Yeah, yeah, settle cowboy. I appreciate you think they're hot but they're useless for working in." He looks like a kids who's just dropped his ice cream. I head for the door, then glance back at him over my shoulder. He's staring at my ass.

"Don't worry. I think you'll like the jeans I'm planning on wearing." I shoot him a smirk, then leave the room.

When I reach my bedroom, I hunt in the back of my dresser for my oldest pair of jeans. I don't even know why I still have them. They're so worn. There's rips in several places, but they hug my ass like no other pants I've ever owned and I haven't quite been able to part with them, or the confidence boost they give me. I slide them up my legs, then head for the kitchen. Dallas is leaning against the counter, staring at his injured arm and running his fingers over the bandage.

"How's it feeling?" I ask, grabbing my house keys and his ute keys off the bench.

"Throbbing like a bitch," he says with a grimace. "It's like my heart beat is actually in my arm."

"We probably didn't exactly help it."

He smirks at me, that cocky look he'd given me the night we met, the one that made me want to take him home and spend the night moaning his name. "I don't regret it."

Heat floods my cheeks. I don't know why I'm suddenly blushing. I'm the one who took this afternoon from an emotional overshare into me grinding on his lap while he buried his face in my cleavage.

"Let's go get Sadie," I say, turning abruptly and heading for the door. I lock it behind us and climb into the driver's seat of the ute as Dallas finds a shirt in the pile of clothing in the back seat. I start the vehicle and turn to back out of the driveway, the empty space beside the spare clothes catching my attention. "Shit. We don't have her car seat." I flop back into my seat, chewing on my bottom lip, trying to find a solution here. I assume Dallas would normally switch the car seat from Violet's car to his on the days he was picking her up.

"It's okay. We leave the car seat at school on the days we aren't sure who's going to make pick up."

I blow out my breath, then resume reversing. "That's a smart idea."

Dallas shrugs. "Having a kid, especially in my situation, you have to be prepared for all sorts of things. Because I never know if I'm actually going to make pick up, but because I really want to be able to do it, Violet suggested leaving the seat with Sadie so we didn't run into that issue." He runs a hand through his hair, then braces his elbow on the door. "Honestly, I don't know what I'd do without Violet and Olivia. I don't know how parents have jobs, let alone single ones."

"Vi and Livvie are pretty amazing, but don't discredit yourself. You're doing an incredible job." Dallas snorts, as if he doesn't believe me. "You've only been here for six months, right?"

"Yeah. What's your point?"

"My point is Sadie was a spectacular kid before you got here. As amazing as Violet and Liv are, their influence can't have been that great on her in such a short amount of time. You raised that little girl. You should give yourself the credit for doing a great job."

Dallas doesn't respond, he doesn't even look my way as we drive slowly through the streets of town. There aren't many. The main street with the majority of retail businesses lining it, including the pub where we first met on the corner. The farm supply store is just down the street, and other industrial or trade businesses are located a block over, taking up twice the area of the retail stores. The town definitely isn't a big one, but supports such a vast rural area, we have all the services we need except a decent clothing store. Unless of course you only want to wear farm brand attire.

The primary school is located on the far side of town to my house, set in a residential area. The high school, weirdly, is on the same side of town as my place, just about as far away from the primary school as possible, something that's never made any sense to me.

I turn down the street the school is on and find an empty parking space in the shade of a massive Puriri tree. We're lucky to get it. We aren't late, but already most of the parking spaces are filled and parents are milling around in front of the school.

Dallas and I join them and a moment later the end of day bell rings. Children pour from the classrooms and I search through them for Sadie. I never went to this school, so I'm not even sure which classes are for junior students as opposed to senior ones.

"Katie!" I turn as a small force collides with me. Apparently I was looking in completely the wrong direction.

"Good afternoon, Lady Sadie." I grin down at her as she hugs my legs, her backpack sliding off one shoulder.

"Why are you here?"

"I was in town with your dad and wanted to surprise you."

"I'm so surprised," she says, beaming up at me. I scoop her into my arms and once she's settled on my hip she seems to notice her dad for the first time. "Daddy!" she exclaims. A small frown creases her forehead. "What happened to your arm?"

Dallas is standing watching us with a soft smile on his face, his arms crossed over his chest. He glances down at the bandage. "I hurt my arm on the farm today. The doctor had to look at it."

"Will it be okay?" Sadie whispers and I hug her tighter against me.

"I'm going to be absolutely fine. Katie looked after me."

Dallas slides Sadie's backpack off her, leaving the little girl in my arms. She leans her head against my shoulder and squeezes her arms around me so tightly I'm not sure I can breathe. "Thank you, Katie," she says softly.

"It was my pleasure, sweetheart," I murmur into her hair. I close my eyes as her scent hits me. Her hair smells like bubblegum. For a moment my brain flashes to what my life would be like if I hadn't lost my own baby, but I push the thoughts away. Now is not the time to dwell on the past.

"My pleasure too," Dallas mutters into my ear as he falls into step beside us heading for the school building.

Heat flares through my cheeks and I shove him with my elbow, careful not to dislodge Sadie who's clearly exhausted and has curled into me. "Shush," I say.

"Let's just grab this car seat and we'll get back to the farm. I think Sadie and I could help you with Scout this afternoon ..." He trails off and runs a hand through his hair. "If you want some assistance."

"I'm not allowed to help with the horses," Sadie says in a sleepy voice.

"You can now," Dallas says. "If you want."

Sadie sits up immediately and almost topples from my arms.

"Really?" she asks, eyes wide and bright as I manage to remain upright.

"Yeah." Dallas scoops up the car seat and heads back for the car. "Scout at least. I feel like we maybe came to an understanding today."

I laugh softly. "Your dad had to ride Scout with me after he hurt himself."

"You did?" Sadie turns back to Dallas. The pride on her face is evident as he nods. "Yay, Daddy!"

"Would you like a little ride on her when we get home?" he asks her and when she nods so enthusiastically she nearly falls from my arms again, he laughs and ruffles her hair. "Let's go then."

I expect him to drop his hand from Sadie's head back to his side, but he doesn't. He meets my eyes over her as she sighs contentedly and presses her face back into my shoulder.

Then he lifts his hand from her blonde curls and brushes it against my cheek in a slow, sensuous stroke, his eyes—burning with desire—never leaving mine. As his hand reaches the edge of my cheek, he twists a lock of hair around his forefinger, lets it slide free, then turns and strides away, leaving me and Sadie to scurry after him.

26

DALLAS

KATIE WAS RIGHT. I'm a huge fan of her jeans. They are spectacular, almost as good as the body inside them.

I fought the urge to hold Katie's hand the entire way back to Wildflower Ridge.

Sadie fell asleep in her car seat in the back of the ute before we left the town boundary, so she wouldn't have seen it, but I couldn't run the risk that she might wake up while Katie's hand was in mine.

Katie also didn't remove her hands from the steering wheel for the entire trip, except to shift the ute into gear, so it wouldn't have been a simple matter of slipping my hand into hers while it rested on the console between us.

Now, she parks my ute beside the main farm house and climbs out of the cab, snagging Sadie's backpack from the back seat, while I unbuckle my daughter and scoop her into my arms, encouraging her to wake up.

A clatter of boots on wood and Olivia races down the porch

steps, sliding to a stop in the gravel in front of us. "Are you okay?"

"I'm fine. They cleaned it out really well and put in a few stitches. But it'll be all good in a few days."

"You'll be all good in a few weeks," Katie says, rolling her eyes at me. "And you're lucky you didn't hit any tendons or anything else important in there."

"I'm fine," I repeat, liking the way Katie has slipped straight back into pushing my buttons and not putting up with my shit.

"Daddy rode Scout today," Sadie pipes up and Olivia's eyes widen.

"He sure did." Katie reaches out and rubs a hand down Sadie's back. "You back with us, Lady Sadie? Why don't you go get changed so you can come help me give Scout some extra special treatment for being the hero today?"

Sadie immediately starts squirming in my arms. I place her on the ground and she takes the backpack from Katie's arms. "I'll make sure to finish my lunch before I have any of Violet's cookies," she says, smiling up at me like the sweetest angel to ever grace the Earth, one that would never pig out on cookies instead of nutritious options I make for her every day.

"Go on." I give her a nudge. "Put on your farm clothes and boots too." Sadie races up the steps and into the house.

"How long are you giving her?" Katie asks.

"About three minutes and she'll be back, cookies in hand," I say sharing a grin with her. Then I glance at Olivia. She's staring at me as though I've lost my mind and she clearly wants to say something, just isn't sure how.

I clear my throat and rub a hand across the back of my neck.

"I've asked Katie to teach Sadie to ride," I say, my voice uncertain.

Olivia blinks a few times, then shoots her best friend a look. Katie scuffs a boot in the gravel. "Are you sure?" Olivia asks after what feels like an eternity of silence.

"Yeah. She wants to be around the horses all the time. It's not fair for my fears to stop her. She needs to learn how to be safe around them. So do I."

Olivia shoots another look in Katie's direction, then back at me. "Okay. She's only allowed near them when an adult is with her though. You, Katie, Me, Mum or Flynn."

"Absolutely," I say.

"I'm ready," Sadie says, interrupting our conversation. She clomps down the steps in her tiny boots. As expected, she's clutching a handful of Violet's chocolate chip cookies. She hands one to me and one to Katie, then looks up at Olivia and down at the single cookie left in her hand. After a moment she holds it up to Olivia.

"It's alright kiddo, I'll go steal my own." Olivia winks. "Have fun you three," she says as she turns and disappears back into the house.

Katie spins on her heel. "Let's go, Lady Sadie," she says through a mouthful of cookie and Sadie giggles, then skips along beside her.

My gaze bounces between them—my girls—walking away, and back to the house where Olivia has disappeared. Something about the way she winked at us and her parting words ... she knows. Somehow, she knows, even though Katie and I barely know.

"You coming, cowboy?" Katie calls over her shoulder and I shove the thought away. I catch up to the girls when they reach the gate to the house paddock. Scout is already heading in our direction.

"Violet said Scout can have this," Sadie says, pulling a carrot from her pocket. "Can she?"

"She sure can," Katie assures Sadie, and when Sadie holds it out for Katie to take, she pauses. "Would you like to feed it to her?" She's asking my daughter but she immediately meets my eyes over Sadie's head. She's already worried she's overstepped.

Sadie glances at me, then slowly nods when I don't bring this whole thing to a screeching halt. Katie takes the carrot and snaps it in half, then shows Sadie how to hold it on her flat palm so Scout can take it off her hand without also taking any of her fingers.

Scout stands patiently at the fence, watching the carrot carefully, until Sadie climbs up on the gate and holds her hand out, exactly the way Katie showed her. She giggles as Scouts lips brush against her palm and she beams at us when the horse is busy crunching away.

"Now, your turn," Katie says, holding out the other half of the carrot ... to me. There's a spark of challenge in her eyes, but as I slowly reach out and take the carrot from her, the challenge softens into reassurance. Our fingers brush as I take the vegetable from her and she catches mine under hers, giving them the briefest squeeze. If I hadn't felt the jolt of electricity that tiny gesture sent straight through my chest, I would have struggled to believe she'd done it, as quick as it'd been.

I step up to the gate beside Sadie and lay the carrot on my

palm. I try to extend it to the horse, who's waiting patiently, letting Sadie stroke her nose right between her nostrils.

My hand shakes, and the carrot falls. I slam my eyes shut in frustration. My five-year-old could do this without any kind of fear. She didn't even hesitate, but for me, just being near this horse, even on the other side of the gate has my pulse racing.

"Here," Katie says quietly in my ear. She presses the carrot back into my hand, then helps me extend my fingers so they're flat. "You good?" she whispers, her fingers still encircling my wrist.

I focus on the feel of her skin and how good she smells, still fresh from her shower, and my heart rate settles—slightly. I give an unsteady nod and expect Katie to release my arm, but she doesn't. She keeps her fingertips pressed into my skin as I offer the carrot to Scout again. My hand shakes again, but Katie steadies it and the carrot doesn't fall. Instead Scout gently picks it up, brushing her big soft lips over my palm, and crunches into it, the look in her eye blissful.

The breath leaves me in a whoosh as I realise I did it, without losing a finger, or my nerve. Katie squeezes my wrist, then lets me go.

"Well done," she says.

"Are you mocking me?"

She turns to face me, so I can see her face. There isn't a trace of mockery or teasing on it. "No," she says, her voice is soft. "I know what it's like to be terrified of something. Now I know why ... well, I'm sorry I ever teased you about this." She chews her lip and I have to resist the urge to reach up and free that full lush bottom lip from her teeth with a brush of my thumb.

I clear my throat. "What's next?"

"How about we go give Scout a little bath?"

"A bath?" Sadie gasps. "Do you have one big enough for her?"

Katie manages to hold in the laugh I know she desperately wants to let loose. I know, because I'm doing the same thing.

"No, Lady Sadie. When Scout has a bath, she doesn't get in a bathtub like we do ..." I tune out as Katie explains how horses have baths. My brain is instantly assaulted by images of Katie in a bath, bubbles piled high around her as she lies back in the steamy water. It seems like something she'd like, but as I recall her bathroom, I realise she doesn't have one. A few comments she's made at the end of long days or dinners at the main house come to mind and I realise she's been using Olivia's bath.

Suddenly, the image of Katie relaxing back in an anonymous bath is replaced by one of Katie in *my* bath. I've got to arrange that ... sooner rather than later.

For now, I shove the thought away before I embarrass myself. I tune back into the conversation Katie and Sadie are having, now about how to safely lead a horse. I should be paying attention.

"The most important thing," Katie is saying, "is never, ever, wrap the rope around your hand. If she got a fright and tried to pull away, and the rope is around your hand, you can get really hurt, so we never want to do that, okay?"

Sadie nods, absorbing everything Katie is saying. "Okay."

"I'll get her halter on and then would you like to lead her to the barn?" Sadie nods so fast I'm concerned for the safety of her neck. "Think your dad's up for carrying a saddle?" The teasing lilt is back in Katie's voice.

"Of course I am, princess," I say.

She gives me a cheeky smirk. "Just making sure you're paying attention." She one hundred percent knows I zoned out.

At least she can't read my thoughts, though maybe I should mention the existence of my bath to her, just so she has to think about it like I am going to be constantly until I can get her in it.

Sadie leads Scout to the barn, while Katie and I carry the tack that Katie had stripped off her and left hanging on the fence when we rushed to the hospital. Sadie is full of confidence with the horse, as she leads her exactly how Katie showed her.

As we walk, Katie explains more to her about how to keep safe around horses. Sadie absorbs every word and asks questions, both sensible and fantastical. I slow my steps, letting them pull slightly ahead of me, then pull out my phone and snap a picture of them together.

This is the kind of moment I want to remember. Sadie, the happiest she's ever been now I've finally gotten over myself, side by side with Katie, the utterly gorgeous woman who's given me a chance.

A chance to take her bruised, broken heart and prove to her I can look after it.

To prove to her that she can be happy here.

To prove to her that she's home.

27

KATIE

SADIE AND DALLAS ace their first horse lesson.

Dallas is still terrified of the animals, but he pushed through it. He helped Sadie and I wash Scout down and give her a thorough groom after Sadie had a quick bareback ride around the arena at the end of the lead rope.

Sadie was in her element, asking a million questions and handling Scout like she's been dealing with horses her whole life.

I return from putting the tack away to find Sadie standing on a mounting block, carefully untangling Scout's mane with a comb as she chats away to the mare at a million miles an hour, telling her all about her day at school.

I come to a stop next to Dallas, who's watching his daughter with a look of blissed out wonder on his face. It's a sight to behold.

So is the way his biceps flex as he crosses his arms.

"Stop by my place before you go home tonight," he murmurs.

"Hmm?" I say, still distracted by his arms.

Dallas chuckles. "Eyes up here, princess." He touches one finger to my chin and lifts my gaze to meet his. "Tonight?"

"Yeah," I breathe, a flurry of nerves churning in my belly. "I guess we've got to figure some stuff out, huh?"

"It's not going to hurt."

"Says you. The talking's the hard part. And I assume you're not going to let me do the *other* hard part until after?"

He laughs again, but smothers it quickly when Sadie glances our way. At least he's not touching me anymore so that won't raise any questions for her.

"One hard thing at a time, princess," he says, voice low. "It's better for us both if we're on the same page."

"Yeah, yeah," I say, trying to brush off the panic I'm feeling at having to bare more of my soul to this man, even though he's been gentle and perfect with every part I've already shown him. "We have terms to renegotiate, I know."

Dallas watches me for a long moment, like he's trying to puzzle me out. It's disconcerting, like he can see right into my brain and pick apart my thoughts. "Is that what you want?" he asks.

"Yes," I whisper. "I'm ready to change the terms of our agreement."

"Good. We'll do that, then we can get to the *real* hard part." He smirks at me, then steps around me to help Sadie while I'm left spluttering over my laugh.

ONCE WE'RE DONE with Scout, Sadie and Dallas head off to do something else, leaving me to work with Aurora for a few hours before dinner.

She's making such good progress, letting me lay the saddle across her back for the first time. I leave it at that, not wanting to push the horse too far, especially when my head is so scattered.

It was easy to push aside my thoughts and feelings about spilling my guts to Dallas when he was here with me and we had Sadie between us, acting as a buffer.

But now that it's just me and Aurora, all the things I said come hurtling back.

I never talk about the miscarriage. Olivia and Toby are the only ones who ever knew I was pregnant. I'm assuming Toby didn't tell anyone, not even after the devastating loss. It wasn't so devastating for him, considering he hadn't wanted to be a father yet.

Losing the baby had been the first blow to our relationship. My grief was vast and while he tried to support me through it, he could never fully understand why I wasn't more relieved.

The months that followed, we tried to regain the relationship we had before we left Kauri Creek, but we never quite managed it.

Two years after we left town, I'd lost hope of ever getting it back. I knew our relationship was over. I just didn't realise his life would be that same day too.

I sigh and lean into Aurora, pressing my face into her warm neck.

This is why I didn't talk about these things—Toby, Max, my lost baby—it brings everything back.

"Katie," Olivia's soft voice calls from the yard fence.

"Yeah?" I pull away from Aurora and slip her halter free. I'm done with working for the day, even if it is with the horses. I trudge towards Olivia, knowing I'm going to have to do even more talking.

"You good?" Olivia reaches out and rubs my arm as we settle onto the top railing.

"I don't really know," I say, avoiding eye contact.

"Is that because you've got a thing for Dallas and are refusing to admit it?"

I shoot my best friend a look and she's grinning at me like the cat who got the cream. "That statement is incorrect."

"So, you *don't* have a thing for Dallas?"

"Oh, no, that part's correct. The refusing to admit it part is what's not correct."

"Shit." Olivia's staring at me with wide eyes. "I really wasn't expecting you to just come out with it like that. Are you feeling okay?"

"Not really." I sigh. "We have to *talk* about things."

Olivia laughs at my disgust. "Honey, that's what people in relationships do."

"I don't know that this is a relationship exactly."

"Why don't you tell me exactly what it is then?"

I climb down from the railing. "Want to walk?"

She jumps down beside me and loops her arm through mine. We head around the corner of the barn, into the paddock and up the hill.

"So the first night I got here, I went into town." I chew on my bottom lip while I fiddle with the gate latch letting us into the paddock. "I met Dallas. And I took him home with me."

I thought Olivia's eyes couldn't get wider than when I admitted I have a thing for Dallas.

I was wrong. They just about bug out of her head.

"It was … incredible," I continue. "I had no idea he worked here. We didn't find out until that morning in the arena when I had Sadie on Scout." I wince, remembering what he told me earlier today about Sadie's accident. God, what that must have done to him. "So things didn't start out well, but …" I shrug. "They've improved."

"Sounds like they started spectacularly, if you ask me," Olivia says with a giggle. "It was after that they got worse. But I'm assuming they're better again now?" She waggles her eyebrows.

"Behave," I say, playfully slapping her hand. Then I take a long breath. "We had an arrangement for one-night only. I once tried to suggest we change the arrangement so we could have a second night. He said he doesn't want that." I come to a stop, turning away from my best friend so I can't see her studying me, analysing everything I'm saying. "He doesn't want another night. He wants lots of nights, and days, and months and years."

"That doesn't surprise me," Olivia says quietly.

"I don't know that I can give him that," I say, my voice as soft as hers. "You know I wasn't planning on staying beyond getting us both some stability again. I don't know that I can change my plans for a guy again. I don't know that I can trust someone with that kind of power over me."

Olivia wraps an arm around me and tugs me down so we're sitting side by side in the grass, her arm around my shoulders. I snuggle into her.

"If you stayed, why would you be staying?"

"For Dallas."

"Would it be? Just for him?"

"Yes?"

"You don't sound convinced. What about for me, for Mum, for Flynn and Scout and Aurora and Sadie? What about for *you*?"

I stare out over the farm. From here we can see the main farmhouse, Dallas's cottage across the paddock from it, tucked away in some trees, the stables and barn, Scout and the other horses grazing in their paddock. We can see the rolling hills and the sheep in the distance. I know behind the far hill is the function centre—Olivia's dream.

Before I left this place with Toby four years ago, I was certain this would be my home forever. Even after Toby passed away, I thought I'd come back here.

Until I did for his funeral and was struck down by memories, now stained with pain, and Max let his feelings be known.

"Don't live your life for anyone else, Katie. Not for Dallas, or any of us, or for Toby or Max. You have to decide what you want to do, without any of our opinions." Olivia tilts her head so it rests against my shoulder. "But for what it's worth, every one of us wants you here, except for Max and since he's a grade-A asshole we don't give a shit about his opinion."

I snort a laugh. "Wasn't he your best friend for like, your whole life?"

"Yeah, when we were kids. Then he lost his shit over something, wouldn't talk to me about it and instead became the bastard we all know and hate today."

I laugh full out this time. "God, I love you," I say, my voice cracking.

"I love you too. I'll love you even more when you tell me more about Dallas." She waggles her eyebrows at me. "The first decent new guy in town in years and you snap him up on your first day back. That's so typical of you."

The giggles over take us and we end up lying in the grass, tears running down our cheeks and bellies aching. "It wasn't on purpose, I swear," I manage to choke out between wheezing breaths.

"I know, but come on girl, give us the goooooods. What's he like?"

I stretch out, enjoying the afternoon sun warming my face. I take a breath of spring air and release it slowly. "What's he like? Fuck me ..." I trail off, trying to think how to describe him.

"No, that's what you need to say to him." She's off giggling again, howling at her own jokes, and despite my best efforts, I'm right there with her.

Eventually I sober, the giggles petering out. "He wants me to go see him tonight. To talk things through. He's worried about Sadie."

"But Sadie adores you."

"Yeah, I don't think me being in her life is what scares him. It's what happens if I can't stay in her life."

"Oh ... well, Sadie can sleep at ours tonight. Give you guys the space you need to ah, clear the air."

I give her a shove. By the time we finish cackling this time, the sun is beginning to drop behind the hills.

"Come on, Katie Kat," Olivia says, helping me to my feet. "Time for you to go get your man."

28

DALLAS

I'M ABOUT to wear a hole through the original Rimu flooring of the tiny farm cottage I call home.

Sadie didn't quite fall asleep over dinner, but it was a pretty close run and as I went to scoop her into my arms to bring her home to bed, Olivia suggested I put her to sleep in the main house.

I hate leaving her over there, because I miss her in the night and hate that I'm relying on Violet and Olivia so much. But Olivia refused to even let me argue about it.

She gave me a stern look and insisted on it, then shot a knowing look towards Katie washing the dinner dishes, and winked.

She knows, and apparently it won't be an issue for our working relationship.

So, I put Sadie to bed in the room she uses at Violet's. When I finished, I expected to find Katie waiting for me, but she was nowhere to be found. The kitchen was spotless. Maybe she'd gone. Maybe she changed her mind.

As I stepped out onto the porch I caught my breath at the sight of her little car, still parked in its usual spot next to my ute. Seeing them side by side gave me a little twinge in my chest. It's how they should be, all the time.

"She's asleep?" Violet asked from her seat on the porch swing, startling me from my weird little daydream about our vehicles, parked next to each other in the driveway of another home somewhere in the future. A home that's ours.

"Yep. Completely passed out. Thanks again for this."

"You don't have to thank me every time, Dallas. I enjoy it, and it helps you. Plus, the girls said they'd see you soon. Or maybe that was just about Katie?" She gave a nonchalant little shrug and settled back in her chair, picking up her book.

She also knows.

I tried not to choke on my breath, said goodnight and headed across the small paddock separating my cottage from the main house. They're so close I don't usually bother to even drive my ute around to the cottage.

I did a quick tidy of the house. I put mine and Sadie's breakfast dishes in the dishwasher, made sure I hadn't left filthy clothes lying around and that the bathroom isn't gross. Luckily I mostly manage to keep all those things in check so there wasn't much to do, but stepping into the bathroom I caught sight of the bath, my earlier thoughts returning to my mind.

So now, I'm pacing the floor, a bathtub full of steamy water and sweet smelling bubbles in the next room, and there's no sign of Katie yet.

I collapse onto the couch. I must have pushed her too hard and now she's freaking out. I let out a frustrated sound, right as there's a knock at the front door.

I leap off the couch and swing the door wide. Katie is on my porch, chewing on her bottom lip and looking up at me with those stunning eyes.

"Hey, cowboy," she says. Her voice is low and throaty and I want to pull her directly into my lap again.

"Heya, princess." I lean against the doorframe, feigning casual and folding my arms across my chest to hide my shaking hands.

"Are you always cocky when you're horny?" she asks and it startles a laugh out of me. I push off the doorframe and step aside, gesturing for her to come inside.

"More like I pretend to be when I'm nervous," I mutter and Katie giggles, turning to face me.

"I like it, you know ... sometimes. Cocky Dallas is pretty hot." She trails a finger along the waistband of my jeans, pausing at the button. Before I have the chance to stop her—because we're supposed to be talking, not undressing each other—she pulls her hand back. Then she steps right into my space and places her hand on my cheek. "You don't need to be nervous. I'm here. I'm sorry I took so long. Livvie thought it would heighten tension or something. I didn't think to tell her we have enough of that."

She shoots me a saucy smirk, then bites her lip again, her confidence wavering.

"It's fine," I say. "Gave me a chance to make sure the house wasn't in total disarray."

"It looks good," she says, turning away and taking in the room. "I haven't been in here in years. This wallpaper is so much better than what was here before."

I laugh at her expression. I love the little house. It's probably because it's part of the farm, belonging to the family that accepted Sadie and I as their own from the day I started working here, but it's also simply a gorgeous house.

The original Rimu timber floors, simple colours on the walls like the colour Katie commented on, a yellow/white that brightens what could be a dark, dreary little cottage.

Sadie also loves the colour, but not as much as the wild-flower patterned wallpaper in her room. Violet let Sadie help choose it when we came by for a meeting prior to moving here and by the time we arrived with our possessions, the room was completely redone, ready for my little girl.

The furniture all came with the house too, from the comfortable, well-loved couch to the battered dining room table. It's not new or fancy, but it's perfect for our needs.

Katie is still exploring, taking in the evidence of my life in the cottage: a picture Sadie drew stuck to the fridge, a photo of the two of us on the shelf, a pot plant that's in desperate need of some kind of attention.

"Last time I was here," she says, "I painted the bathroom." She pushes the door open and freezes. "Oh, was I interrupting?"

I'd forgotten about the bath. Seeing her standing on my porch in those jeans—she was right, I really do appreciate them —had wiped my brain.

I clear my throat. "No. It's for you." Clearing my throat hadn't worked and my voice still came out rough.

She blinks at me and I wait for her reaction. Was I being presumptuous? Have I overstepped?

She crosses the room in a few long strides, reaches up and presses her mouth to mine. It takes me a moment to catch up on what's going on, then I thread my fingers through her long hair and open my mouth to kiss her back. She immediately slides her tongue against mine and makes a sound in the back of her throat.

She breaks off as quickly as she started, then presses a single chaste kiss to my cheek. "Thank you. I love baths," she whispers in my ear.

"Good, I was hoping so." I slide my hand from her hair and instead tangle my fingers with hers, then lead her back to the bathroom. I check the bath temperature and add a little more hot water. I press a kiss to her cheek when I'm done. "I'll leave you to it."

"Dallas," she says, not releasing my fingers. "Will you stay? Please."

"This isn't a way for me to get your clothes off," I say. "I just thought you'd like it."

"And I do. We also both know you don't need a bath as a guise to get my clothes off. I'll take them off for you anytime, cowboy." She gives me another one of her looks that sends blood rushing south and weakens my knees. "But aren't we supposed to have a conversation?" She pulls a face like Sadie does when I ask her to eat kumara—her least favourite food.

"Yeah, that was supposed to be the point of tonight. But we can do that after your bath if you want."

"No, stay. If you want. We can talk while I wallow about in

there." She steps close to me again and trails her fingers down my chest. "At least help me get ready for it." She bites her lip and this time it's not from nerves.

My hands find her hips, then the hem of her t-shirt and when she raises her arms I pull it up over her head. The hot pink sports bra is even better than my foggy memory from before. I reach out and run my fingers across the fabric, causing Katie to shiver when my skin brushes hers.

My fingers slip to the band of the bra and slide underneath.

"This part isn't going to be sexy," she mutters. "You're going to have to wrangle it off me."

I press a kiss to her cleavage, then commit to removing her bra.

She's right. I do have to wrangle it but when it's off over her head I toss it to the ground. "You're wrong. Everything you do is sexy." I press my mouth to the spot just below her ear and gently suck. She moans and sways. I chuckle and pull away.

I drag my fingers down her chest, between her breasts and across the smooth expanse of her belly, pausing on the button of her jeans.

A nod from her and I flick it open, then slide the zipper down. It's all playing out in slow motion, as I begin to work the jeans over her hips.

"You were right about the jeans," I murmur. "Spectacular."

Katie laughs, a little breathlessly. "Liv and I call them my booty jeans."

"I can see why." I use the slightest pressure of my hand against her hip to turn her around, admiring her ass and the stretch of denim over it. I palm the full curve and feel her press back into my hand.

Another tug on the waistband of her jeans and they slip down, taking her underwear with them. A guttural sound escapes me.

"Like what you see, cowboy?"

"Oh, fuck yes." I can't help myself and bend down, nipping at her ass, then pressing a kiss to the spot, now slightly reddened by my teeth. "We need to get you in that bath before I forget how to talk, let alone what we're supposed to be talking about."

Katie laughs, the bright sound echoing around the tiny bathroom. Then she pushes my hands out of the way and strips her jeans off. She stands naked in front of me, the most glorious sight I've ever seen. "Care to join me?" She reaches out and pops two buttons on my shirt before I have a chance to respond.

I lift my injured arm. "Probably shouldn't get this wet."

She shrugs. "We'll be careful. But your choice." She turns away and steps into the bath, hissing slightly.

"Is it okay?" I ask, suddenly worried I'm going to boil her in my over hot bath.

"It's perfect," she says, scooping her hair into the messy pile on her hair and securing it with a hair tie from her wrist. Then she slowly sinks down into the bubbles.

When all that's left visible of her is her head and shoulders, my brain reengages.

"Do you need anything? Something to drink?"

"Just stay, Dallas," she says softly, reaching up to tug at my hand. I kneel beside the bath and let her weave our fingers together. "We need to talk about Sadie."

"I know." I close my eyes and hope my next words don't hurt her too much. "I don't want her to know about whatever this is yet."

She squeezes my fingers. "I know." She signs and leans back in the water. I crack my eyes open and take in the sight. My dick twitches, because hot damn.

"I know I'm too much of a flight risk for us to tell Sadie anything yet." She sounds disappointed and it's my turn to squeeze her fingers. "I don't want to be," she whispers, so quiet I'm not sure I've heard her properly. "I want this to be the place I can put down my roots and grow ... I want to be here with my family." She waves her free hand in the direction of the main house. "I want to be here with you. I want to try." Her voice cracks on the last word and I surge forward, capturing my mouth with hers. Her free hand lands on the back of my neck and she clings to me like she's desperate. I don't want to let her go. She breaks off panting and presses her forehead to mine. "I understand not telling Sadie until we've figured out what there is between us. I'm not offended. I don't want to hurt her ... or you."

I kiss her again. "We'll figure it out," I mumble against her lips.

"Cowboy," she says, a slight growl in her tone. "Get in this bath with me. Right now."

I pull back slightly and take in the sight of her flushed cheeks, the swell of her breasts moving with each heaving breath she pulls in and the desire flaring in her eyes.

I push up to my feet and flick open the rest of the buttons on my shirt, never taking my eyes off her face as she lets hers roam over my body.

"What ever you say, princess."

29

KATIE

WHAT IS THIS LIFE?

I lie back in the bath, the sweet scented bubbles piled up around me and watch as Dallas strips in front of me.

He's not being seductive about it. In fact he's being brisk and to the point, like he is with so many things, except handling me apparently, if the way he just undressed me was any indication.

But despite his efficiency, it's still the hottest thing I've ever seen.

I slip my fingers beneath the water and trail them up and down my thigh. He watches the movement of my arm, his eyes darkening with a flare of lust so desperate it has me clenching my legs together.

"Go on, princess," he rasps. "Get ready for me."

I bite back a moan and relax my legs. "Thought you liked putting in the work."

"Fuck." He shoves his jeans down his legs, releasing his already hard cock.

Truly, I'd have been disappointed if he wasn't hard from what we've done so far, because I am *desperate* already. He steps forward, out of his jeans and closer to the bath.

I know he's going to bypass me and climb straight into the water, but I reach up and wrap my fingers around his length before he has the chance.

He freezes. I pump my fist once, then twice.

A groan escapes from somewhere deep in his chest. He's staring down at me, chest heaving. I lean in and swipe my tongue across the tip of his erection. His hand settles in my hair.

"This isn't like last time, Katie."

"I know," I say, before sliding my mouth down his length. I sit back, my fingers still wrapped around him. "I know who you are this time, Dean."

His hand tightens in my hair at the use of his name and I don't even think he's aware the movement brings my face closer to him again.

I swirl my tongue around him, pumping the rest of his length with my hand. He holds still, either frozen by my brazenness—which at this point shouldn't still be surprising him—or because he simply wants to let me set my own pace.

"Fuck. God, that's good," he mutters. He tips his head back and groans, long and low. Then steps away.

He bends down. His hand is still in my hair, controlling my movements, so he can tilt my head at the perfect angle to plant a scorching kiss on my mouth. "You have a filthy mouth, princess."

"From memory, so do you," I say, moving back as his fingers slip free from my hair. "Now, get in here with me."

I slide forward in the tub and Dallas gingerly climbs in behind me. When he settles back, he wraps his uninjured arm around my waist and hauls me back into him. His rock hard shaft presses into my ass and he wriggles so it's not poking me quite so aggressively. Time for that later.

I lean back against his hard body, resting my head on his shoulder and revel in the feeling that flows through me as he presses a gentle kiss to my temple.

"We can take this as fast or as slow as you like," he says into my hair, the breath of his words whispering along my temple. "I just need you to be a little more sure before we tell Sadie."

I nestle into him. "I understand about Sadie, but I hope we don't have to take things too slowly." I jerk my hips back, feeling the pressure of his cock press into me.

Dallas lets out a low grunt. "You know the best thing about hurting my arm?"

"What's that?" I ask, confused at the abrupt change in topic.

"That it was my left arm." With that, his right hand clamps down on my thigh. He lifts my leg, hooking it over his, spreading me wide open.

Dallas keeps his bandaged arm out of the water, and instead threads his fingers into my hair, holding my head in place against his shoulder.

I whimper as his right hand leisurely strokes between my knee and hip, straying ever closer to where I want it. He teases me relentlessly, until I turn my head and bite the soft skin of his neck, sucking it into my mouth to soothe the pain away.

"I thought you'd be accomplished enough to use either arm," I say into his ear, my voice a breathless moan.

"Oh, I am, princess. I'm just better with my right."

And finally, he places his hand flat over my pussy and presses down.

I moan and thrust my hips up, chasing the pressure, chasing the release I'm going to find from it.

He brushes another gentle kiss across my forehead. It's a stark contrast to the two fingers that find my clit and twirl in a tight circle.

"More," I pant.

"Not yet," he whispers back. "We have time."

"I've waited long enough," I say. "Either fuck me with your hand, or I'm going to have to do it myself ... on your cock."

His grips tightens in my hair, until it's almost painful, but I relish the way I affect him, especially when he slides his hand lower and slides a finger inside me.

"More," I say again.

"Impatient, are we?"

"Obviously."

He chuckles in my ear and the warm sound, the affection in it, shoots straight to the spot his hand is, right as he adds a second finger.

I arch back, the sound I make incoherent and raw.

"Ride them," he whispers.

I bear down and twist my hips, rolling them until the pressure is just right and I'm a shaking, sobbing mess, only upright because Dallas is holding me tight against him.

"Good girl," he murmurs, between more soft, gentle kisses. "Now, up."

He withdraws his hand and I moan at the loss.

Immediately, he's helping me up and turning me with sure but gentle hands until my ass is on the edge of this fancy antique bathtub, Dallas kneeling between my legs.

"You good?" he murmurs, pressing more kisses to my skin, this time along my thigh. I nod shakily. "Don't slip," he says.

He picks up my leg, brands a searing kiss to the inside of my knee, then slings it over his shoulder and licks straight up the centre of me.

I cry out and my fingers knot in his hair. His injured arm is wound around behind my ass, holding me in place. His good hand is resting on my thigh, but after several long, slow licks, he slides his fingers back where they belong.

The pressure and dual sensations send waves of want and desire and lust through me as I stare down at this man, who's opened his heart to me, and left it open, even with me trying to slam that door closed at every turn.

His eyes lock with mine as he twists his fingers and the orgasm hits me like I've run into a wall at full speed. I cry out again as Dallas holds me to him, his face against my thigh as I ride it out.

When the tremors subside, he peers up at me, his smile sheepish. "Sorry, this bath isn't very relaxing," he says, not looking at all sorry.

I run my fingers through his hair. "I don't know. I'm feeling pretty fucking relaxed."

He laughs and stands. Miraculously, we still haven't got his bandage wet. He steps out of the bath, avoiding my grasping hands. "Do you want to finish your bath?"

"No," I snap. "I want to finish you."

He wraps a towel around his waist, hiding the goods. Only when it's secure does he come near me again. "There's time for that later. Enjoy your bath." His hand settles on my shoulder and he gives a gentle push, encouraging me to slide back into the water. "I'll see you soon. When you're ready," he says, then leaves the room and pulls the door closed behind him.

"How the fuck am I supposed to enjoy my bath now?" I shout, petulantly slapping the water.

I hear his deep laugh rumble through the walls and again, the affection in it does something funny to my insides.

It's not the cocky cowboy laugh he used with me the first night. Not the one he used at work those first few weeks when it was obvious he was just tolerating me. This is the laugh he uses with his friends, his family. The laugh he uses with the people he cares about most.

I step out of the bath and grab a towel, drying off the excess water and wrapping the fluffy fabric loosely around me. Leaving my clothes scattered across the bathroom floor, I swing the door wide open.

Dallas is across the room on the couch, facing away from me. He turns at the sound of the door, sending me a mock scowl. "You're supposed to be enjoying the bath."

"Yeah, well, now I want to enjoy your bed." I saunter across the room, push the door open to the room I know must be his and head inside, dropping the towel as I cross the threshold.

His room is exactly how I imagined it would be. Calm grey

walls, a navy blue duvet with dark sheets, the bare minimum of pillows. A wooden dresser in the corner has more of Sadie's artwork and pictures of her displayed on the top, along with a couple of men's toiletries.

I crawl onto the bed and flop down, right in the centre. A moment later Dallas is leaning against the doorframe, his arms crossed against his chest. The stance shows off everything, from his biceps, strong chest and narrow waist to the decidedly delicious bulge under the towel he's still wearing.

"You're going to be the death of me," he mutters as he stalks across the room.

I laugh. "Come here, cowboy." I pat the bed beside me, then stretch languidly. I know exactly what I'm doing and it's nothing that's going to help what's under that towel, unless he lets me near him.

Still grumbling, Dallas climbs onto the bed and lies on his side, facing me.

"Improved, but could be better." I tug at the towel until it comes free, then slide my hand down his thigh. The muscle is hot and hard under my palm. I glance up, my eyes locking with his and something in his gaze brings my wandering fingers to a halt. "What's going on, cowboy?"

He sighs and rolls onto his back. "It's stupid." He rubs a hand across his eyes.

"Hey," I reach up and tug his hand away, rolling up onto an elbow so I can look him in the eye. "Dallas, what's going on?"

"You're here, laid out in my bed, naked, looking like a god damn dream come true ... and my brain just keeps freaking out over what happens if I lose you."

I cup his face, stroking my thumb over his cheek, the touch comforting rather than sensual. "We both know I haven't exactly been settled about being back here," I say. "Your caution is warranted. But ..." I take a deep breath. I need to say the next words, for him and for me. "I'm in this, Dallas. I really am. We can slow things down if you want, but I promise. I'm right here with you."

Dallas draws in a slow breath, closing his eyes and absorbing my words. He turns his head and presses a kiss to the inside of my wrist. A tiny gasp releases from somewhere in my chest and when he turns his face back to me again his eyes are clear and determined.

He traces a line across my eyebrow, down my cheek, then sweeps a finger over my lips. "I don't want to slow things down," he says. "Because I'm pretty convinced you're it for me. I want you to stay here, because I love it here and Sadie loves it here, and your family—our family—is here. I think you can love it here, but really, in the end ... I don't think it'll matter where we are."

Heat races down my cheek and Dallas brushes his thumb across it, swiping away the tear.

"Sorry," I mutter, more heat flooding my cheeks, but this time it's embarrassment, not tears.

"Don't be sorry, princess." His voice is too soft over the stupid nickname he's always said with a mocking lilt to his voice.

"I want that too. I want to be here, with you and Sadie. Please."

He surges up off the bed and captures my mouth with his. I

immediately open for him and he draws at my tongue. He pushes me back down onto the bed and rolls over me. His towel has been left behind and the fiery heat of his bare skin connects with mine.

I gasp out a breath and hook my leg around him, pulling him closer.

"We do have to slow down for just a second right now," he says, breaking off another scorching kiss.

"What? No. Why?" I whine, wriggling underneath him as he reaches for the bedside table, pulling out a foil packet.

"I have a kid and although I love her to death, I didn't exactly plan for her so I'm a bit paranoid about protection." He waves the packet in my face while I laugh.

"Okay, fair. But hurry up. You've made me wait long enough."

He kisses me, then pulls back and rolls the condom on. I expect him to resume his position on top of me immediately, but he doesn't. He pauses there, hard length resting against my thigh and he just stares at me for a long moment while I pant and try not to writhe desperately while he admires whatever he's seeing. His hand wanders across my body and when it grazes my nipple I lose all control, grasping for his hips and pulling him flush with mine.

"You can look later," I growl in his ear as I lift my legs and wrap them around his waist.

He lets out a breathless, throaty chuckle, then thrusts his hips forward, sliding all the way in. We moan together and when I open my eyes I'm staring directly into his.

This is new. Our first night we never ended up like this. We used hands and mouths and finally, I straddled his lap and rode him while he lay on my bed, encouraging me with words and his hands on my hips. But this ... this kind of closeness, between our bodies and hearts. This kind of intimacy. We didn't have any of *this*.

He fuses our mouths together and draws his hips back. He holds himself with just the tip of his cock still in me until I'm whimpering against him, clawing at his back.

I unlock my mouth from his. "Just fuck me already."

He meets my eyes and there's some kind of uncertainty there, like he's not sure this is the right way to be doing things. I run my hand down his face, cupping his cheek. I brush my lips across his cheek. "It's already special, because it's you," I whisper.

His eyes slam closed at my words and he thrusts forward, causing us both to utter desperate groans again. This time he doesn't stop, not until I'm shaking and trembling, teetering on the edge, his hand thrust into my hair and his hips pounding into mine.

"You're mine, cowboy," I whisper into his ear and he drives into me, pressing me down into the bed. At the guttural moan coming from his throat, his hand tugging at my hair and the possessive way his hand curls under my ass and squeezes, I shatter.

30

DALLAS

MY PHONE IS RINGING, but I don't know where it is. Sunlight is filtering in from behind my curtains and I can hear the birds in the trees outside the cottage.

I had an exceptional sleep, despite the aching and throbbing in my arm.

Katie's hot body is pressed against me, her back to my front and as I try to wriggle away her arm snakes out and latches onto my hip, hauling me back to her.

"Phone," I mutter. "Need to answer it."

She huffs her disapproval as I stumble from the room.

My phone is sitting in the middle of the couch cushion, where I discarded it last night when Katie dropped her towel in front of me and spread herself across my bed, utterly naked and the sexiest thing I'd ever seen.

Olivia's name flashes across the screen.

"Hey boss," I say as I lift it to my ear.

"Just giving you some warning that we've delayed Sadie as long as possible. She's heading your way in about three minutes, so I suggest you get clothes on and my bestie out of your bed unless you want Sadie to witness it."

I spin around and glance at the wall clock in the kitchen. It's after seven-thirty.

"Shit. Sorry. Thank you." I hang up the call, but not before Olivia's laughter echoes down the line.

"Time to get up," I call to Katie, who's still snuggled so far down in my bed I'm not sure I'll ever get her out. "Sadie's on her way."

"Fuck!" Katie throws the blankets back and is on her feet in a flash, searching for her clothes. I guess getting her up wasn't so hard after all.

"Bathroom," I say, pointing uselessly because she knows where it is.

She runs, while I pull on fresh underwear and pants. A moment later Katie is in front of me, hoisting her jeans up her legs. "My shirt's soaked. Apparently I dripped all over it when I got out last night."

"In a hurry for something were we?" I smirk at her.

"Shut up and find me something I can wear unless you want your little girl to ask why I'm in your house in my bra."

That snaps me back into the moment. I pull a plain grey t-shirt from my drawer and toss it at her, grab one for myself, then head for the kitchen, flicking the jug on to make us coffee and hopefully give us a cover story Sadie will buy.

A moment later Katie disappears back into the bathroom.

The sounds of water draining from the bath echo through the house as she tidies up our mess.

I'm spooning coffee into mugs when she slides onto the barstool across from me, right as the front door opens and Sadie bounces inside.

"Morning, Daddy." She greets me with her usual smile and leap into my arms for a hug. "Hiya, Katie. How come you're here?"

"Came to ask your dad what jobs I need to do today," she says. It's so convincing I almost buy it. I let out a breath and relax. It was good save.

Olivia follows Sadie into the house, a look of relief washing over her face as she sees us both fully clothed. "Go get ready for school, Sadie," Olivia says. "Then I can take you when I go into town."

"Okay, Livvie," Sadie agrees and skips off to her room, completely oblivious.

Olivia smiles after her. "She only started calling me that after she heard you do it," she says to Katie. Then gives her a playful punch in the shoulder and a wink. "Have a good night you two?"

I cough and choke on my first sip of coffee.

"You know it," Katie grins at me as I continue to splutter. She turns back to Olivia. "Can you come help with Aurora later? I think today's the day we try a proper ride."

"Sounds good. Sadie's all sorted for today," Olivia says, directing the trail end to me. "I'll take her to school. Flynn can pick her up, if you're happy with that."

I nod. "Of course. And thank you."

Sadie rushes back into the room wearing a clean outfit and her hairbrush in hand. "Katie, can you do my hair like you do yours?"

Katie smiles down at the little girl and takes the brush before instructing Sadie to climb up on the stool next to her. A few minutes later and Sadie has two perfect French braids in her hair.

"Right kiddo. You all ready? Let's go and leave Dad and Katie to their boring work."

Sadie kisses me goodbye, then turns to Katie and does the same. My heart swells at the sight of Katie's arms wrapped around my little girl.

"Bye, Lady Sadie," Katie says, waving them off from the door. "Have a good day at school."

She closes the door and I half collapse onto the kitchen counter.

"That was close," Katie says mildly, like my five-year-old didn't nearly just catch us both stark naked, asleep in my bed, thoroughly fucked out.

I groan into my hands, my elbows propped on the bench. Katie hops up so she's sitting beside me and rubs my shoulder.

"We'll be more careful next time," she says. "Olivia's got our backs."

"Yeah, I'm not sure I feel super great about my boss having to phone me and tell me to get her best friend out of my bed at seven-thirty in the morning."

Katie tips her head back and howls a laugh. "Don't worry, I know someone who can put in a good word with her."

I shake my head and step between Katie's knees. My hand

finds her nape and I pull her in for a kiss. She melts into it, her hands slipping under my t-shirt to trail across my abs.

"Any regrets?" I murmur when we take a breather.

She pulls back, far enough that she can get a good look at my face, but not so far I'm not still touching her with almost every part of me. "Not a single one."

IT IS NEARLY impossible to get anything done at work when you're in a relationship with your boss.

We've managed to keep it quiet around Sadie for two weeks now, but every adult on the property knows exactly what's been going on.

Flynn has caught us in compromising positions more than once and is constantly wolf-whistling in our direction, even when we aren't making out against the side of the barn.

At least both Dallas and I have kept our heads enough to not do anything more than kissing on the farm, so no one has caught us with our pants down.

We're also lucky that Olivia is in full support of us, or she'd be getting way more annoyed about how long our lunch breaks at the cottage are running. Especially when we don't actually eat any food while there and still raid the main house kitchen for sustenance.

Progress with Aurora has been as swift as progress with

Dallas. She now stands quietly while I saddle and bridle her and will let me ride her around the yard. She's also spending the majority of her time in the small paddock beside the yard, getting used to more typical fences, rather than the sturdy yard railings.

Today, Flynn is keeping an eye on us as I take Aurora into the main arena to ride for the first time. She's wary and skittish, but eventually relaxes into our work. I'm grinning widely when I finally stop in front of Flynn and dismount.

"She's doing great," he says, reaching out to ruffle the horses mane. She doesn't even flinch at his touch like she would have a month ago.

"She is."

"So are you," Flynn says quietly.

I freeze where I am, running the stirrups up their leathers so they don't bang against Aurora's sides as I lead her back the barn to untack her.

Flynn tugs on my ponytail. "You okay there, Katie Kat? I didn't mean to break you."

I smile, but it's watery. "I know you didn't. But you're right. I'm doing good."

"Does this thing with Dallas mean you're staying?" His eyes are so hopeful that I'm relieved at the truth.

"Yeah, I think so. I mean, I want to. I really do. I missed this place."

Flynn steps forward, his eyes uncharacteristically wet, and wraps me in a hug. "This place missed you, Katie Kat."

I push away from my friend's embrace. "Damnit Flynn." I wipe at my eyes. "No crying on the job."

He laughs. "I told you Dallas was a good one."

"You were right." I turn and lead Aurora towards the gate.

"Could I have that in writing?" Flynn asks, jogging to catch up, then opening and closing the gate as we pass through.

"No. But do you know what Dallas does with most of that time we spend at his place?"

"Um, I'm really not sure I want to," he says, lifting his hands as if to cover his ears. "Innocent little ears over here."

"Yeah right," I laugh and shove him.

"More than you'd think," he mutters, so low I'm not sure I was supposed to hear. "What does Dallas do?" he asks at normal volume.

"He braids my hair. Over and over."

"Well, that's ... different. I guess whatever gets your rocks off."

"So he can do it for Sadie." I roll my eyes. "He spends half an hour a day with me in his house alone so he can learn to braid his daughter's hair."

Flynn slings his arm around my shoulder. "Told ya. Good one." When I don't respond, Flynn notices my hesitation. "What is it?"

"I thought Toby was a good one too."

He stiffens beside me. "He was ... wasn't he?" Flynn pulls me to a stop, turning me to face him. He doesn't know what happened the day of the car accident. He doesn't know how hard I fought for my relationship with Toby. I never felt like it was worth bringing it all up and airing the dirty laundry with anyone other than Olivia, who only heard about it because she caught me in a weak moment and I spilled my guts before I could stop myself.

"I thought so. At the start he was. He was perfect. I thought he was the love of my life. But, even before the accident, I'd lost him."

"I'm so sorry," Flynn said, tugging me in and wrapping his arms around me.

The warm embrace triggers something in me and before I know it, I'm sobbing against Flynn's shirt. He stands rigid, his hand carefully rubbing my back as I heave in shaking breath after shaking breath.

Eventually I step back and wipe at my eyes. Aurora gently nudges my shoulder and I give her a soft pat, thanking her for her silent support.

"I thought it was weird you never mentioned him. Ever," he says as we resume walking. "I figured it was just your way of handling the grief."

"It is, but there's too many layers to it, so much anger and hurt. I thought I was okay with it all, until I saw Max again for the first time. They're just so alike, in looks and personality as it turns out."

"Fucking Max," Flynn grumbles. "No one gives a shit about Max, okay? Or Toby. The bastard. God, he was like my best friend. I can't believe I didn't know he was an asshole."

I squeeze Flynn's arm. "Flynny, I was with him for years. I lived with him for *years*. I didn't find out until the day he died what he was really like."

"Do I even want to know?"

I shake my head. "No. I'm kind of sorry I told you he wasn't the guy you thought he was. That I ruined that for you."

He shrugs. "You're who matters, Katie Kat. You're the one who's here."

"Yeah, which makes it sound like I'm blaming a guy who can't defend himself."

"Well, then the idiot shouldn't have got into a car after drinking. I've always been mad at him about that. Even if you're not supposed to be angry with your old bestie who's no longer with us, I still am. I can't even imagine how you must be feeling with whatever his betrayal to you was." He lets out a long breath. "But, let's refocus. Dallas is not like that. And if he is, I'll have my pitchfork handy to run him out of town. We'll keep Sadie though. I like her."

I laugh. "Deal. I like her too. She did a barrel race yesterday."

"Really? Man, sucks I missed it. How did she do?"

"Well, it wasn't the slowest race I've ever seen," I say with a laugh.

"Oh yeah?" Flynn knows there's more to the story.

"Yeah. That accolade goes to her father."

That sends Flynn into fits of giggles. "Hey, he's trying his best."

"That he is." The warm, cozy glow I've grown accustomed to over the past couple of weeks settles over me again at the thought. I always expected that he'd blow off the riding lessons before long, but he's sticking them out.

"Well, let me know next time Sadie's going to do something

cool. Geez, next she'll be Grand Prix show jumping and I won't even know she can handle trotting poles."

I laugh and begin to untack Aurora, slipping the saddle and bridle from her body, then picking up a brush. Flynn picks up another brush and begins working on her other side.

"Flynny, what'd you mean before?" I ask.

"About what?"

"About your innocent ears and 'more than you'd think'."

"Oh." He's quiet for a long moment, studying the horse's coat carefully. "I'm just being bitchy and jealous."

"Jealous?"

"Yeah. You guys are a great couple. You're so perfect for each other and with Sadie it's like, instant family." He lets out a long sigh. "I want that. I've never had it, not even close."

"Never?"

"Nope. No girlfriend, no boyfriend. No partner of any kind. Not even hook ups. Just me. Alone."

The addition of hook ups stuns me for a second. I thought Flynn was living it up with a variety of people, especially when he's off on his regular surf trips. But it's the last word that tears at my heart.

I drop the brush and step around the horse. This time it's my turn to wrap my arms around Flynn and pull him in for a tight hug. "Not alone, Flynn, okay? Never alone."

He hugs me back. "I know. Having you and Livvie is obviously incredible. But it's not the same as having someone who wants to sleep in the same bed as you every night."

"Dude, I've slept in the same bed as you. I don't blame them."

He slaps me on the ass with his brush. "Shut up." But he laughs.

"Come here," I say and reach out for another hug. "It'll happen for you, Flynny."

"Yeah, I suppose. I guess I never really noticed how much I wanted that until I saw you with it." He squeezes me tight, then lets me go.

"The right person will come along for you," I say, reaching up to ruffle his hair.

He bats my hand away. "Speaking of the right person." He tilts his head in the direction of the barn door to where Dallas is standing.

"Hey," I call and he takes a hesitant step forward.

"I'm not interrupting anything?" He asks. "I can catch up with you later."

"It's all good," Flynn says, handing me his brush. "I'll leave you two to it. But think of Aurora, okay? She has innocent ears too."

I laugh and toss the brush at his head. He catches it deftly and drops it in the grooming bucket.

"I'm going to go fix that fence in the Kauri paddock, okay, boss?"

"Sounds good. Give me a call if you need a hand." Dallas pats him on the shoulder as he passes

"Should be right. Looks like you'll have your hands full." Flynn shoots me a smirk.

"Oh, I wasn't offering me. I'd find someone else to help you."

Flynn fires finger guns in Dallas's direction. "Good call

boss. I'll catch you later, Katie Kat." As Dallas turns back to me, Flynn points at him then shoots me a thumbs up. A moment later his motorbike flares to life and Flynn speeds off down the farm.

"That guy is chaos," Dallas says, shaking his head.

"That he is. But we love him for it."

Dallas smiles and nods agreement, then wraps an arm around my waist and pulls me to him. "Afternoon, gorgeous," he says against my lips.

I lick his mouth and he opens, sliding our tongues together. I melt into him, like I do every time his lips connect with my body.

"You two okay?" He asks as he rubs his nose to the spot right under my ear, which he knows always causes shivers.

"We're good," I say and nip at his throat.

"Have plans for the next few hours?"

"Dunno, boss, do I?" I swipe the cap off his head and slide it over my hair, wearing it backwards.

"Punk. And yeah, you've got plans with me. I'll pick you up from your place in an hour. I'm taking you on a date."

"What're we doing?"

"It's a surprise." He's pressing open mouthed kisses down my neck and it's making me think I should be wearing nothing when he picks me up.

"I need to know what to wear."

"Something you like, but it's only Kauri Creek so it doesn't need to be red carpet. Something pretty, or sexy, or not. I don't really care. You look stunning in everything."

"Alright, cowboy. That's super helpful. I'm sure I can find something."

"Good. I'll see you in an hour. I'll put Aurora in the paddock for you."

That snaps me out of the lusty haze his mouth has trapped me in. "You will?"

"Yeah, I will. If you think she'll be okay."

"She'll be fine." I press a final kiss to his cheek. "Thank you."

"See you soon, princess," he says, releasing the knot holding Aurora in place and leading her from the barn, leaving me feeling a little unsettled, and a lot like I'm in love.

32

____

DALLAS

KATIE OPENS her front door and steps onto the porch as I pull into her driveway. At the sight of her I'm tempted to cancel our first official date and spend the rest of the afternoon locked inside her room.

She's wearing an oversized white shirt with the sleeves rolled back and it's questionable if she has any of the buttons done up, so when she leans on the porch railing I catch an eyeful of white lace bra.

My brain stutters as memories from our first night hit me. Of her wearing a white lace bra and riding me, never taking the bra off, but me scooping her tits out of the cups when I wanted to get my mouth on them.

I've only made it halfway up her front path and I'm frozen to the spot with a raging boner. I haven't even made it past looking at her shirt. I'm not sure my heart—or my dick—is going to cope with whatever she's dressed her lower half in.

I force myself to keep walking forward and hope my strides

hide the readjustment I have to do of my pants. I hear her laugh softly and know I've been busted.

I step onto the porch and take in the full outfit. The oversized shirt, with no buttons holding it closed, just the way it's tucked into her tight, dark red mini skirt keeping it in place. The skirt shows off the muscles in her thighs, a long expanse of leg that ends at knee high boots.

At least they're not the over the knee ones, or I really wouldn't be able to leave her place tonight.

"Suitable?" she asks, a small smirk playing at her lips. I step forward and slip my hands into her loose hair, finding the back of her neck and pulling her into me.

Our mouths collide in a searing kiss. Katie lets out a little gasp and I swallow it down, almost choking when her fingers find my throat and she trails her fingernails down it.

"I'll take that as a yes," she says when I finally pull away.

"I told you, you look stunning in everything. But this," I say, pushing aside the collar of her shirt to expose the white elastic of her bra strap and a touch of the lace. "Is this the one I think it is?"

"Yeah," she breathes.

"The matching set?" My hand drops to her ass, then lower until I'm toying with the hem of her skirt.

"Mmhmm. Want confirmation?" she mumbles, then bites her bottom lip.

"Later," I manage to croak out.

A flash of disappointment crosses her face. "Later?"

"Yeah." I press a kiss to her forehead. "We have all night, princess. First, we've got a date to go on."

"A proper date?"

"Yeah, if that's okay with you."

Suddenly I'm hesitant. Maybe she's not ready for this. Maybe she wants to keep it to sneaking lunchtime rendezvous and talking on the phone for hours at night after Sadie is asleep. Maybe she doesn't want this to be public.

"That sounds perfect." She reaches up and brushes her lips across mine. The movement causes my hand to slip from the edge of her skirt to her thigh and I pull away before I have the chance to caress her skin. If that happens, I'll lose all self-control and end up doing something to her that's better saved for behind closed doors, not on the front porch of her house.

"Let me get my jacket," she says as I reluctantly step away from her. She disappears inside the house for a moment, returning with a handbag and denim jacket, that she holds over her arm. Then she hesitates. "Are you sure this is suitable?"

"It's perfect," I say, wrapping my arm around her and leading her to my ute.

Five minutes later we pull up outside the farm supply store and a look of confusion crosses Katie's face.

"Come on," I say, climbing out of the vehicle.

"You're taking me on a date to the farm store?"

"Well, this is the first part of it. I need to pick something up." A 'what the fuck' look crosses her face, but she shrugs and follows me while I struggle to suppress my laughter. "Just trust me, princess," I murmur, linking my fingers with hers. She snags my keys from my other hand and drops them into the handbag she's wearing slung across her body.

"Hey, Dallas, Katie," Trevor, the store manager greets us as we enter the store. "Need any help today?"

"Yeah, I had an order come in."

"Righto, of course." Trevor fishes around under the counter for a moment, then pulls out a brown paper bag with the store logo on it. "All paid for. Anything else?"

"Not for now, thanks Trev." I tug at Katie's hand. "Come on." Then, instead of leading her out of the store like she's clearly expecting, I head towards the back corner where the women's clothing is displayed. "Anything you like?"

"What?" Katie asks, turning to face me, confusion on her face.

I chuckle. "You sacrificed your favourite shirt to stop me bleeding out in that paddock. I figured the least I can do is replace it for you."

"Oh." Her face softens. "You don't have to do that."

"I know." A shrug. "But I want to. So, is there anything here you like?"

Katie studies the clothing on the racks before us. Most of it is boring utility farm clothes and not really Katie's style. "Not really," she says, sounding disappointed. "Sorry."

I shrug again, then hold out the bag to her. "I guess it's a good thing I got this for you then." My cheeks ache from trying to smother the grin desperate to break free as she cautiously takes the bag from my hand.

Katie opens it, still watching me warily, then peers inside, emitting a soft gasp when she catches sight of what's inside.

"How did you get this? They don't even sell them here," she

says, pulling the shirt out of the bag. It's exactly the same as the shirt she used to stop my arm bleeding.

"I had them order it in."

"How did you even know what brand it was? Or what size?"

"I looked at the label while it was wrapped around my arm."

Katie's still looking at the shirt, rubbing her thumb over the lilac fabric that's butter soft. I know because I saw it earlier when I dropped in the other part of her gift. She lifts her eyes to meet mine.

"Thank you," she whispers. "I didn't know you could get them anymore. That shirt ... my grandma used to buy me one every year for my birthday. That one ... it was the last one she gave me before she died. I can't believe you could get the same colour and everything."

"Well, it took some time," I say, rubbing at the back of my neck as heat finds my cheeks. I didn't understand the significance of it, but now I'm glad I spent hours trawling the internet to find that particular style and colour. "There's something else in the bag, but you don't have to look at it now."

She drops the shirt back into the bag and pulls out the sheet of paper. "Oh my gosh," she whispers, her eyes immediately going glassy.

"That one isn't actually from me. Sadie wanted to give it to you and I asked if I could pass it along."

"I love it so much." Her voice cracks mid-sentence as she stares down at the colourful drawing.

In it, Sadie drew herself sitting on Scout, and beside the horse are two people. Despite the rough drawing skills of my five-year-old, anyone can see that one of the people is me. The other is Katie.

"Is this ..." Katie trails off, then clears her throat and tries again. "Is this our first family portrait?"

The breath stops in my chest. Our first family portrait.

Family.

The world goes a little fuzzy at the edges as the word hits me. I suck in a deep breath and realise Katie is staring up at me with wide, timid eyes and her bottom lip caught between her teeth. She's freaking out. Internally. Silently. But I can still tell.

"Yes," I manage to say, my voice a hoarse rasp. "If you want it to be."

She flings herself at me and I catch her as she wraps her arms around my neck. "Yes. So much yes," she whispers, voice thick with emotion.

"So, you'd be okay with telling Sadie about us?" I ask into her hair.

She pulls back and stares into my eyes for a long moment, studying me. "Are you sure?"

"If you are," I say and lean in for a kiss. "This isn't some spur of the moment thing. I've been thinking about it for a while now. So if you're okay with what that means, then I want her to know."

"I am," she says softly, then her face lights up. "Can we tell her now?"

The joy on her face sets my insides on fire and I laugh. "Well, we can. Or we can finish our date and I can take you home ..." I trail a finger down the gap between the front of her shirt. "And we can see Sadie tomorrow."

"Tomorrow is probably okay," she whispers.

"I thought so. I may have some plans for then too. For a family hang out."

Her eyes flash with emotion as I say the word family back to her and she crushes me to her with a visceral hug. My arms wrap around her, holding her close, where I want her to be forever.

"Okay, so what else is planned today? Or do I get to take you home yet?"

"Always in such a rush."

She smiles coyly. "You know me." It's her turn to run her hand down the gap in her shirt, except this time she pushes the two sides apart, exposing even more of her bra.

"Fucking hell. This is not the place." I step forward and crush my lips to hers, opening for her as her tongue swipes over my mouth, drawing her into me. My hands grasp her ass and pull her into me where she can no doubt feel my cock pressing into her stomach.

She lifts a foot off the ground and somehow knowing exactly what she means with that move, I hoist her up. Her legs wrap around me and she breaks the kiss, giggling against my mouth.

"You're right. This is definitely not the place," she says, then presses another kiss against my mouth. "I can be patient."

"Good girl. I'm going to put you down now before we flash the whole store because your skirt is too short."

"Too short?" She leans back, trusting me to support her while her hands come to cup my neck. She arches an eyebrow at me. "Please tell me you didn't just tell me my skirt's too short." She says it with a mocking tease in her voice. "That's not what you indicated earlier when you almost lost your shit over it on my front porch." She smirks at me.

"It's absolutely not too short for anything except this position in a public place," I say. "I am in full support of the length of this skirt and I'd love to evaluate it further later, especially what's under it, but I'm currently holding it firmly in place. We wouldn't want to give poor Trev a heart attack with those white lace panties you've got on under here." I tease my finger along the edge of the skirt where it's tucked around her ass.

She tips her head back and laughs, her loose hair cascading down her back. "This is a fair point." She kisses me and begins to unwrap her legs when movement at the end of the aisle startles me.

Then a voice cuts through our bubble of heat and lust, stripping away any and all happiness from Katie in an instant.

33

———

KATIE

"OH, FOR FUCK'S SAKE." Max Sheridan's voice echoes around the store right as I'm about to unwrap my legs from Dallas's waist and slide to the ground.

I freeze as his voice hits me, but Dallas strokes a hand down my back and I manage to function enough to get my feet back on the ground. I hope he has enough cognisance to keep my skirt in place because if I'm going to be flashing anyone, I really don't want it to be Max.

"Dude, I warned you about her," Max snaps at Dallas. "She's a snake in the grass."

"Not interested in your opinion," Dallas growls, his hand curling protectively over my shoulder as he steps closer to me.

"I shouldn't be surprised she got to you, too."

Ice fills my veins, a sharp contrast to the red hot heat that's flaring behind my eyes. Not heat like I'm about to cry. Heat like I'm going to rage out and completely lose my shit. "Shut up, Max," I growl. "You don't know what you're talking about." My hands shake and my knees feel wobbly. Without Dallas here beside me I'm sure I'd be a puddle on the ground.

"I can't believe you're letting her near your kid." Max keeps talking, completely ignoring me. "Sadie's a sweet girl and you're asking for her to be hurt."

"Come on, Katie. Let's go." Dallas strokes his hand down my back again. "You don't need to listen to this."

I shake my head. If I'm going to live here, I need to end this thing with Max. I can't keep hiding from him.

"I don't know what you think I did to you," I say, willing my voice not to shatter. "But you have to stop."

"Stop what? Telling people the truth about you?"

"What truth?" I snap.

"It's your fault my brother is dead." His voice is low and filled with venom. "You made him leave. He hated it in the city. He hated it with you. But you wormed your way into his head so fully he didn't know how to get himself out. For years he put up with your bullshit."

I stare at him dumbly. "That's not what happened."

"Isn't it? Why the hell would my brother lie to me about that? Why would he lie to me that you threatened to hurt yourself if he left?"

"I have no idea ..." I trail off. I try to remember back through the years, if at any point I said something like that.

Things weren't good after I lost the baby, but they weren't that bad. I don't ever remember wanting to hurt myself, or telling him I was going to.

Even after I discovered the truth about Toby, I still couldn't reconcile this version with the man I knew. Or thought I knew. Why would he say things like that about me?

"I know you only wanted him for the money you thought he would have. He was too good for you though, wasn't he, and you ended up with nothing. You didn't care that he died. You only cared about his money."

Max keeps snarling at me and every word cuts me a little deeper. He turns to Dallas. "Keep her out of your bank accounts. I'd say keep her out of your pants but it's clearly too late for that."

"That's enough," Dallas says, voice steady and quiet, but firm.

I reach out and squeeze his hand and with a subtle shake of my head tell him we need to finish this properly.

"Do you know what really happened?" I ask, my voice low and lethal now.

"Yeah, I do. Toby told me everything."

"So he told you it was his choice to leave Kauri Creek and a few months after we left, he started fucking his way through the women he worked with? That eventually, he lost his job because someone accused him of harassment? Then, he couldn't get a new job and he spent every afternoon drinking and finding more random women to sleep with?"

Max was ready with a retort on his lips before I started speaking, but it slowly fades as I tell him the harsh reality of his brother's actions.

I stop speaking and haul in a few deep breaths, trying to centre myself. Dallas's hand is back gripping my shoulder and I use the heat and pressure to ground myself.

"If he was so awful, why were you still with him?" Max finally asks, the potent fury gone, but his voice is still laced with poison. He doesn't believe me. And why would he, if Toby spent all that time telling him awful things about me?

"Because I didn't know," I say, lowering my voice too.

Max snorts. "How could you not know?" he asks, exasperation causing his voice to rise.

"Because I was too busy working two jobs to keep our flat. I didn't find out until the day he died."

"The day he died you bitched and moaned and nagged at him and he finally decided he'd had enough of you. He called me right before his accident and told me he was going to leave you and come home. That's where he was going. He was on his way home."

"No, he wasn't." I draw a deep breath. "He was drunk when I got home early from my shift. I left work early because a woman he'd been screwing showed up and offered me all the evidence I needed to know the relationship I'd been trying to save was a sham. He admitted everything and yeah, he was leaving. But not to come here. He was going to find another of his women. Because that's what he did."

"You screamed at him until he got in the car and drove drunk," Max yells in my face.

"Yeah, I screamed in his fucking face. I gave him *every-thing* and the bastard screwed me over, time and time again. But it was his choice to get in that car. I tried to stop him, but he shoved past me anyway, pushing me into a wall as he went."

A gasp catches my attention and I turn woodenly to find

Tilly, Max and Toby's younger sister, standing between us, her face pale and eyes wide.

I've always adored Tilly. She's a total sweetheart and I never, ever wanted her to know these things about Toby. I especially didn't want her to learn them like this.

"Tilly," I rasp out.

"Don't speak to her," Max snaps.

"I'm so sorry," I whisper to Tilly.

Then I drop the bag containing the shirt and Sadie's picture, and I run.

I rush through the store, tears already streaking down my cheeks and blurring my vision. I skid around the corner by the counter, my boots slipping on the polished concrete floors.

There's a woman in front of me, waiting at the counter, and I manage to twist my body to avoid hitting her.

"Are you okay?" she asks, grabbing at my arm, trying to slow me down.

I take in the sight of her. She's wearing a pair of slim fit charcoal dress pants and a green blouse that perfectly matches the colour of her eyes. Her make up is flawless and her dark hair tumbles in waves down her back. She's so completely out of place in Kauri Creek. That's the only thing I can think as I take her in.

I snatch my arm away from her and rush through the door.

I'm sure Dallas will be coming after me. I'm sure he'll meet me outside and I slow my steps as I head for the street, expecting to hear his footsteps, his voice, anything.

But I don't.

Dallas doesn't follow me.

34

DALLAS

I REACH the end of the aisle, my long strides eating up the distance between me and the door, and hopefully Katie.

The confrontation with Max was too much. Katie tried to keep it calm, but in the end, she shouted at Max, right as Tilly appeared around the corner.

The devastation on both their faces made me want to go back in time and eviscerate Toby Sheridan for what he did to Katie.

No wonder she hates this town, and Max. No wonder she took so long to let her guard down with me.

She wanted to face Max though. She wanted to settle whatever was between them, so she could move on.

So she could be here with me.

I reach the counter and skid to a stop.

A woman is standing in front of it, staring out the door with confusion written all over her face.

She turns to face me and the world slows down, each second that passes feels like a year.

"Dallas?" she asks, stunned.

"Abi." I choke out the single word. I stand and stare at her, both of us frozen to the spot. I wasn't sure I'd ever see Sadie's mum again. I sure as hell didn't expect to find her standing in the middle of a farm supply store in Kauri Creek.

"I — I didn't expect to see you," she says, stumbling over her words. She looks fantastic, not at all like the last time I saw her, when she was heartbroken and exhausted.

"You knew where we were, though. You know we live here. Why are you here?"

Something flashes across her face and I want to punch myself for how that came across.

"I have a job interview," she says. "I was going to see how that went, then get in touch."

"I'm sorry. I didn't mean it like that." I run a hand through my hair. "A lot of stuff has just happened."

"That girl, is she okay?"

Katie. "No. I don't think so."

"Are you going after her?"

"Yes, I have to, but ... God, Abi, we need to talk."

"I know we do, but it looks like you need to go after her first." I nod. "First though, can you give me some directions?"

"Of course, walk with me. I need to catch up to Katie." I turn and head for the door, hoping Abi will keep pace beside me. She does.

We head out into the sunshine. There's no sign of Katie. I

expect to see her waiting beside my ute, but the carpark is empty.

My ute is gone.

My heart rate spikes, adrenaline flooding my body.

"Shit," I curse and kick at the gravel. I took too long. I was too slow. She thinks I wasn't coming after her.

I go to pull my phone out of my back pocket, but it's not there. Because I left it in the centre console of the ute when we went inside.

"Shit, shit, shit, shit." I thrust my hands into my hair and grip the strands so tightly it stings.

"Dallas." Abi presses a hand to my forearm, dragging it down. "Take a breath. Where's she gone?"

"I don't know. Maybe to her house, maybe the farm."

"Come on, I'll drive you."

"You have your interview."

"I'll let them know I'm running late due to an emergency and if they have a problem with that then I really don't want to work with them anyway."

I crack a tiny smile. That little bite of sass is so much like the old Abi, the one I first fell in love with. It's nice to see the part of her we lost after Sadie's accident.

"It's so good to see you," I say and wrap an arm around her in a quick, tight hug.

"You don't hate me?"

I blink down at her and shake my head. "I don't hate you Abi, but we do have to sort some things out, especially if you're hanging around. Sadie's going to have a lot to process."

I slide into the passenger seat of her car. It's nothing flashy, but it's clean and relatively modern. She must be doing alright for herself. I'm relieved. I always worried where she was at and if she was okay.

"I know she is. Does she know about you and ...?"

"Katie." I sigh and run a hand through my hair again as Abi pulls onto the road. "Not yet." I twist to face her. "You're not ..." I trail off, unsure how to phrase the question without sounding like a total jackass. Instead of finishing my question, I show Abi where to turn so we can drive past Katie's house. If she's there, then perfect. If not, I have to hope she's seeking refuge with Olivia and Flynn at the farm.

"No, Dallas. I'm not back to cause trouble in your relationship." She gives me a soft smile. "I want you to be happy, and I know I lost my chance with you when I left you and Sadie."

"But you'd like to see Sadie?" I hold my breath as I wait for her answer.

"Yes. If you think that's a good idea. It's totally in your court." Her voice wobbles.

"She's not here," I mutter as we approach Katie's house. It's just her car in the driveway, right where we left it earlier. "Keep driving, take the next left," I say.

Abi resettles her hands on the steering wheel and accelerates as we leave the town boundary and enter a higher speed zone. "Can I ask why Sadie doesn't know about Katie?"

I sigh and rest my head against the window. "Because it's new. Katie wasn't sure she was sticking around and we didn't want to tell Sadie anything until she was sure." My voice cracks and I heave in a strangled breath, fighting against a sob that's threatening to escape.

A pain stabs through my chest as I realise the potential repercussions of the altercation with Max. Will Katie want to stay? Or is she going to leave me after everything anyway?

Abi doesn't respond. She must know me well enough from our history to understand I'm out of words and need to stew in my feelings for a bit. I close my eyes and rest my head against the glass of the window. There's silence in the car, just the rumble of tyres on the rough road surface.

After a while, I feel the car slow and crack my eyes open. We're approaching the Wildflower Ridge gate.

"It's this one," I say, my voice rough.

Abi slows further and turns into the driveway, pulling to a stop and staring up at the wooden sign announcing the property name. There's a matching one hanging over the function centre door—handmade gifts from Henry to Violet after he renamed the farm for her.

"This is where she works?"

"Yeah, and me."

"You've got to be kidding me. Of all the places."

She accelerates again, still muttering under her breath about coincidences and chances and how it's a small fucking world.

I'm too distracted looking for any sign of Katie to pay her much attention. The main house comes into view, but my ute isn't parked outside. Olivia is just climbing out of the side-by-side though, and we come to a stop beside it.

I jump out of Abi's car and glance at my cottage. No sign of the ute over there either. I'm sure I'd be able to see it through the trees.

She's not here.

My heart plummets.

Olivia is staring at me open mouthed. "Dallas. Why are you here?"

I spin to face her. "Do you know where Katie is?" The desperation in my voice is clear and she snaps out of her confusion.

"No. She's supposed to be with you. What happened?"

"Max happened," I rasp and Olivia's eyes slam closed as she takes a deep breath. "Did you know all the things Toby did to her?" I ask.

"I know some of them," she whispers. "What happened today?"

"Max had a go at her again. She told him the truth, but Tilly was there and she heard everything."

Olivia lets out a long sigh. "Oh, the poor kid."

"Yeah. Katie was horrified. I think Tilly overhearing was more upsetting for her than having it out with Max. Katie took off and before I had a chance to catch up, she'd taken my ute and gone. She isn't at home. She isn't here. Where else could she be?" My words spill out of me, tumbling over each other so fast I'm amazed they even sound like words anymore.

A hand on my back slows my rapid breathing. "Take a breath, Dal," Abi says softly. "You'll find her."

Olivia has her phone out and she's tapping the screen so ferociously I think she might be about to smash right through the device. A moment later a motorbike skids to a stop beside us and Flynn climbs off, looking harried and panicked.

"What's the SOS?"

"We can't find Katie," Olivia whispers and Flynn's face goes white.

"Wasn't she with you?" He turns on me and the always cheerful, loveable Flynn I've always known has vanished. He's looking at me like something gross he stepped in. Like I've done something to hurt his best friend and he's going to murder me for it.

"She was. But we had a run in with Max."

Flynn clenches his fists. "That bastard. I'm going to—"

"No, you're not. Focus." Olivia snaps and we both turn back to her. "My interview just flaked, so I've got plenty of time and Mum's picking up Sadie this afternoon so she's taken care of. We'll find her."

"Um," Abi says, voice hesitant. "I'm sorry, but if you're Olivia, I'm your interview."

Olivia stares at Abi and so do I.

"Your interview is *here*?" I say and now I understand all the mutterings about coincidences.

"Yeah, managing the function venue."

"Wait, wait, wait." Olivia waves her hands in the air. "You're Abigail?" Abi nods. "And you happened to run into Dallas and give him a ride? He's the emergency."

"Yeah, except, well … I won't be able to work here. I'm sorry to mess you around."

There's too much going on in my brain. I need to find Katie. I need to deal with the Abi situation and Sadie. Shit. Sadie.

"You can't be here when Sadie gets home," I blurt and all eyes land on me.

"Dallas," Abi says, one hand landing on my shoulder, the other reaching up to cup my cheek. "Take some more breaths ... slow ... that's it." I focus on her eyes and let her voice wash over me. She's always had a way with calming me down when I get panicked. I've always regretted not being able to do the same for her, especially when she needed me most after Sadie's accident.

"I won't be here when Sadie gets home," she says. "Olivia has my phone number, or use the email address you send the updates to, and get hold of me later. Go and find Katie." She reaches up and presses a kiss against my cheek, then turns to Olivia. "I'm really sorry to have wasted your time." Then she turns, climbs back into her car and heads down the driveway.

"Who was that?" Flynn breaks the silence that's hanging over us as we watch the dust from the car settle.

"Sadie's mum," I say, voice strangled.

Flynn's eyes almost bug out of his head. "Holy shit. She's—"

"Focus, Flynny. Where would Katie go?" Olivia snaps her fingers in front of his face.

"The waterfall," he says abruptly. "She'll have gone to the waterfall to throw rocks at it and echo-scream." He moves to swing his leg over his motorbike but I grab it in midair.

"Waterfall? Echo-scream?" I gently push him out of the way and climb on the bike myself.

"The bush block above the back stream paddock. There's a waterfall in there. If you stand in just the right place and yell, it echoes around you. We used to go there and scream when we were upset," Olivia explains.

"I can't believe I didn't know there was a waterfall in there," I mutter.

"You do now. If she's anywhere, I'll bet she's there," Flynn says. "I'm not even going to be offended that you're stealing my bike right now. But go, make sure she's okay and bring her home safe."

I kickstart the bike and rev it to get the motor running. "I will." Then I release the clutch and I'm gone.

35

DALLAS

THE WIND WHIPS at my face and pulls at my clothes as I tear through the farm, pushing Flynn's bike to its limit.

I should be taking it slower because the last thing I need is to come off the bike. I need to get to Katie as soon as possible, not end up in a ditch.

But every time I try to ease off the throttle my hand won't let me.

It feels like I ride forever. Why does this waterfall have to be at the far reaches of the farm. I hope Flynn recently refuelled his bike.

Eventually the bush block comes into view. It's a fenced off area of native trees and shrubs that sits on the back boundary of the property. The stream that gives the back stream paddock its very original name emerges from the bush block, but I've never ventured past the fence line to explore further.

I skid to a stop beside the fence where the stream passes

under it and kick down the bike stand. Leaving it there, I scramble over the fence and follow the stream up the hill.

It's gorgeous in here, everything is lush and green. Sweeping fern fronds crowd the ground while towering trees dapple sunlight over mossy rocks. The sun is starting to fade, so the light is slightly gloomy, but I imagine in the middle of the day this place is a haven, especially for someone in the middle of an emotional upheaval.

As I work my way up the stream, the trickling sound slowly gives way to crashing water. I step around a bend in the creek, careful not to slip on a particularly mossy rock, and the waterfall comes into view.

I stop and stare at it. How have I been here all this time and not known about it?

When Flynn said waterfall I assumed he was meaning a little fall, half a metre or so with a small trickle of water. The reality is over two metres tall. The water spills over the edge of a boulder and plummets into a small pool at the bottom before swirling down past where I stand. It doesn't look like the flow is usually very high, but after the rain we had earlier in the week, it's currently gushing fast and free, the splashing echoing through the trees.

I tear my gaze away from the sight, making a note somewhere in my brain to bring Sadie here one day.

I need to find Katie. She isn't immediately obvious. She's not screaming into the rock face or standing out in the open waiting for me.

After a moment of scanning, I spot her, the white of her shirt out of place in the greens and browns of nature.

She's sitting on the ground near the pool, curled into a tight ball with her knees pulled up to her chest. Her head is across her knees as she stares into the tumbling waterfall.

I slow as I approach her, not wanting to startle her. My plan fails when I'm too busy watching her and I step on one of those extra slippery rocks I've been so careful to avoid. I shift my weight to it and my foot disappears from under me, ending up in the creek. The splash and my muttered curse breaks Katie from her zoned out stupor and she lifts her head.

I drag myself out of the stream, shaking off the worst of the water. Luckily I managed to stay upright so it's only my foot that got wet. I'll have to deal with my soaked boot later.

"Katie," I say as I approach her.

Her eyes are following my movements, but I don't think she's fully registering my presence.

I kneel on the ground in front of her. She's sitting close enough to the waterfall that the spray is hitting us and the side of her body is soaked and chilled. Her white shirt is plastered to her arm.

"Katie," I say again, reaching out to rest my hand on her arm.

She flinches at my touch and I try not to let that shatter my heart completely. I pull my hand away and settle back on my heels. The knees of my jeans are already soaked through.

"Why're you here?" she asks in a harsh whisper, her voice raw and raspy.

"I needed to find you," I say.

"You didn't follow me." Her voice cracks and a tear runs down her already tearstained cheeks.

"I did," I say, running a hand through my hair. "I told Max what I thought of him, then followed you."

"I waited but you didn't come outside," she says. "I understand though. It's okay." She sucks in a breath and I can hear it shaking.

"There was a ... complication that delayed me. I was coming after you, Katie. I promise." I reach out and lace my fingers through hers, squeezing tight. It's a relief when she lets me touch her, but she doesn't respond in any way and it causes my heart to clench.

"It's okay," she says again. "I figured you just realised the same thing I did."

"What's that?"

"That I can't stay here. I was right from the start. I can't stay here, even though I really want to." The waver in her voice collapses and she's sobbing, pressing her face into her knees. She cries and cries, never releasing my hands, which I take as a good sign. I want to take the pain away, but there is nothing I can do right now except hold onto her. I need to wait until she can hear me properly before I start talking.

Eventually her sobs subside and she lets out several huge, body wracking breaths. "I'm so sorry," she says.

"Can you tell me why you think you can't stay?" I reach up and use our joined hands to wipe the fresh tears from her cheeks.

"I can't live here having to see Max all the time. You know him and Toby were identical? Every time I see Max I'm reminded of everything Toby did and how I stupidly went along with it all. I just bought all his lies and manipulations. That was the worst of it. That I could be so stupid." She spits the word. "I thought he was the love of my life, so I let him get away with all of that."

"You're not stupid, Katie. Far from it. And he wasn't the love of your life, princess," I say, my voice rough. "Because you're mine and the world isn't cruel enough to make you that, if I wasn't the same for you."

Her breath stutters and catches. A fresh wave of tears spilling from her eyes. "You can't say things like that to me."

"Why not? It's the truth."

"Because, didn't you hear me? I can't stay here."

I shrug and slide a little closer to her. "Katie." I wait until she meets my eyes. "Remember that picture of Sadie's? Our family portrait? That's what I want ... It doesn't matter where."

Her mouth drops open, shock striking her silent for a long moment. But I'm not shocked about my statement. It's the truth: I'll follow her anywhere, if she'll let me.

Katie works her jaw, as if trying to find the words to respond to my admission. Finally, she whispers, "I can't ask you to give up your lives because I'm a complete mess."

"We wouldn't be giving up our lives. We'd be getting you and I can one hundred percent guarantee that Sadie will agree with me on this one. You belong with us, no matter where we are."

Katie slips her fingers from mine and I'm bereft at the loss. She presses her hands to her face, hiding her expression from me.

Seconds pass, stretching into minutes, and with each one, my heart slowly begins to disintegrate.

I thought we'd be enough for her, but I was wrong. She doesn't want this. She probably wants a clean break with no reminders of Kauri Creek or the Sheridan brothers.

I'm about to push up to my feet, to give us both some space when she drops her hands, twists around so her knees are no longer pulled up between us, then she throws herself into my arms.

I barely manage to catch her—and myself—before we go tumbling backwards.

"I want that more than anything," she whispers against my chest as she buries her face in my shirt.

I exhale a long, hard breathe. Thank fuck for that.

She makes a sound halfway between a sob and a giggle and I realise I've said it aloud.

I hold her close as she clings to me and I breathe in the scent of her. To hold her is all I want for eternity, but this kneeling position is about to break me.

"Princess, as much as I always love having you in my lap, perhaps we could reposition, otherwise my legs are going to riot on me."

She giggles again, the sound still thick with tears, and shifts away. I spin around and settle in the spot beside where she was sitting, my back resting against the rock wall, then I scoop her up and place her back in my lap. I expect she'll curl into me sideways, but she turns herself so her knees fall to either side of my hips. The position pushes her skirt up and my cock proves it's incapable of reading the room when it goes hard. "God, you're going to be the death of me, princess," I grumble as she leans her head against my shoulder and presses a soft kiss to my throat.

"I'm sure you'll be fine. I haven't managed it yet."

"You've damn well tried though, haven't you?"

She snorts out a laugh and the lightness in it shoots me straight through the heart. She's back with me. I haven't lost her.

But I need the certainty.

"Katie, I need to know for sure … are you in this with me?"

She sits up and I try not to notice the way her weight shifts in my lap and what it does to me. Her face is tear-stained, with smudged makeup beneath her eyes, which are still watery. She looks exhausted, but also beautiful, because this woman never looks anything other than beautiful. She studies my face, takes several deep breaths and then nods.

"You'd move for me? You and Sadie?" Her voice is hesitant, like she can't quite believe I'm being straight with her. Maybe after the things Toby did to her she doesn't trust anyone's word.

I nod and Katie releases a shaky breath.

"I'm all in, Dallas. I want you more than anything. You and Sadie." She cups my cheeks with her palms and looks me straight in the eye. There's determination there, but also a whole lot of fear.

I hope my next question doesn't change her answer. "So, even when I tell you things you probably don't want to hear, you'll stay with me?"

She sighs and bites her lip. Her eyes drop away for a moment and I stay stock still, waiting for her decision. "Yes," she whispers finally. Then her serious expression fades and the sassy, confident, sexy-as-hell one slips onto her features. "I still might not listen though."

I shake my head and press a kiss to her forehead, my lips curved by a smile. "I wouldn't expect anything less from you."

"What awful truth are you going to tell me?" She's trying to be teasing, but I can see the fear in her eyes, feel it in the way her body is lined with tension, hear it in the slight wobble of her voice.

I lift my hands and rest them on her hips. "I think we ... should stay here."

She flinches, then her mouth slowly curves into a smart-ass smirk. "We could stay out here all night, cowboy." She gives her hips a quick twist and I catch my breath as heat shoots down my spine.

I suppress my instinctive groan and despite really, really wanting to let her run the show, I shove the feelings away and refocus on my point. "I'm serious, Katie." I hold up a hand to forestall her objections. "Please, just hear me out." After a long moment she nods and I gently cup her cheek, brushing my thumb over her lips. "You love this place. You've told me over and over. The only issue here are the Sheridan's and they're just going to have to get over it. Your family is here, Katie, and while Sadie and I will follow you anywhere, the rest of your family can't. This is their home, like it should be yours."

Katie keeps opening her mouth to interrupt me, but never actually goes through with it. I take it as a good sign so I continue.

"You told me once that you wanted a place you could put

down roots and grow. This is that place, surrounded by people who love you. You can live here, at Wildflower Ridge, in full bloom."

36

KATIE

DALLAS'S WORDS hit me and I take a moment just to absorb them.

It's more than I ever wanted, which was to be settled somewhere—to have a home. A place to call my own. That's all I wanted, the basics. A family didn't really come into it, especially not after Toby, but a place to settle, that was the dream.

But to live in full bloom ... that's something else entirely.

I imagine what my life could be like, living here with Olivia and Flynn and Violet, working on the farm, or maybe ...maybe finding something else to do with my life if I wanted too.

I imagine a future with Dallas and Sadie, one that already feels certain, wherever we are, because I know Dallas means what he said. He'll move with me, even if he doesn't really want to. He'll do that for me.

But I imagine waking up each day in the farm cottage, Dallas at my side.

I think about teaching Sadie to barrel race on Scout, and

spending evenings riding out on the farm with my family; Dallas and Sadie, but also Olivia, Violet and Flynn.

They're all here, and while Dallas will go wherever I go, he's happy here. So is Sadie and I know they've needed as much security and stability as I've always longed for. Can I uproot them from the place they call home?

But then, I think of Max and how every time I see him it's like that final day with Toby, when I finally realised the truth and the devastation hits me all over again.

I think of Tilly and the horrified expression on her face as I destroyed the memories she had of her brother. More than anything, that's what I regret the most. I never wanted the Sheridan's to find out what Toby did, especially not sweet Tilly and most definitely not like that.

I close my eyes and try to push that memory away.

"Katie," Dallas whispers, his hands still caressing my face with the most gentle care. "You can't let what happened with the Sheridan's ruin your life. It wasn't your fault what Toby did to you. It's not your fault that Tilly found out the way she did. Whatever problems Max has, that's up to Max to deal with. Don't let them take away the life you deserve, the life you've always deserved."

I sigh and lean into Dallas, inhaling his scent and feeling his arms come around me. This is home. Right here, in his arms. None of the rest of it matters.

"You don't have to decide right away, and if you choose to go, please give us a chance to make plans with you. Don't just run from us."

I sit back and study his face. His expression is careful and the story he told me about his ex comes crashing back into my mind. He's been abandoned before.

"I'm sorry," I say. "I didn't mean to just take off on you. I thought you weren't coming." I take a deep breath. "I wanted to stay, before we saw Max today, I decided I was going to stay, but all of that," I wave my hand in the air, encompassing the confrontation, the realities of my relationship with Toby and everything else that happened, "it shook me. I thought you were right behind me ... but you weren't."

"Yeah," he shifts my weight in his lap slightly, then tips his head back to rest it against the rock wall. "I mentioned there was a complication."

"A complication?"

"Did you see a woman as you left the store?"

"She was kind of hard to miss. She's gorgeous."

"That's Abigail ... Sadie's mum."

I choke on my breath. "Holy shit." I want to scramble off his lap. I don't know why but the urge to run again hits me like a truck. Maybe Dallas doesn't even want me in his lap anymore. He must sense my panic because he reaches out and tugs on my shoulders, pulling me into him and wrapping his arms around me. His fingers begin to work their way through my hair, untangling the snarls in it.

"She's not here for me." The panic in me ebbs a little at his words. Dallas presses a kiss to my temple. "I didn't know she was coming, but she was interviewing for a job and was going to see how that played out before she got in touch. I guess she needed to know if she'd be settled before she reconnects with Sadie—if that's what I want." His hands separate my hair into three sections and he weaves them into a loose braid, like he does most days when we sneak off to the cottage for lunch.

My thoughts are spinning. Abigail is here. What does this mean? For Dallas, for me? For Sadie?

Based on my history, Dallas wanting to get back with his ex the moment I fall in love with him wouldn't be unexpected.

Based on current evidence, with me wrapped in Dallas's arms while straddling his lap and him talking about moving wherever I go, Abigail's arrival doesn't appear to have altered our situation at all.

I take reassurance from the fact that he's here, right now, with me. His delay in following me from the farm store makes sense if he was confronted with his past on his way to the door.

But the reality is he still followed me. He's here with me now, making promises to me about the life we're going to have. And that is what matters.

"Is that what you want, for Abigail to be a part of Sadie's life?" I murmur, blissed out from the gentle pressure his braiding is putting on my scalp.

"Yeah, I think so. I want Sadie to know her mum, but I have to see where Abi's at before I let her near Sadie. I'm not running the risk of her bailing again. I don't want to put Sadie through that. Abi has to be all in, or not at all." He finishes the braid and gives it a little tug. "It's a lot to think about and not top of my priority list."

"It's not?"

"No. Abi's going to wait until I get in touch with her and Sadie's being taken care of by Violet at the moment. My main concern right now is you."

I sit back and stare down at him. He drops his hands from my shoulders down to my hips, then slightly lower, to the bare expanse of my thighs.

I shiver as he brushes his fingertips up the outside of my legs, until he reaches the hem of my skirt which is right up around my ass. I'm essentially sitting in his lap wearing just a pair of lace underwear.

His head is tilted back against the rock and he gazes up at me, his blue eyes filled with love and adoration.

"You don't have to be concerned about me," I whisper, then I take a deep breath and lay my heart out for him. "I love you. I want to be with you, wherever that is. But ... I really, really want it to be here."

Dallas surges forward in a movement so fast I almost topple off his lap, but his strong arms are around me, holding me to him as his mouth crashes down onto mine.

I release a startled gasp and he uses the opportunity to slide his tongue into my mouth. He lets out a low groan and his hands fall to my hips again, now I'm not in danger of falling off him.

Where his touch before was a gentle caress, this time it's burning with desire. His calloused hands are firm on my thighs as he tugs me forward. His kisses slip from my mouth and trail along my jaw until he's nipping at my pulse point.

I moan and shiver.

"Are you cold?" he asks, his mouth still pressed against my skin.

"No. Yes. Don't know. Probably just the wet clothes," I mutter, unable to even fully comprehend his question with his tongue on my neck.

He glances up at me, his eyes flashing dark with lust. "Should probably take them off."

"Yes, please," I breathe as his mouth reconnects with my neck and I slide my fingers into his hair.

He reaches up and pulls the shirt apart at the front, untucking it from where it's held in place by my skirt. He pulls back and watches as the shirt gives way to reveal the same white lace bra I wore the first night we were together. He lets out a satisfied sigh.

"I've had to wait so long to see this again," he says, tracing the edge of the lace with one fingertip.

I lean in and nibble on his earlobe, then drag my tongue down his neck. "Your shirt's a little damp too," I whisper, then undo each button in swift succession, exposing the hard planes of his chest and stomach. As I reach the last button, I spread the sides apart and trace a line from the hollow of his throat to the line of hair disappearing beneath his belt buckle.

He shivers at my touch. "This isn't exactly how our first date was supposed to go," he says, his voice a breathless pant.

"Maybe this is better," I reply, shooting him a little smirk.

"It's better," he says. "God, I can't believe you're mine."

"All yours," I whisper against his mouth, leaning in for a slow, languid kiss. "Do you want the rest of my clothes off?"

He moans. "I can't decide." He sits back to take in the sight of me. I must be a mess with tangled hair and smudged make up. My shirt is hanging off my shoulders, my skirt around my waist. "This whole look is so fucking hot." He tugs on the hem of the skirt. "But fuck, I want to see that full set again."

I laugh and roll my hips forward until I feel the press of his dick on the inside of my thigh. "Well, we have forever, so I'm more than happy to remain clothed for now, and later, you can spend as long as you like admiring what's underneath."

"Fuck." He presses his forehead against mine, holding me in place with a hand on the back of my neck. "I don't know what my favourite part of that sentence was."

"I do," I whisper. "The forever part."

"You're right. We do have forever, and that's the best part."

With no further preamble he slips a hand between us and drags it across the lace covering my pussy. I jerk at the sudden contact, the desire that's been slowly spooling in me rushing to the single place his fingers touch.

"What do you need, princess?" He mutters against me. "I'll give you anything you want."

"I want to feel you inside me. Right now." I press a kiss against his mouth.

"I'm not exactly prepared for this eventuality," he says, brushing against me again. He hooks his finger around my underwear and pushes it to the side. Sensation explodes as he touches my bare skin, then slides a finger inside me. I bear down with a guttural moan. Another finger joins the first.

"I'm on the pill, but I understand if you don't want to." I bite my lip and grind down harder. I reach clumsily for the front of his jeans, releasing his belt, then the button and zipper. I reach inside and wrap my fingers around his dick.

Dallas makes a sound in the back of his throat, then lifts his ass to shimmy his jeans down out of my way.

"This is a shit time for this conversation," he grits out as I pump my fist around his length to the same tempo I'm now riding his hand. His eyes are fixed on the point his fingers meet my body. "But if something happens, are you with me?"

"I'm always with you, cowboy," I whisper. "Family, remember. Forever." I brace my free hand against his neck, brushing my thumb against his jaw as his gaze locks with mine. "But we don't have to, I can get you off just as good like this." Then I lift my hand to my mouth, drag my tongue across it and return it to his shaft, sliding it firmly over his head.

"Family." He repeats, timing the words with the thrust of his hand. His blazing eyes haven't left mine. "Forever."

He withdraws his fingers and I almost keel over from the loss, but he scoops his hands under my ass and lifts me so I'm lined up directly over him.

He lowers me down and we groan simultaneously as we connect, then again when he bottoms out inside me, my ass resting against his thighs.

"I'm not going to last," he mutters into my neck. "I'm sorry." One hand reaches up and wraps itself around the braid that's somehow still half formed in my hair. He gently pulls back, forcing me to lift my hips, arch my back, and present my tits to his face. He leans forward and sucks a nipple into his mouth, his tongue tracing over the pattern of the lace.

I gasp. "It's okay. Neither am I if you keep that up."

"Good, because I want you to come with me."

Then he somehow thrusts his hips straight up. He fucks up into me over and over, until I'm seeing stars. One hand is wrapped in my hair, the other roaming between my nipples and my clit, toying with each and sending white hot pleasure spearing through my body as he alternates soft brushes with firm pressure and the occasional pinch. With his hands and his cock, he builds me up, until I'm trembling and the tension is coiled so tight I don't know how it'll ever unravel.

"Now, princess. Come now."

His command, and his thumb pressing against my clit, is all it takes as he slams into me one more time. I grind down onto him, riding the wave of my orgasm while the world fractures around me. He presses his face into my neck as shudders wrack his body.

We shatter together, clinging to each other, body against body as we come down from the high.

"I love you, Katie," he says into my cleavage and I can't help myself, I tip my head back and laugh.

"Me, cowboy, or my tits?"

"Fuck, both." He glances up at me, a sheepish smile on his gorgeous lips. Then he drops his eyes back down and licks his lips. "We should get you home and dry."

"And ready for later?" I smirk at him and he laughs, then sobers quickly.

"We should also let Olivia and Flynn know you're okay. They'll be worried about you."

I sigh and lean into him, resting my head on his shoulder. His arms immediately come around me. "Did I completely freak them out?"

"Little bit," he says and guilt stabs through me. "But they aren't going to be upset with you. Max should probably watch his back, but you don't have anything to worry about." He presses a kiss to my temple. "Come on. Let's go home."

37

———

DALLAS

I BRING the motorbike around and meet Katie where she left the ute on a barely used gravel road that borders the bush block. She helps me lift the bike onto the back tray, then I find her a fleece pullover in the back seat that she slips over her ruined outfit.

The skirt may never recover from its adventure and the time Katie spent sitting on the ground in it, but I'm hoping the shirt will be fine and I get to enjoy it for a while longer.

Katie climbs into the passenger seat and while I get the engine started and heater blowing, she texts Olivia and Flynn, letting them know she's okay.

"Where do you want to go?" I ask as she drops her phone back into her lap.

"The cottage," she replies without hesitation. "Please."

I nod and make the turn to head towards the Wildflower Ridge driveway.

She's quiet the rest of the drive, but she reaches out and twines our fingers together, resting them between our seats.

We turn into the driveway and for some reason, it feels different this time with Katie beside me, even though we've gone in and out this gateway multiple times while working together. Instead of following the road towards the main house and parking in my usual spot, I turn off and head for the cottage.

We climb out of the vehicle and I look at Flynn's bike in the back tray. I should get it back to him.

"Flynn said not to worry about the bike," Katie says behind me. "Said he'll just use yours until you return his baby to him."

I laugh and usher her into the house. The moment the door is closed I pull her to me. I wanted to outside, but Sadie will be at the main house by now and I can't run the risk of her catching us out.

"Do you want a shower?"

"Please."

"Or a bath?"

"Oh, that sounds good."

I peel myself off her and head for the bathroom, turning on the hot water and dumping a load of bubblebath under the stream. I dig a fresh towel out of the cupboard and set it on the counter.

"Are you joining me?" she asks, that coy little smirk playing on her mouth again.

"Not this time," I say and she pouts. "I thought I'd go, uh, have a chat with Sadie."

Katie's eyes go wide. "Oh."

"If you're okay with that?"

She nods. "I'd love that. Are you okay with that?"

"God, yes. Do you know how many times I've almost blown it by kissing you in front of her already?"

Katie laughs. "Alright, cowboy. I'll have my bath alone. You go take care of your girl."

I reach out and brush a lock of hair back from her face. "Our girl."

"Our girl," she echoes, a small smile tugging at her lips. "I hope it goes okay. I'll be here when you get back ... Or I can be gone too if you need." She runs a hand across my cheek. "If you and Sadie need some space."

"Thank you." I cover her mouth with mine for the softest of kisses, then leave her to her giant bubble bath and go to find my daughter.

Olivia meets me on the front porch of the main house, with Flynn barely two steps behind her.

"She's fine," I say before they can even ask. "I promise. She's good. She's at the cottage right now."

"Then why the hell are you here?" Flynn asks.

"Because I thought now was a good time to have a chat with Sadie about some things."

Flynn's eyes go wide. "Oh. Shit. Yeah, I suppose there are some things to cover."

I laugh, but it doesn't sound amused. "Just a few minor details. Nothing life changing at all."

Olivia rubs my arm in a comforting gesture. "You guys will figure it out. Should we go see Katie?"

"She's in the bath right now, so probably not. But she really is okay."

"I'm so glad she has you," Olivia says and I swear her eyes are getting a little misty before she turns away and calls for Sadie.

"We'll leave you to it," Flynn says, giving me a pat on the back as he heads back into the house, followed by Olivia. A moment later Sadie skids down the hall, sliding in her socks.

"I thought you were busy tonight?" she asks as she comes to a stop in front of me.

"I sort of am. But I need to go check on Aurora and thought you might want to come with me."

"Of course. Is Aurora okay?" She jams her feet into her boots and skips down the steps, pausing to wait for me as she asks her question.

"I'm sure she is."

As we walk down the driveway to the barn, Sadie slips her hand into mine. I'm trying to figure out how to start the conversation in which I have to tell my child I'm in love with someone and that her mother is also back on the scene—but also that they're two different women.

"Is Katie okay?"

"Yes," I say slowly, drawing out the word. "Why do you ask?"

"I heard Flynn and Olivia talking about her. They said she got in a fight with someone." Her eyes suddenly go round and her expression shifts. "I didn't listen on purpose," she says. "It was an accident. But also, she normally checks on the horses."

"I know but I wanted to do it for her. She did have a fight with someone. He said some pretty mean things, but Katie is absolutely fine."

"That's good. Did he apologise to her?"

"Not yet. But that doesn't matter right now. I wanted to talk to you about Katie actually." I draw in a deep breath. "We've been spending a lot of time together."

Sadie kicks at a loose piece of gravel. "I know. You spend all day together on the farm."

"I've also been seeing her outside of working. I guess ... she's my girlfriend."

"Oh." Sadie stops walking and stares up at me as understanding settles on her face. "Are you going to get married?"

"Ah, I'm not actually sure," I say, rubbing at the back of my neck. "It's still pretty new, but we wanted you to know."

"Okay." She looks a little puzzled, but continues walking towards the paddock Aurora is in.

"You like Katie, don't you?"

"Yeah."

"You don't sound convinced." I bend down and scoop her up into my arms, propping her on my hip. "It's okay, Sadie. It's going to take all of us some time to get used to."

"But why aren't you marrying her? Isn't that what you're supposed to do? Cinderella only met the prince for one-night and wanted to marry him. Why don't you want to marry Katie? She's *amazing*."

Understanding dawns. Freaking fairytales. I ruffle Sadie's hair and set her down on the fence railings so we're at even height.

"She is amazing. And maybe one day we'll get married. But real life isn't like *Cinderella*, or any of those other fairy tales. It takes time. But we love each other, and we both love you."

Sadie wraps her arms around my neck, squeezing me so tight I can hardly draw breath. "I love you both too." She lets me go as another idea fires through her brain. "Did you give her my picture? Is that why she loves you?"

I chuckle. "I think your picture helped, Lady Sadie."

I don't tell her that both Katie and I left the bag containing the picture on the floor in the back of the farm supply store. I have no idea if we'll ever see it again.

"I want you to know," I say, smoothing Sadie's hair back from her face. "You're number one, okay? If you're ever worried about something, you can come and talk to me. I love you so much."

She leans in for another breath stealing hug. "I love you too, Daddy. Can we go tell Katie I love her too?"

I laugh. "Alright, alright. You can tell her, but then are you okay going back to stay at Violet's tonight?"

"Yep, I've got to finish beating Flynn at Go Fish." She jumps to the ground and takes my hand again. "Is Katie living with us now?"

"She's not living with us yet, but is it okay if she stays over sometimes?"

"Yeah. But if she lived here then she wouldn't have to drive to work every day. She could have my room. I don't mind sharing."

Warmth floods me. This whole conversation has been wild, but in the best way. "If Katie stays over, she'll be staying in my room, sweetie."

Sadie scrunches up her nose. "But I love her too, so don't we get to share her? Plus you snore."

I laugh until tears fill my eyes. "We'll figure it out."

"Come on," Sadie tugs on my hand. "I have to tell Katie and go beat Flynn. I'll bet he's looked at all my cards by now."

"I'll race ya," I say, dropping her hand and speeding up. A moment later, Sadie racing past me, cackling maniacally.

"I'm going to beat you," she screeches.

Of course she is. I always let her.

38

———

KATIE

THE BATH ISN'T EVEN FINISHED RUNNING when I hear a vehicle outside the cottage. I turn off the water and head for the front door, peering through the window as I do.

There's a small red hatchback parked in front of the house. I open the door, relieved I haven't bothered to start undressing yet. I haven't seen the car before and I don't know who I'm expecting to see climb out of it. Maybe Dallas's ex Abi, even though he told me she was waiting to hear from him.

A person I definitely wasn't expecting to see get out of the car is Tilly Sheridan.

My breath catches at the sight of her, as memories fire through my brain.

She glances up at the house and spots me, leaning against the door frame. She hesitates, then straightens up and takes purposeful strides across the gravel. She stops at the bottom of the porch steps and holds out a brown paper bag.

"I'm sorry about my brother," she says, her voice wobbling.

"*Both* my brothers. You left this behind. I thought you might miss it."

"I'm so sorry, Tilly," I say. My voice is haggard and tears threaten to spill over again. The emotional rollercoaster of the day has almost wiped me out completely.

"It's not your fault," Tilly assures me, gesturing at the bag. I step forward and take it, knowing it contains the shirt and Sadie's picture. "I always really liked you and I never understood what Max was on about. But Toby could be a real jerk sometimes, especially to Max. I think it really messed him up." She takes a few steps back. "I'm not making excuses for Max, because he was a jackass too, but I am sorry."

"Thank you, Tilly," I rasp. "I appreciate that. And you bringing this all the way out here."

She shrugs. "I'll see you around sometime. I hope." She shoots me a little smile, then climbs back into her car and disappears down the driveway.

She doesn't hate me. She wants me to stay too.

I sit down on the step and pull out the contents of the bag. The shirt spills into my lap, but it's the picture I'm after.

My family.

I don't know how long I sit there and stare at the drawing, but the sound of running boots on gravel causes me to look up, right before Sadie plows into me.

"I love you, Katie," she says, words bursting out of her along with an enormous grin. "I told Daddy we can share a room when you stay over, but he wants you to share with him." She leans in close. "He snores though, so you might not want to, but don't be mean to him about it. He really likes you so it might hurt his feelings."

I wrap my arms around her and pull her onto my lap, carefully setting the picture down beside me.

Dallas sits on the step beside me and I lean into him. "How?" He asks, picking up the drawing.

"Tilly," I say simply, then I turn my focus back to Sadie. "I love you too, Lady Sadie, and I really like your dad, so I'll do my very best not to hurt his feelings."

She leans in close again and I inhale the bubblegum scent of her hair. "He told me he loves you."

"Did he now? That's good, because I love him too."

She giggles like I've told her a secret and snuggles into me. I lean into Dallas's side as he wraps an arm around me. It's a moment of pure bliss.

"Let's get you back to the main house," Dallas says to Sadie after a few perfect minutes pass and Sadie starts wriggling in my lap. I'm impressed she's stayed still this long. "Katie can have her bath."

"Then I'll come over. Maybe see if Vi has space for a couple of extras for dinner?"

"You sure?" he asks, eyes gentle with affection and concern.

"Yeah. It seems like a good day to be with family."

"That it does." He kisses my temple and helps Sadie up. "We'll see you soon."

∼

I SOAK in the bath until the water is cold and my fingers are pruned. I climb out, wrap myself in the fluffy towel Dallas left for me, then sit on the edge of the bath contemplating my choices.

I have no spare clothes, only the shirt Dallas gifted me, so either I put back on my ruined skirt, or I find something of Dallas's to wear. I eye the crumpled pile of my wet, dirty clothes. I'm reluctant to put them back on, but I'm even more reluctant to rifle through Dallas's things. We may be together, but I'm not comfortable searching his drawers.

The front door opens just as I'm shaking out my skirt and Dallas appears, knocking on the bathroom door before pushing it open. He has a bag in hand and holds it out to me.

"Olivia suggested I bring these over. Something for you to wear."

I exhale a breath and take the bag. "Oh, thank you. I was not looking forward to putting this back on." I wave the skirt at him, then drop it on the floor.

"I'm sorry about that. Is the shirt salvageable? Maybe after we've washed it we could have an encore," he says, eyes flashing.

"I can get behind that." I smirk at him and lift my hand to the fold where my towel is held in place. "But maybe for now ..."

"I wish, princess. But dinner's almost ready." He steps closer, his hand coming to rest on my cheek as he gently tilts my chin to look up at him. "It's okay. We've got all the time in the world."

He's right. "We do," I say as I turn my head and kiss his palm.

He leaves the bathroom while I pull on Olivia's clothes, a pair of comfy jeans and a sweatshirt. I finger comb my hair and use one of Sadie's hair ties to secure it in a messy ponytail and finally wipe the remnants of my makeup from my face.

It's a stark difference to me preparing for my date with Dallas earlier, but for a family dinner, I feel perfect.

We walk to the main house hand in hand and when we enter the kitchen Sadie promptly drops her hand of cards—leaving Flynn looking rather put out—and bounces over to greet us. She immediately, and proudly, announces to the room that her daddy and I love each other.

Flynn applauds, Violet gives us a warm smile, but while Olivia is smiling, there's something else in her expression. She's wary.

"Sadie, my love, can you come and help me get something from the garden?" Violet says, and when Sadie nods vigorously, leads the way out the back door.

When it's just the four of us—me, Dallas, Flynn and Olivia—silence falls as everyone glances furtively from one to the other, wondering who's going to be the first to speak.

"Are you staying?" Olivia asks finally, resignation in her tone. "Or are you both leaving?" Her voice wavers as I cross the room to her. "I'm sorry," she whispers as I take her hands. "I'm so happy for you, but I just need to know."

"We're staying, Livvie." I squeeze her hands tight and she raises her watery eyes to look at me. "I want to be here. All of my family is here, and they're more important than anything Max Sheridan has to say to me."

A sob bursts free from her, and she flings her arms around me. She clings to me until she manages to get her breathing under control. "Thank god, I didn't want to lose you. Either of you."

"Never again, Livvie. I'm home now."

Another set of arms comes around us and squeezes us tight.

"Group hug," Flynn says. Even his voice sounds a little choked up. "So glad you're staying, Katie Kat."

Eventually we break apart and take seats at the table while Olivia passes around a pitcher of Violet's fruit punch.

"I haven't told Sadie about Abi yet," Dallas says, his hand finding mine on the table. "So if you could keep that to yourselves for now."

Flynn and Olivia both nod, then Olivia hesitantly breaches the subject.

"Do you think she said she couldn't work here because of you? She didn't want to encroach on your turf?"

Dallas runs his hand through his hair. "Probably. I don't really know. We're going to have to talk through some things."

"Would you be okay if I went through with the interview? And potentially offered her the job? Her work won't really cross over with yours." She traces a line through the condensation on her glass. She's nervous. "She's just the only decent applicant I've had and I desperately need help if I want the venue to operate this summer," she blurts out, then falls back in her seat, like she's preparing for us to rage at her.

I study her, then glance at Dallas. "I have no issues with it," I say. Sadie deserves to know her mum, and I know Abi's arrival won't affect my relationship with Dallas, because he loves me, as much as I love him. "So long as you're okay with it." I squeeze Dallas's hand. "And Sadie is number one."

"Absolutely," Olivia says. "Sadie's always number one."

Dallas chuckles. "Don't let her hear you say that. That kid's ego is big enough already. But yeah, I'm okay with it. I want to talk to her first though, if that's alright."

"Of course," Olivia says, the tension draining from her. "And like I said, you won't really have to work with her. Flynn can do any of the work needed at the venue if you'd prefer to keep your distance."

"I feel like I'm the only one not getting a choice here," Flynn grumbles, but there's a small satisfied smile tugging at his mouth. I study him closer. Is he ... blushing?

Olivia drags my attention away from Flynn when she continues the conversation. "We'll see how it all plays out, but for now, is it safe to let Mum bring Sadie back inside? I'm pretty sure she's going to run out of delay tactics in a moment."

"I'll go get them," Flynn says, striding to the door. "Hey, Sadie! You ready to finish losing yet?"

"In your dreams," she shouts back and a moment later races back through the door and takes up her hand of cards. Flynn grins, ruffles her hair and collapses into the seat opposite her, collecting his own cards.

Five minutes later, dinner is ready and Flynn has been annihilated in the most intense game of Go Fish I've ever seen.

After dinner, Dallas and I cross the paddock back to the little cottage, Sadie swinging on our hands between us. Neither of us could bear to leave her at Violet's for the night.

We tuck Sadie into her bed and kiss her goodnight.

Then we crawl into Dallas's bed and as he curls his strong, hot body around mine, pulling me in close he whispers into my ear. "Welcome home, Katie."

"COME ON, WAKE UP," the little voice repeats close to my ear. The bed moves and a small weight lands on me. "Katie. It's time to wake up."

I groan and try to roll over, but there's a solid wall of heat behind me.

"Morning, princess," Dallas murmurs into my ear, brushing a kiss against my hair as Sadie climbs over us both.

"It's today. Scout will be waiting for us."

"Alright, I'm up," I say. "Wouldn't want to keep Scout waiting. Go get some breakfast and I'll be right out."

Sadie scrambles off the bed and disappears into the kitchen of the little farm cottage that's now my home.

After our mishap of a first date, I never really went back to my house in town. I finally rented it out around Christmas-time and officially moved into the cottage with Dallas and Sadie. In a way, it feels too fast, but at the same time, I know there's nowhere else I ever want to be.

"Ready for today, cowboy?" I ask as I roll over, into Dallas's waiting arms.

"I'll never be ready for today," he says, then brushes his lips against mine for a long, slow kiss.

"Dad! Katie! Stop kissing, we'll be late."

"Uh, fine," Dallas grumbles as I pull away from him, overtaken by laughter.

"Come on, cowboy. You promised her."

TWO HOURS LATER, we're pulling into the Kauri Creek Showgrounds where the annual rodeo is held at the end of every summer.

Olivia and Flynn have saved us a parking spot and Sadie scrambles from the horse truck the moment Dallas stops.

We unload the horses—Scout, an elderly gelding named Paddy, Olivia's mount Bruno, and Aurora, ready for her first event.

"Team's race is at ten-thirty, so we better get you ready and over to the arena," Olivia says, handing me Aurora's lead.

We tack up and head for the main arena.

"You good?" I ask Dallas, as we watch Sadie trotting Scout around the warm up arena.

"Absolutely not. I can't believe I let you talk me into this."

"You got this, cowboy." I reach up for a kiss, then give him a little shove of encouragement as he turns and swings up into Paddy's saddle.

When Sadie first learned of the team's barrel race she

desperately wanted to compete, despite me explaining it's an open class and everyone else will be racing at a full gallop. There's no way she'd be competitive.

I suggested the individual race, where she'd be pitted against other kids her age. She agreed to that, but wanted to race with me too.

When she learned about the requirement for three riders in a team, her little heart had almost broken. I was ready to suggest Olivia, who herself is a champion racer, but before I had the chance to open my mouth, Sadie decided Dallas should be our third.

Completely incapable of saying no to his daughter, he reluctantly agreed and now the day is here.

Both Sadie and Dallas have come a long way with their riding in the past few months and Dallas is mostly over his fear of horses, but it doesn't mean he's really up for a competition barrel race.

We warm our horses up, Aurora keeping a watchful eye on every new sight she comes across, but staying calm and relaxed under me. She's come a long way too and now that Sadie is riding Scout most days, Aurora has become my main mount.

We watch some of the other teams race, Sadie's eyes wide with wonder as the horses streak by. Dallas's hands grip his rein's tighter and tighter, until his knuckles are white.

"It's all good," I murmur, running my fingers over his hands. "It's just for fun."

"I know." He blows out a breath as the announcer calls our names, playing up our local connection and family team.

"Our youngest competitor in her first ever race, Sadie

McLeod," he booms over the loud speaker as Sadie and Scout trot into the arena, waiting in the starting area like I explained to her. "And her dad, Dallas, also in his first race." The crowd cheers and claps as we ride side by side into the arena. "And rounding out their team from Wildflower Ridge, Katie Barton— soon to be McLeod, no doubt." The crowd makes even more noise and I ignore the heat in my cheeks, instead running a soothing hand down Aurora's neck as she skitters at the ruckus.

The race starter counts us down and as the flag drops, Sadie claps her legs against Scout's sides and the horse trots through the starting gate.

Despite being the slowest racer in the competition, the crowd is fully behind Sadie as she reaches each barrel, carefully guiding Scout in the correct pattern and breaking into a canter in a few places between the barrels. On the final stretch home, she stands in her stirrups and pushes Scout even faster until the crowd is whooping and hollering.

"You got this, cowboy," I say as Dallas fidgets by my side. I give his thigh a rub, then smack my hand across his ass as he repositions himself in the saddle and moves forward, ready for his run as soon as Sadie crosses the line.

If I thought the crowd was cheering loudly for Sadie, I was wrong. The noise goes to a whole other level as Dallas carefully makes his way around the course, everyone knowing he's only doing this to make his daughter happy.

Sadie bounces in Scout's saddle, screaming her head off for her dad as happiness and pride glow from her.

He canters home, laughing and a fist in the air in celebration of a successful ride.

Then, it's my turn.

Aurora blazes through the starting gate, powering towards the first barrel. She's laser focussed on the task at hand, not even registering the crowd cheering or the flags waving in the breeze all around the arena. We reach the first barrel and I sit back, guiding her through the turn. Aurora spins and powers forward again, then again as we reach the third barrel.

A straight gallop home, where my family waits for me, their arms in the air cheering and screaming.

We cross the finish line in a flash and come to a stop beside them. Dallas reaches out and wraps his arms around me as Aurora leans into Paddy.

He kisses me square on the mouth.

The crowd whoops and hollers.

"Fucking incredible," Dallas says.

I TUCK Sadie into bed that night, her third place ribbon from the individual barrel race already hanging on her bedroom wall.

"Goodnight, Lady Sadie," I say.

"Night, Katie," she murmurs, already half asleep. "So excited you're going to be my stepmum. The ring is so pretty and sparkly."

I smile at her words. She hasn't been shy about encouraging Dallas and I to get married, and she's often talked about the ring her dad will one day give me. She's also mentioned a tiara a few times.

I pull her door closed behind me and head for the lounge

where Dallas is waiting for me on the couch. I curl into him the moment he opens his arm for me.

"Sadie is apparently excited for me to be her stepmum," I say. "She mentioned the ring. She said it'll be sparkly."

Dallas's arm tightens around me, then he lets out a sigh. "I should have known she'd be shit at keeping the secret."

"What?" I push away from him and sit up. "What secret?"

"This secret." He reaches behind him and pulls out a dark blue velvet box. He holds it out to me. "We chose it yesterday."

I take the box, my hands shaking, and flip the top open. My breath catches at the ring inside. It is indeed very sparkly.

"Yes," I breathe.

Dallas laughs. "I didn't ask you anything yet."

"Do you need to? Of course it's yes. Yes to you, yes to Sadie. It always has been."

He takes the box from me, pulls the ring free and slides it into place on my finger.

"I guess that pretty much covers everything then," he says, pulling me in for a kiss.

I throw myself at him, climbing into his lap so my knees are on either side of his hips. "There's one more thing we could cover," I say as I press kisses down his throat.

"Oh, yeah. What's that?"

"I need to show you what I bought yesterday too."

I reach for the hem of my t-shirt and pull it over my head, revealing the lilac coloured bra.

Dallas's eyes flare with lust and desire and I press my hips forward, feeling his cock already hard in his jeans. "Matching set?" He says, his voice a thick rasp.

I nod.

"You'll be the death of me." He leans forward and mouths at my breast, right along the edge of the lace.

"Well, it's 'til death do us part now, cowboy."

He lets out a low moan.

"Bedroom, now."

He stands, hauling me up with him and carries me, giggling to our room.

Being home has never been this perfect.

ACKNOWLEDGMENTS

There aren't enough words to express my gratitude to everyone who has helped me produce this book.

I'll start with my publishing team:

Ashleigh van Arkkels from AVA Book Editing - your feedback was invaluable and working with you was a fantastic experience. Thank you for helping making Dallas and Katie's story so wonderful.

Jenn Rackham, cover designer extraordinaire - I feel like I really put you through it with this cover, but we made it and I love it!

Kelsey, Natalie and Mon who were the earliest readers of this book. Thank you for your feedback and insight on how to make this story so much better than my scrappy first draft!

Special thanks to Mon for coaching me through writing this entire book, especially the spicy scenes. I hope I made you proud.

My friends from the book world - I appreciate you so, so much. I wouldn't be doing this if it weren't for your support.

And lastly, I've got to thank my wonderful husband and daughters. Your support of my career choice has been unwavering. I love you so much.

ABOUT THE AUTHOR

Elle Ashwell has always been a hopeless romantic.

Dedicated to the swoon and happily ever afters, it makes perfect sense to combine her love of all things romance with the charm of small town life in New Zealand.

Her romances are sweet and a little spicy, with green flag guys and ride-or-die friendships.

When not lost in fictional small towns, Elle works in administration, is a farmer's wife and mum of three girls in rural New Zealand.